Gables of Legacy

VOLUME SIX

Full
CIRCLE

OTHER BOOKS AND AUDIO BOOKS
BY ANITA STANSFIELD:

First Love and Forever

First Love, Second Chances

Now and Forever

By Love and Grace

A Promise of Forever

When Forever Comes

For Love Alone

The Three Gifts of Christmas

Towers of Brierley

Where the Heart Leads

When Hearts Meet

Someone to Hold

Reflections: A Collection of Personal Essays

Gables of Legacy, Vol. 1: The Guardian

Gables of Legacy, Vol. 2: A Guiding Star

Gables of Legacy, Vol. 3: The Silver Linings

Gables of Legacy, Vol. 4: An Eternal Bond

Gables of Legacy, Vol. 5: The Miracle

Gables of Legacy

VOLUME SIX

Full CIRCLE

a novel

ANITA STANSFIELD

Covenant Communications, Inc.

Published by Covenant Communications, Inc.
American Fork, Utah

Printed in Canada
First Printing: May 2005

11 10 09 08 07 06 05   10 9 8 7 6 5 4 3 2 1

ISBN 1-59156-966-4

This book is dedicated to every reader
who has felt an increase of hope as they have shared
the struggles and challenges and triumphs of the Hamilton family.
Thanks for sharing the journey!

Chapter One

South Queensland, Australia

Emily Hamilton stared through the darkness toward the ceiling, longing for sleep to overtake her. During the busy hours of the day her loneliness was manageable. She shared her home with children and grandchildren who kept her delightfully occupied. Her life was blest and full and good—and she was grateful. But in the darkest hours of the night the ongoing absence of her husband was difficult to accept. Michael's death, nearly six years ago, had not been the hardest thing she'd ever faced. She had known then, as she knew now, that it had been his time to go. She knew they would be reunited when the time came, as she lived for that blessing. She had lost loved ones before and had endured much heartache in her life. No, losing Michael had not been the most difficult thing she'd ever faced, but living without him—year after year—was proving to be far more of a challenge than she had imagined.

The history Emily had shared with Michael and the trials they'd endured together were incomprehensible. Even beyond his death, Emily had often felt him close by, well aware of the challenges being faced by their loved ones. Michael's death had deeply strengthened her testimony of the ministering of angels, and shown her how thin the veil could be at times. But life had reached a more even plane for her and her family. While little difficulties came up, the family hadn't faced any significant crisis for quite some time. Emily was grateful to see her children and grandchildren content and healthy and doing well. But as the challenges of life had lessened, the evidence of Michael's presence had done the same. She sensed that he was busy elsewhere now that his family didn't need him nearby. And Emily found herself having to adjust to a new level of distance and separation from her husband, and, subsequently, a new level of loneliness. And she hated it!

Emily turned to look at the red digital numbers of the clock. Two-forty-three A.M. Realizing that it was pointless to just wrestle with the bed, she got up and went into the bathroom. She splashed water on her face, then dried it before she became distracted by her reflection. While her eyes adjusted to the light and managed to focus, she pressed a hand over her cheeks and forehead, amazed at how the signs of age seemed to show themselves more every week. Without her glasses the tiny details were fuzzy, but she thought that might be just as well. Her skin was more firm than that of many women her age, a benefit she had gratefully inherited from her mother. Still, her hair was more gray than ash-blonde, and she had given up on trying to fight the signs of age with a monthly bottle of hair color. Though her hair was thinner than it used to be, it was still thick enough to look fairly decent. She wore it shoulder length and naturally curly, just as she had for years. It was boring perhaps, but maintenance free. Taking a step back to look at herself overall, she wondered if Michael would still find her attractive were he still around. She felt relatively certain that he would, but then, he had loved her from her youth. He would likely love her no matter what she looked like. The next thought that popped into her mind caught her so off guard that she gasped. But she had to admit that she was actually wondering whether or not any other man in the world might find her attractive. She was a grandmother of many years, for heaven's sake, and seeking out male companionship had never once crossed her mind since Michael's death. Others had suggested the possibility; well-meaning friends had dropped hints. Ward members had politely steered her toward socializing among the older singles. But she had never felt single; she'd felt attached and still very much married.

Emily fingered the gold band on her left hand. It had been there for so many years that it had practically grown to be a part of her finger. While she had never felt even mildly inclined to take it off, suddenly it just didn't look right. She tugged at it but couldn't get it to move beyond the knuckle. Looking at the ring again, she was struck with a clear memory of the moment Michael had put it there, the day they'd been married. The years were so many that she'd actually lost track. She gave it another tug before she was struck with an unexpected rush of tears. After crying a few minutes, she concluded that she was nothing but confused and muddled and she just needed to get some sleep. Not certain she could sleep even if she wanted to, Emily pulled the Book of Mormon off the bedside table, made herself comfortable against the pillows, and read until she was finally able to relax. Reading in Second Nephi, chapter four, she became unexpectedly distracted with thoughts of how Michael had loved this particular passage of scripture. In fact, she had first heard his voice while sitting in a Book of Mormon class at Brigham Young University, where he'd sat right behind her. And he'd made a comment on that very passage of scripture.

* * *

Michael Hamilton was an easy man to notice as he filtered in and out of the class they shared, where he seemed to silently absorb the knowledge as if he thrived on it. Emily had heard him described as "the nonmember who got straight As in the class, even though he only took it because religion classes were a requirement at BYU." She'd only realized he was Australian weeks into the term, when he finally decided to make a comment in class—a very insightful remark about 2 Nephi, chapter 4. After class Emily mustered the courage to speak to him as he gathered his books. "That's quite a brogue you've got, Mr. Hamilton," she said in reference to his accent. She'd meant it as a compliment and felt relieved to see his eyes catch a sparkle of humor.

"It is not a brogue," he stated as if he were telling her the reason the sky was blue. "What I speak is perfect Australian prose."

Emily introduced herself, to which he quickly responded by saying, "It's a pleasure, Miss Emily Ladd." He blended her two names together as if they were one note of an Australian folk song. Then for the first time in her life, Emily's hand was kissed rather than shaken.

Emily couldn't recall exactly how the conversation went beyond that; she only knew that he left a deep impression. She felt completely fascinated with this six-foot, one-inch man who dressed in a studied simplicity that seemed to astutely express his manner. She was thoroughly intrigued with his slightly waved brown hair that looked neatly styled and windblown at the same time, and with his hazel eyes that changed hues according to his mood.

The following day she returned to her Book of Mormon class with a delightful little tremor hovering in her stomach. It had been slightly less than twenty-four hours since she'd officially met Michael Hamilton, but their brief interaction had triggered a sensation inside her that she'd simply never experienced. Never had she been so thoroughly enchanted with another human being. While something inside of her was tempted to be afraid of treading into uncharted territory, she felt more inclined to succumb to the thrill of this sudden infatuation.

Sliding into her seat, with no sign of Michael in the room, Emily tried to convince herself that just because she was intrigued with him didn't necessarily mean he would be equally intrigued with her. Handsome as he was, and being foreign, she felt certain he wouldn't have any trouble finding women willing to go out with him. And she was a simple farm girl from Idaho. Distracted by her thoughts, she was startled to hear Michael's delicious voice whisper near her ear, "Hello there, Emily Ladd."

Emily tried to suppress the excitement that filled her every nerve as she turned to look into his smiling eyes. Seeing his smile deepen, she felt certain he knew the effect he had on her. "Hello, Michael Hamilton," she said.

He smiled deeper still, and while she was attempting to figure out if he was truly interested in her, or just being polite, he leaned forward a little and said, "If you tell me there's a chance that you might go out with me, I could possibly make it through this class."

Emily couldn't keep her smile from widening. "I think there's a fairly good chance of that."

Class began and the conversation ended, but Emily could barely contain her excitement as she realized that Michael Hamilton wanted to take her out. When class finally ended, Michael immediately said, "So, when? Tonight? Right now?" He laughed and she couldn't help laughing with him. She loved the way he laughed.

"Well . . . right now I have another class, and I suspect you do as well. Tonight I've committed to helping a friend. The next two evenings I have to work, and I'm going home for the weekend."

She started walking toward the door as she spoke, and he walked alongside her. His disappointment was evident, but she appreciated his straightforward manner when he said, "You're not just putting me off, are you? Because if you really don't want to go out with me all you have to do is—"

"Oh, no," she insisted and put a hand over his arm. He glanced down to where she was touching him and smiled slightly. "I really *do* want to go out with you. How about . . . a week from tonight?"

"Done!" he said like an auctioneer finalizing a bid before anyone else could take what he wanted. "Tell me what you'd like to do," he added, holding the door open for her. "Dinner, movie, the ballet, all of the above?"

Emily laughed again. "Perhaps one at a time," she said, and he laughed too. *She loved the way he laughed.* "Truthfully, dinner sounds nice. It doesn't have to be anything fancy, but . . . it's difficult to get to know someone in a theater."

"How right you are," he said as if he liked her theory very much. "We'll plan on it, then. I'll be counting the hours."

"Me too," she said as he hurried away. The memory of his words still lingered in her mind. She loved his accent. In fact, she loved everything about him. She wondered if that meant she was falling in love with him. Reminding herself that she knew practically nothing about him, she cautioned herself against being a fool and settled on enjoying this attraction she felt.

That night, as Emily lay in bed contemplating her fascination with Michael Hamilton, the reality struck her like a splash of cold water. *Michael was not a member of the Church.* She'd known it all along, but until he'd actually asked her on a date, it was a fact that had little consequence to her. She'd never dated anyone who didn't share her faith. Her goal to marry in the temple was firm. She could tell herself it was only one date, but if she were completely honest, she couldn't deny that she hoped it went far beyond one date. Michael Hamilton was the most attractive, intriguing man she'd ever met. She didn't want to offend him by telling him she had a policy to only date those of her own religion, but on the other hand, eternal marriage was high on her list of priorities. She reasoned that her influence in his life could possibly bring him into the Church. They'd met in a Book of Mormon class, for heaven's sake. Surely she needed to be open-minded enough to not slam the door in his face because of a technicality.

Emily slept with a hovering confusion that clung to her the following day. When she saw Michael and exchanged simple conversation with him before and after class, she felt somehow as if just being in his presence made her more complete. But through the remainder of the day, the confusion returned. As her sleep was impeded once again, Emily prayed for direction and came to only one conclusion. She needed the guidance of the Spirit in this matter, just as she did with every decision in her life—however large or small. And while this decision technically *seemed* small, she knew well enough that little choices could easily turn into big ones.

Emily began her weekend with a twenty-four hour fast. Her drive to Idaho was pleasant, and the time she spent with her family the same. As she ended her fast and prayed fervently, Emily knew that when she did get married, it needed to be in the temple, but she knew just as firmly that dating Michael was the right thing to do. In truth, her answer came with such conviction that she felt almost certain that she and Michael were meant to be together forever. Driving home from Idaho, she contemplated the idea more deeply and felt as if she'd been given a little glimpse of eternity. She cried silently for a few brief and tender moments, and then she laughed— an eruption of pure joy as she considered the very idea that this incredible man might actually be a permanent part of her future.

By the time Emily had returned home, her spirit had settled back into the reality of existing in this world. She made a firm resolve to approach this relationship as she would have done anyway. She would be appropriate and cautious while she took every possible opportunity to get to know Michael better. Whatever spiritual insights she might have received were far beyond her own comprehension, and she knew well enough that God's interpretation could likely be much different from her own. Still, she felt certain that Michael would play a significant part in her life—and she in his.

On Monday when Emily saw Michael coming into the class they shared, she became briefly distracted by the thoughts and feelings she'd had over the weekend. She felt embarrassed when he chuckled, and she realized she'd been staring at him, almost dazed, while her mind had wandered.

"You okay?" he asked with that distinct Australian drawl.

"Oh yes," she said. "How about you?"

"As long as we still have a date, then I'm fantastic." Emily laughed softly and forced herself to look away. "How was your weekend?" he added.

"Good, and yours?"

"Tolerable," he said. "The highlight was my traditional phone call home."

"To Australia?"

"That's right," he said. She wanted to ask more about that, but class began.

The only conversation they shared beyond that was the arrangements for their date. He smiled when he told her the time he'd pick her up, and Emily felt butterflies swarming inside of her. Just thinking of him almost caused her to swoon. And now she had a date with him.

When it finally came time for him to arrive at her apartment, she wondered if she'd ever been so excited in her life. He knocked at the door two minutes early, and he smiled when she pulled it open.

"Well hello, Emily Ladd," he said. She loved the way he said her name.

"Hello," she said.

"You ready?" he asked, holding out a hand.

Emily eagerly took it and closed the door behind her. As he opened the passenger door of a Chevy Blazer, she decided that it suited him. "I like the Blazer," she said when he got in and turned the key. "You have good taste, Mr. Hamilton."

He grinned. "I'm going out with you, aren't I?" She gave him a timid smile. "And my name is Michael." Pulling out onto the road, he asked, "So, where to?"

"You're driving," she said.

"I hope you trust my judgment."

"You're going out with me, aren't you?" she said, and he laughed.

Following a stretch of silence he asked, "So where are you from, Miss Ladd?"

"I grew up on a farm in central Idaho, in the middle of hundreds of acres of wheat, miles from the nearest town. It was a good life." Michael smiled at her as if he understood her appreciation of simple things. "And what about you, Mr. Hamilton? Where are you from . . . more specifically? Australia is an awfully big place."

"Yes, it is," he stated. "I come from an area in southern Queensland, which is a province in the east end of the country."

"That's nice." She gave an embarrassed chuckle. "But I have no idea where you're talking about."

"I'll show you on a map sometime."

"I'll look forward to it," she said. "Is all of Australia as dry and desolate as rumor has it?"

Michael laughed. "Not hardly. My family's land is partly dry and flat, but it moves into a mountain range nearby that is incredibly beautiful. I like the mountains, which is one of many reasons that I like it here in Utah."

"And what does your family do with this land?" she asked.

"Until the early 1900s, we ran a great many sheep on it, but now it's mostly just land. We use a portion of it to keep horses and give them room to run." She made an interested noise, and he asked, "Do you like horses, Miss Ladd?"

"I can't say that I've ever touched one," she admitted, and he chuckled. "I take it you have."

"A time or two." He smiled.

"Well?" she said when he didn't go on.

"Well what?"

"Aren't you going to tell me about these horses?"

"My family has been breeding and racing horses since the 1870s."

"Really? Wow."

"I must confess, horses are a big part of my life. Well, at least when I'm not going to BYU."

"And what brought you here?" she asked. "Utah is a long way from Queensland."

"Yes, it is," he agreed emphatically. "But what brought me here is kind of a long story, and we're here."

Emily looked up to see that he'd parked the Blazer next to JB's. "Is this all right?" he asked.

"It's great," she said. "I told you that I trust your judgment."

Michael opened the door and helped her step down, then he kept her hand in his as they walked inside and were shown to a table. They were given menus, but Emily left hers on the table. He glanced at it in question, and she shrugged and smiled. "I trust your judgment. I'll have whatever you have."

Michael ordered steak and shrimp dinners with baked potatoes and salads, then he looked at her and said, "You're not a vegetarian, are you?"

"No," she laughed.

"Boy, that's a relief. I was raised on home-grown beef."

"And horses," she said.

"Yeah, but we didn't eat the horses."

"I didn't figure you would." She laughed softly. "But why don't you tell me what exactly you do with these horses."

"I already did."

"How many do you have?"

"A few."

"Is that three or four?" she asked, knowing he meant much more.

Michael chuckled. "Well, we have several brood mares and a few fine studs. And then there are a number of racing animals in many stages of training. I work with the jockeys and the handlers . . . when I'm home. And then we have some workhorses, though not as many as there used to be when horses were the only transportation available. And we have horses to ride just for the fun of it, and then there are the horses used by the boys at the boys' home."

"It sounds like you have a few horses," she said, "but I don't believe you've mentioned the boys' home before."

"Oh, that's the other part of our family business. It was founded in the nineteenth century. It's just kind of . . . an orphanage I suppose, although most of the boys are actually fostered from difficult situations. We average between twenty and thirty boys at a time. The profit from the horses supports the boys' home, and the boys work with the horses for therapeutic reasons. It works out rather nicely."

"It sounds fascinating, Mr. Hamilton," she said, meaning it.

"Enough about me," he said. "Tell me more about you."

"I haven't heard *anything* about you. I've only heard about boys and horses."

"There's little to tell."

"Tell me about Australia."

Michael leaned forward with eager eyes. "Not until you tell me about Idaho."

Over their meal they shared bits and pieces of their lives, their homes, their childhoods. And over dessert Michael entertained her with stories about his grandfather, who was reputed to be a rogue. Emily didn't realize how little she'd eaten until Michael pointed at her barely touched sundae and said, "You'll never get fat eating like that."

"Are you trying to fatten me up?" she asked lightly.

"No, just keep you healthy. You're going to need your strength to . . ." He hesitated and looked slightly nervous. "Well . . . I was going to ask you out again, but I suppose I shouldn't take for granted that you would go."

"Why wouldn't I?" she asked.

His nervousness increased visibly, and his expression turned grave. Emily's heart quickened just before he said, "I'm not a member of the Church, Emily."

She felt indescribably grateful that she had already pondered this, and that she knew exactly where she stood. She felt certain that with time the issue of religion would no longer be a problem. Wanting to dispel his obvious concern, she hurried to say, "I know. And I'm not an Australian."

Michael smiled, his relief as evident as his concern had been a moment ago. "Does that mean you'll go out with me again?"

"Only if you ask me. I'm a little old-fashioned that way."

"Well then." He reached across the table and took her hand. "I have two tickets for the game Saturday. Now, I'll be honest, I'm not much into football, but I am a dedicated fan of my college team."

Emily smiled. "My sentiments exactly."

"So, are you busy Saturday?"

"Yes," she said, thoroughly enjoying the disappointment in his eyes that fled when she added, "I'm going to the game with Michael Hamilton."

He laughed and squeezed her hand. The waitress brought the check, and they left the restaurant, holding hands. As Michael pulled the Blazer out onto a darkened University Avenue, he said quietly, "Would you like to do something else, or should I take you home?"

"You're driving," she said easily, feeling completely comfortable and safe. "Although, if we could find a map of Australia, you could show me Queensland."

Michael grinned and took her to his apartment where they sat together at the kitchen table as he opened a world atlas. He found the map of Australia and pointed to the area of his home, telling her briefly about the physical features surrounding it and answering her questions about the country in general.

"Show me where you had to travel to get here," she said.

He turned back to the world view at the beginning of the atlas and traced his journey with a closed pen. "I fly by private plane from home to Brisbane, then by jet to New Zealand, then to Hawaii, and on to Los Angeles, and to Salt Lake City. With stopovers, it takes about twenty-four hours."

"Wow," she said. "You're a long way from home, Mr. Hamilton. What was it about BYU that made it worth all the trouble and expense to be here?"

"You," he said with no hesitation—and no indication of humor. Meeting his eyes she couldn't help wondering if he too believed that this might be the beginning of something eternal. He glanced away and cleared his throat tensely, then added, "I simply wanted to attend college in the States. It was a dream of mine from my youth. But I wanted a good college, and I wanted one with some standards. I met some missionaries who suggested BYU, and I just knew it was right."

"What are you studying?" she asked. "Besides the Book of Mormon."

"My major is English Lit, and my minor is . . . well, food."

"Food?" she chuckled.

"Food is one of my hobbies. Cooking, to be more specific."

"Are you any good?" she asked.

"I don't know. Why don't you find out for yourself one of these days? I could use a guinea pig."

"I think I'd like that," she said, liking any allusion to sharing more time with him. She felt more fascinated with him by the minute. "Why English Lit?"

"Because I want to be a writer. I don't know why; I've just always wanted to do it."

"How very intriguing," she said.

"It's like . . . I just have this story in my head that needs to be written down, but I'd like to know a little more about writing before I attempt it."

"Just one story?"

"For the moment; maybe there will be more eventually. I suppose I'll just take it one at a time."

The conversation went on and on, winding from one topic to another. Emily's exhaustion was the only thing that made her willing to bring an end to her date with Michael. She felt as if they could have talked forever. She looked forward to going to the game with him, and when Saturday came she felt as if her life could be close to perfect so long as he was in it. The game was thoroughly enjoyable, especially since BYU won. Once it was over, they decided to just sit in the stands and visit rather than fighting the crowds. They filled the time with more conversation, and the more that she learned about Michael Hamilton, the more she loved him. Or did she? Attempting to look at the situation from a completely reasonable, logical viewpoint, she concluded that she needed more time. She could admit to being thoroughly intrigued and attracted, but love was something she'd never admitted to regarding any of her previous dating experiences. Yes, it would take time to be certain. Still, no one had ever made her feel the way Michael did.

Leaving the nearly empty stadium, Michael said, "If I had any food in the house, I'd cook you some dinner."

"Sounds like you need to go grocery shopping," she said, "unless you're like me and you've run out of grocery money until payday."

"I've got a little money kicking around," he said. "I just don't get excited about grocery shopping for one person."

"Well, we'd better go do it because you can't go tomorrow." He looked at her in question, and she clarified as if it were obvious. "Tomorrow is Sunday, Michael."

"Of course," he said and smiled. "We mustn't go shopping on Sunday." Emily smiled back, appreciating the way he accepted and respected her religion. He added, "You really want to go grocery shopping?"

"Sure. Then you can make dinner . . . if you're up to it. And I'll make dessert."

He grinned. "You've got a deal."

While Michael pushed a cart down the first aisle, Emily asked, "Are we stocking up or just getting by for a few days?"

"Stocking up would be a good idea," he replied, winking at her.

A few good laughs and a full grocery cart later they waited in the checkout line while Emily browsed through a fashion magazine. She glanced up and caught him looking at her, his eyes full of interest and adoration, an expression that made her stomach quiver.

At his apartment, she helped him carry the groceries inside and put them away. Once that was done, she watched him tuck a dish towel into the front of his jeans and begin working efficiently in the kitchen. They visited as he prepared lasagna, garlic bread, and a green salad. Once in a while he would ask her to hand him something, but he wouldn't let her help beyond that. While the lasagna was baking, Emily put together a dessert called stacked pudding that her mother made frequently. With that in the fridge, they sat together at the little kitchen table where he held her hand and asked her probing questions about life and her theories on the world, taking in her answers as if he could thrive on them. Their conversation went on through the meal they shared. Emily was so impressed with his cooking that she insisted he needed to come and cook for her roommates. And Michael eagerly agreed. His easy willingness made her wonder if he truly wanted to spend every minute with her the way she wanted to spend them with him.

Late in the evening, after the dishes were all washed and the kitchen in order, Michael finally took Emily back to her apartment. As he walked her to the door, holding her hand possessively in his, Emily took a deep breath and asked him what she'd been longing to all day. "Are you busy tomorrow?"

"Are you kidding?" he chuckled. "Everything stops in this town on Sunday."

"Not everything," she said, and the look he gave her was almost skeptical. She felt suddenly nervous as she glanced down and added, "I'm trying to ask you on a date . . . unless of course you wouldn't feel comfortable going to church with me." Emily's nervousness increased when he stared at her incredulously, as if he'd been stunned into silence. She nearly expected him to get angry and tell her that he had no interest in her religion beyond his need to take classes that met his graduation requirements at a Mormon college. Unable to bear the silence, she stammered, "It's okay if you don't want to . . . I mean . . . I'm sorry if I put you on the spot . . . or maybe—"

"Forgive me," he said. "I'm just . . . surprised, maybe even flattered." Emily looked up at him, trying to gauge what he meant. He went on to say, "I've been going to school here for three years, and not once has anyone ever invited me to go to church."

"You're joking," Emily said. Knowing how important it was for Latter-day Saints to actively share the gospel, she could hardly believe that no one he'd encountered would have ever extended the invitation. She took a deep breath of relief, realizing he wasn't offended or angry. "Well," she said, "it's a good thing I came along when I did. It would be a pleasure and an honor to have you come with me."

"Really?" he asked with a dubious chuckle, as if he couldn't quite believe what he was hearing.

"Really," she said firmly, squeezing his hand. "But it starts early. You'll have to pick me up about 8:30 if you want to get a good seat."

"Oh, we must get a good seat," he said, bringing her hand to his lips, kissing it much the way he had when she'd first introduced herself to him. "I'll see you in the morning, then."

"Thank you for a wonderful day, Michael."

"My pleasure, Emily Ladd," he said, and walked away. *She loved the way he said her name.*

The following morning he picked her up right on time, wearing slacks, a blue button-up shirt, and a tie. He seemed to enjoy the meeting, and she enjoyed being there with him, holding his hand in hers. After church they shared a sandwich at Emily's apartment, visited through the afternoon, and attended a fireside together that evening. The following day they met for lunch at the cafeteria and walked hand in hand into the class they shared. From that day forward Emily's schedule quickly became filled with Michael Hamilton. Beyond keeping up with her studies and putting in her hours at work, she was with him every possible minute. His cooking dinner for her and her roommates quickly became a Tuesday-night ritual, as did his going to church with her every Sunday. He fit in so beautifully that she couldn't help wondering why he wasn't already a Mormon. She initiated many spiritual conversations with him, and they even studied the scriptures together on occasion. But when she asked him if he would be interested in taking the missionary discussions, he simply said that he'd already done that. He frankly told her that he respected her beliefs, and he would support her completely in them. He enjoyed being a part of them, but he had no interest in joining the Church. Emily felt so deeply disappointed that she was overcome with some serious confusion. Then she recalled how clearly she had felt the guidance of the Spirit in her initial decision to date Michael. As if to echo what she had felt then, the thought came clearly to her mind: *Dating Michael is the right thing to do; he'll come around.* With that idea reconfirmed, Emily stopped worrying about his lack of interest in becoming a Latter-day Saint. She simply relaxed and enjoyed every minute she spent with him.

On a brisk Saturday in late October, more than five weeks after their first date, Michael parked the Blazer next to the Provo Tabernacle. They got out and walked hand in hand around the perimeter of the building, then through the carpet of crisp leaves covering the lawn on the north side. Emily commented on what a beautiful day it was for that time of year, then they sat together on one of the benches there. They remained in silence for a few minutes while she watched him toying with her fingers as if they were completely fascinating.

"Emily," he said in a severe tone that caught her attention. She stole a glance at his face, then had to look again. The intensity in his eyes took her breath away. Returning his gaze, she felt her heart quicken and realized she knew what he was going to say even before he said it. She'd seen it in him for weeks now, felt it in the way he treated her. In truth, she'd expected him to admit it long before now, but her respect for him had deepened with the evidence of his caution. Without a word spoken, she knew that he had been weighing and measuring his feelings very carefully, and he would not verbalize them until he was absolutely certain.

When their gaze grew long and the tension became deep, Emily said, "You were going to say something?"

He smiled warmly while the serenity in his eyes deepened. "I was," he said. His expression sobered and he lifted a hand to touch her face. "I love you, Emily Ladd," he declared firmly.

Emily took a sharp breath before she could fully absorb his declaration. While his admission wasn't a surprise, hearing it spoken felt somehow magical, as if his words had entirely awakened something inside of her that had been dormant from before her birth. It was easy for her to say, "I love you too, Michael." She pressed a hand to his face as well and watched him close his eyes as if to more fully enjoy her touch, then he pressed his lips into the palm of her hand. "In a way I think I always did," she added in a quiet voice. He opened his eyes to look at her, but put his hand over hers against his face, as if to hold it there. "I think I fell for you the minute you introduced yourself, but I was afraid that what I felt was simply too good to be true."

"But it is true," he said and for a moment she wondered if he would kiss her. Oh, she wanted him to! He only pressed a kiss to her brow while her disappointment mingled with a growing respect. He was truly a gentleman.

Nearly a month later, Michael picked Emily up at work, then drove the Blazer around the Provo Temple and through Oak Hills, stopping at a place where they could look out over the lights of the city. The view was beautiful, but Emily found Michael watching her instead.

"Emily," he said softly, "have you ever just felt that something was right, or good, even though you didn't really understand why?"

"Oh, yes," she said with fervency. "Are you referring to something in particular?"

"Well, like my reasons for coming to BYU. I couldn't ever pinpoint a reason why I felt I should attend college in the States; it's just like I always knew I should. And then when I learned about BYU, I just knew it was the school for me. Simple as that. It was right and I knew it."

"I can relate to that," Emily said.

"Well," he said, hesitating a long moment, "I have felt that way about you, Emily." She turned to look at him through the darkness, her heart pounding as he continued. "I can't define it any more than that. I only know that being with you feels more right to me than anything I have ever known before."

Emily momentarily became too emotional to speak. She turned away and tried to discreetly wipe her tears, but he asked, "Are you crying?"

Emily just sniffled and said, "I know exactly how you feel, Michael."

She heard him let out a long, deep breath, as if her words were a great relief to him. She wasn't sure who initiated the embrace; she only knew that it happened. Stretching across the space between the bucket seats, Michael held her close and laughed softly near her ear. He drew back slightly and touched the tears on her face. Feeling embarrassed by her emotion, she attempted to turn away, but he took her chin into his fingers and brought her back to face him. With gentle purpose he meekly touched his lips to hers, then he eased back as if to gauge her reaction. It wasn't until she drew a deep breath that she realized she hadn't breathed for several seconds. She put her hand to his face, and he kissed her again. It began timidly, then softened and turned warm. Still, she felt him holding back, as if he didn't want any hint of aggression to mar this moment. When their kiss ended, he touched her face, her hair, her face again, like a blind man absorbing something rare and lovely. Never had she felt more beautiful!

"I think I'd better take you home," he muttered close to her ear.

Emily heard an unfamiliar dreaminess in her own voice as she replied, "That would likely be the wise thing to do."

She felt his reluctance in easing away, then he cleared his throat and chuckled before he drove toward her apartment. On the doorstep he kissed her again. Once alone Emily crawled into her bed, Michael's kiss still lingering on her lips. Oh, how she loved him! She felt as if she had loved him from the beginning of time, and she would love him forever.

* * *

Emily snuggled deeper into her bed, pondering how thoroughly familiar Michael's kiss had become to her, and how lost she had felt without it through the years since his death. She missed him perhaps more than she ever had, but she couldn't deny feeling a deep contentment with her sure knowledge of the love they shared. She loved him no less than the day he'd died, and she felt certain his love for her was equally strong. One day, she reminded herself, they would be together again. And with that she drifted to sleep.

Chapter Two

Emily woke to find dawn's light filling the room. She contemplated the memories that had serenaded her to sleep. She actually chuckled to recall the firm conviction she'd felt from the Spirit telling her, *Dating Michael is the right thing to do; he'll come around.* Well, he had certainly come around, but not for more than a decade. Looking back it was easy to see that dating him truly had been the right thing to do, just as marrying another man had been right at the time. She and Michael had been foreordained to be together; they'd both been told as much in priesthood blessings. But they'd both had much to learn and many experiences that had been necessary for both of them. If she had known then what she knew now, oh the grief it could have saved them! But such a wish was futile, and in her heart she knew that the struggles they had blindly waded through had been a necessary part of their earth-life experience.

Emily drifted back to sleep and dreamt that Michael was sitting beside her on the edge of the bed, holding her hand just as he'd done countless times through their years together.

"Are you going to sleep all day?" he asked, bending over to kiss her cheek.

"Oh, Michael," she said as she sat to face him, and he sat up straight, pulling her into his arms. They shared a long embrace while she muttered near his ear how she loved him, how she missed him and longed to be with him.

"I love you too," he whispered, "more than ever." He looked into her eyes and touched her face, just as he'd done the first time he'd kissed her, just as he'd done more than a thousand times in the years since. "I wish we could be together, darlin', but the time's just not right. One day . . . soon, we will be together again. I promise."

He kissed her once more then hurried away, glancing at his watch on his way out the door. Emily looked at the closed door, thinking she should just get out of bed and go with him. She didn't care where he might be going; she only wanted to be with him.

A baby crying in the distance woke Emily, and she gasped as the reality of the present struck her. The closed door looked just the same as it had in her dream. She found it somehow symbolic of the veil between this life and the next that separated her from her husband.

Emily stayed in bed for a long while with clear images of her dreams lingering in her mind, feeling almost as if she'd truly been with Michael. She longed to just huddle beneath the covers and hold the memories close, but she was left with a feeling that their brief visit had been crammed into a very busy schedule, and he'd hurried away to meet other obligations. She was reminded of the time Michael had served as a branch president, and later, as a bishop. He'd always been in a hurry to get to a meeting or to help someone in need. Emily had remained mostly ignorant of what he'd been doing, since much of it fell under the confidentiality of his calling. And that's how it seemed now. She could clearly imagine the responsibilities he might be about on the other side of the veil. And while he might want to be close to her, he simply had more important matters that required his attention; matters that she could never understand from her perspective. Feeling that empty, lonely sensation deepen inside of her, Emily forced herself out of bed, certain that keeping herself busy would ease much of her ailment.

In the shower Emily tried again to remove her wedding ring, feeling torn even as she did. When it wouldn't budge she thought that perhaps it was a sign. Maybe it was right and good that she continue to wear it, and she just needed to rid herself of this silly feeling.

Once dressed and prepared to meet the day, Emily went down to the kitchen and felt immediately better when she entered the room. She shared her home with two families, which added up to a total of five adults, beyond herself, and six children. The home was huge with plenty of room to spread out and allow her son's family, and her daughter's family, to have their own living quarters and separate activities—but they all shared the kitchen. She was often amazed at how well they all got along—for the most part, anyway. They had schedules worked out for meals and dishes, and it was always flexible contingent upon illness, unexpected occurrences, or bad days.

"Good morning, Mother," Jess smiled, being the first to notice her.

"Good morning," she replied, smiling back at a near replica of his father. Jess was her fourth child but her oldest son, and the first child born to Michael. Jess Michael Hamilton, the fourth—to be exact. He ran the boys' home, which was literally connected to the house, and it had been a family business for generations. At the moment he was busy at the stove, flipping pancakes—animal pancakes, she noticed; it was something his father had taught him. Jess's wife, Tamra, was busy at the counter stirring a pitcher of orange juice. Tamra's Aunt Rhea, who also lived in the home, was putting Jess and Tamra's youngest child, Claire, into a highchair. Two-year-old Claire had three older brothers, who were already seated at the table, impatient for their pancakes. Evelyn was the oldest child in the house; she was the daughter of James and Krista, who had been killed when Evelyn was a baby. Jess and Tamra had adopted her before they'd had children of their own, and she was now an official part of their family. Michael was the first born to Jess and Tamra, and he was now six. Like his forebears he was actually named Jess Michael Hamilton—the fifth, in his case. At the table with Michael were the twins, Joshua and Tyson. They were not identical and looked barely like brothers, although they were both equally rambunctious at the age of five.

"Have a seat, Mom," Emily's daughter, Emma, said as she closed the fridge and set the milk on the table. Her husband, Scott, was seated at the table with their infant daughter, Laura, on his lap. She wasn't quite crawling yet, but capable of sitting up and being very responsive.

"I will, thank you," Emily said, reaching out for little Laura, who gave her grandmother a big grin. "I heard you making a fuss this morning," Emily said to the baby, who just grinned again and kicked her chubby little feet. Laura was a miracle baby, considering that her mother, Emma, had gone through pregnancy and childbirth with only one kidney—a kidney that had been donated to her by her brother, Jess. The kidney transplant had been one of many traumatic events the family had endured, but Emma's pregnancy had gone rather smoothly, and life had been good for the family for quite some time.

Everyone was seated, and Scott offered a blessing on the food. Like Tamra, Scott was American and a great asset to the family. He oversaw the stables and everything to do with the horses, which kept him busy with one aspect of the family business, while Jess handled the other at the boys' home. Jess and Scott were great friends, and in fact Scott had moved into the home as Jess's friend long before anything romantic had ever developed between Scott and Emma.

Emily played with the baby while Jess provided animal pancakes for the children, then ordinary round ones for the adults. She found great delight in being with her family, but for reasons she couldn't define, this morning she felt empty. Perhaps she'd been lingering too much in the past—and yet she felt lured to it in a way.

"You look tired, Mom," Tamra said, bringing Emily from her thoughts.

"Oh, I'm alright," Emily said. "Just had trouble falling asleep last night, for some reason."

"Any reason in particular?" Scott asked with mild concern.

Emily hesitated and Jess added, "Be honest, Mother. Isn't that what you taught us?" He raised his voice to mimic her. "We're family and we talk about our feelings."

"Who taught you to be so insolent?" Emily asked with a little laugh.

"It must have been my father," Jess said with light sarcasm.

"Oh, yeah," Scott said, "that's his reputation, all right. Insolent. Huh!"

"He was the finest man who ever lived," Emma said.

"Well . . . yeah," Jess countered. "Don't you know sarcasm when you hear it?"

"Just making it clear," Emma said. "I mean . . . he could be in the room for all we know, and here you are talking about him that way."

"I'm sure his sense of humor lives on," Jess said with a sly smirk toward his sister, who comically stuck her tongue out at him, making him laugh.

"I'm afraid he's too busy to be hovering around the breakfast table," Emily said. She hadn't realized how severe it must have sounded until they all turned toward her with wide, concerned eyes.

"What makes you think so?" Jess asked in a voice that was tender, perhaps worried.

"Just a hunch," she said, wishing she'd not brought it up.

"Your hunches on such things are something I pay attention to," Scott said. More lightly he added, "Come on; we're family. We talk about our feelings."

Emily chuckled but it came out sounding forced. "I just . . . think he's busy elsewhere. I mean . . . when there were challenges he often seemed nearby, supporting and helping us through. But things have been better lately, and . . . I think he's needed elsewhere."

"You're saying he feels more distant," Tamra said gently.

"Yes, I suppose so," Emily said.

"Well, what we need is a good catastrophe to bring in the angelic cavalry," Scott said with drama.

"Heaven forbid!" Emily said. "I've had enough trauma for two lifetimes. I'm going to enjoy the peace, thank you very much."

"I know I'm enjoying it," Emma said just before the twins began fighting over who had finished their pancake first.

Jess broke it up, then said to his mother, "Are you okay, Mom? I mean if—"

He was interrupted by Laura spitting up. Scott grabbed a towel and lunged for the baby, which spared Emily's clothes, but the baby's clothes were covered with the strained fruit she'd eaten twenty minutes ago. While Scott was managing the mess, Claire dumped her plate on the floor, and little Michael spilled his juice.

"Yeah, enjoy the peace," Rhea said, helping wipe up the spills, and they all laughed.

Emily was glad that Jess's inquiry had been lost in a typical meal-time disaster. She had no desire to try to explain how disconcerted she felt, when she had trouble understanding it herself. Within minutes the men were off to see to their work. Tamra was washing the dishes while Emma and Rhea took the children outside to play. Emily took little Laura out to the veranda to watch the other children. She loved to sit in this spot and look out over the huge lawn that sloped down toward the stables and corrals. It was a beautiful place to live, and she often thought of the generations of women before her who had sat in this very place and observed the years passing as family members came and went and found joy in calling this home.

Through the day Emily went about her usual routine, feeling almost as if she were in some kind of fog. A formless confusion continued to hover in her mind. She felt drawn to holding onto her love for Michael, their marriage, their history, all they had shared and would continue to share. But a large part of her felt drawn to move away, to let go, to press forward. Three more times through the day she attempted to remove her wedding ring with no success. Again she wondered if that was a sign or simply an extension of her habitual feelings. Over the next few days she managed to stay cheerful enough around the family to avoid any inquiries that she had no desire to try and justify, but eventually Jess cornered her one evening after supper. He found her on the veranda where she had been sitting for nearly an hour, lost in thought.

Jess came through the library doors to see his mother sitting in her favorite spot, but there was a cloud hovering in her expression that wasn't normal. And he felt concerned. Her comments a few days ago at the breakfast table had lingered in his mind, and he couldn't help wondering what might be going on in her personal struggle to live without his father. Taking a moment to watch her sitting there, he found it difficult to think of her as even being old enough to have teenaged grandchildren. His older sisters were spread out from Australia to California to Utah, with children much older than his own. But Emily Hamilton had a youthful aura about her that always surprised people when she told them she had grandchildren who were dating. The way she dressed and wore her hair, the way she carried herself and the things she did—there was nothing old about her. Except for that look in her eyes. For the first time in her life, Emily's eyes looked old— or at the very least, tired and weary. And he felt concerned.

"Hello, Mom," he said, and she looked up.

"Hello," she said, smiling brightly. But it didn't dispel the clouds in her eyes. "What are you up to?"

"That's what I came to ask you," he said, sitting close beside her.

"I'm just . . . enjoying the evening air."

Following a minute of silence, Jess put a hand over hers and asked gently, "What's wrong, Mom?"

"I don't know how to answer that question," she said.

"Is that why you've been avoiding me?"

"Was I?"

"Sort of," he said with a chuckle. "Try anyway."

"What?"

"To answer the question," he said. When she didn't respond, he added, "Does it have something to do with Dad?" Still she said nothing. Jess sighed and leaned his forearms on his thighs. "You would think after six years we'd get used to being without him, but . . . well, we've adjusted, but I don't think I'll ever stop missing him." Jess heard his mother sniffle and looked over his shoulder to see her holding a tissue beneath her nose while tears leaked from beneath her closed eyelids. "That's it, isn't it," he said, wiping at her tears. "You miss him."

"More than I can believe," she admitted, and the tears burst out of her. Jess turned his chair and eased her into his arms, holding her tightly while she cried. "Oh, Jess, I love him so much!"

"I know you do."

"But . . . it's like I said the other day. He just feels more . . . distant. I mean . . . it's not like I felt him with me all the time. It was only an occasional thing, and most of the time it was subtle. But, somehow I knew he was aware of us, and I didn't feel alone. But recently, it's just like . . . the separation has become more . . . painful, more difficult somehow."

Jess listened to his mother's words, mingled with her tears. He held her close and let her cry, unable to hold back his own tears. It wasn't like her to fall apart and break down this way. He wondered how long she'd been holding her emotions inside, with no husband to cry to.

"Oh, I'm sorry," she said, easing away and wiping at her face. "I really didn't need to—"

"Maybe you did need to," he said. "You have every right in the world to have a good cry once in a while. When I think how much I miss him, I can't even imagine how difficult it must be for you to live without him." He adjusted his chair and put his arm around her; she settled her head on his shoulder. "I mean . . . the two of you are like peanut butter and jelly."

Emily laughed softly. "That's a terribly American thing to say."

"Well, my mother is American, you know. She's an amazing woman."

"Oh, I don't feel amazing, Jess. I feel . . . old."

"You're not old," he insisted.

"Well, I don't want to be old, I just *feel* old. I don't want to be without him anymore, Jess."

Jess let that statement settle into him and felt decidedly panicked. He leaned forward to look at her face. "What are you saying?"

"I'm saying that I'm tired of this . . . separation. I miss him. I want to be with him."

"But you can't leave us. You've got years left to . . . be here, to be a part of our lives."

"I'm not telling you that I'm going to die anytime soon, Jess. I'm just telling you how I feel. It's hard. That doesn't mean I can do anything about it. He's living in one place, and I'm living in another. I'm sure my time on earth is predetermined, just as his was. I just . . . miss him."

Jess relaxed again. "Well . . . that's understandable, but . . . what are your options?"

"I don't have any. I have to make the most of the life I have left. And in order to do that I need to stop feeling sorry for myself. I mean . . . look at my life. Beyond being without Michael, I have everything I could ever ask for. Millions of women would kill to live my life. I'm so richly blessed."

"Yes, we have a good life," he said, "but don't forget the perspective here, Mom. We've been through some pretty tough things—you especially. You've worked hard to have this life; you deserve to be richly blessed."

Emily looked at him and smiled. She pressed her hand to his face. "You're so precious to me, Jess."

"It's the other way around, Mother."

"You're so much like him in so many ways."

Jess glanced down and had to admit, "Sometimes I wonder if that's good."

"Why wouldn't it be?"

"Well . . . you've admitted more than once that having me look so much like him is difficult in some ways."

"But not as difficult as it is a blessing. I'm so grateful for you." She smiled again. "Thank you for letting me have a good cry."

"A pleasure, any time," he said, and came to his feet. "Come along." He held out a hand for her. "It's past your bedtime, young lady."

Emily laughed softly and walked into the house with Jess's arm about her shoulders. They walked up the stairs together and he kissed her goodnight, leaving her alone. That was always the hard part, being left alone at the end of the day. She took something mild to help her sleep, but still woke at dawn and felt restless. She got up and put on a bathrobe before she tiptoed down the stairs, finding the house eerily quiet. She was drawn to her favorite spot on the veranda and made herself comfortable in her favorite chair. Since she was facing west, she couldn't see the sun come up, but she loved the way the view changed hues as it did. She'd first noticed the effect more years ago than she could count, when she had come here for the first time between college semesters. How clearly she remembered the night that she and Michael had sat in this very spot, talking all through the night. They'd both been surprised when the sky began to grow light, then they'd gone to their separate rooms to sleep most of the day. Never in her youth would she have imagined having such an adventure as traveling to Australia with a dashing young man. Traveling at all had hardly entered into her mind, and even through the first few months of dating Michael, the idea of going to his home-land had never occurred to her. Even knowing he was Australian, and hearing him talk often of his home and family, she never imagined going there herself. He'd often joked about taking her there, but she had always taken it as just that—a joke.

"What is this?" Emily asked, staring into the flat box that she'd just unwrapped.

"It's your Christmas present," Michael said.

"Since it had Christmas paper on it, I had figured that much." She giggled. "But . . . what is it?"

"It's a passport application," he said, and it took Emily thirty seconds to even conceive the connection. She looked up at him and felt her mouth fall open. He let out a delighted laugh, as if her reaction was exactly what he'd hoped for. "It's time to get a passport,

Emily. And then we have to get the visa. If you're going to come home with me to meet my family, we need to get started."

"You're serious," she said breathlessly.

"Of course I'm serious," he said, almost sounding offended. "I've been talking about it for weeks."

"But I thought . . ."

"What?"

"That you were just . . . joking or something."

"Emily?" He laughed again. "How could I possibly marry a woman who hasn't even seen my home? We'll go this summer, because it will be winter back home, and the weather will be perfectly pleasant, not so hot."

Emily let out a chuckle of disbelief. "I can't believe it. What are you going to do? Just . . . cart me away for a week?"

"A month, more like," he said. "If we're taking the trip, we're going to make it worthwhile."

Days later Emily was still stunned by the idea of traveling to the other side of the world, where even the seasons were backwards. Michael helped her fill out the application, and took her to get an appropriate picture taken. Once a copy of her birth certificate had been located, he took her to the passport office and paid all the fees. Weeks passed and she became immersed in life as usual. When the passport actually arrived, she was stunned all over again. It took more time to get the visa taken care of, but when that came through she began to realize that she was actually going to Australia. As of yet she hadn't mentioned the idea to her parents. It had felt so ridiculous and out of reach. She knew Michael was right when he said that she was an adult and the decision to go was up to her. Still, she felt better about asking her parents' permission for such an endeavor, and Michael respected her wishes completely. She knew that in spite of their traveling a great distance together, there would be no concern about their remaining chaste. Through all their months of dating he had never done anything more than kiss her, and never once had his affection made her feel uncomfortable. The flights to his home would be long, but they wouldn't actually be staying anywhere until they arrived at the house, where his mother had a room prepared for her.

As the time to make travel arrangements drew closer, Michael traveled with Emily to her home in Idaho where he conscientiously requested permission of Mr. and Mrs. Ladd to escort their daughter to his homeland to meet his family. He phoned with reverse charges to his home and introduced Mrs. Ladd to his mother. The two mothers found much in common and talked for nearly an hour, after which permission was given. Two days later Michael booked the flights and Emily started counting the days until she would embark upon the adventure of a lifetime. She hardly dared entertain the idea that if she truly ended up marrying Michael, Australia could become her permanent home. While she'd not yet seen his home, she felt relatively certain that she could handle it. Still, she was keeping an open mind. More and more she couldn't imagine her future without Michael in it. They were as close as two people could be and still remain chaste. She loved him deeply, and she knew he loved her. He was everything she had ever dreamed of in a husband—except for that one big neon problem. He wasn't a member of the Church, and she had very strong convictions about marrying in the temple. She kept reminding herself that the Spirit had told her clearly Michael would come around. Emily did her best to put her trust in the Lord and have the faith that it would all work out for the best.

When the day finally came to begin their journey, Emily was so full of nervous excitement she could hardly breathe. She'd never flown before at all, and she had no idea what to expect. A friend took them to the airport in Salt Lake City and they were soon underway. Michael often looked at her and chuckled, as if her nervousness and blatant awe over the experience were simply a delight.

They had some time in the airport in Hawaii, where they wandered around and got something to eat. Emily asked Michael to tell her what they would do when they arrived at his home. "Well, first of all, we're both going to take a very long nap and see if we can adjust to the jet lag. And then the possibilities are endless. Most importantly is that I'm going to teach you to ride."

"To what?" she asked, trying to sound serious.

"To ride," he explained. "You know, ride horses."

"Oh," she said with mock enlightenment. "*Ride.* Why didn't you say so?"

"I did," he said, letting out a baffled chuckle.

"No," she pointed a finger at him, "you said 'roid.'" She mimicked his accent; he laughed and threw a napkin at her.

They were soon en route again. Michael had told her the flights were long, and he'd even shown her the flight itinerary, stating how many hours each leg of the journey would last. But the reality of actually being on the plane all through the night and into the next day left her stunned. She couldn't comprehend the vast miles of ocean they were passing over. She tried to rest but had trouble relaxing. But Michael was always right beside her, often holding her hand, making her feel that she could take on any obstacle so long as he was at her side.

"You okay?" he asked at one point when she had been staring out the window for several minutes.

"I'm just a little . . . nervous. What if your family doesn't like me?"

"Oh, Emily. They will love you. After all, I do."

"And I love you," she said, touching his face.

"Yes, but you're blind to my faults."

"I'm not blind to your faults," she insisted. "If you must know, I've tried to pick you apart with a fine-tooth comb in search of your faults."

"And what did you find?" he asked, seeming amused.

"You used to leave the sink dirty after you cooked at my apartment," she said. "But after I said something about it, you never left it dirty again."

"My mother wouldn't be happy with my leaving the sink dirty," he said with mock severity. "But surely you found something more than that wrong with me."

Emily wanted to say that the only flaw in him was that he didn't share her religious beliefs, but his unquestionable support made it hardly justified. She just smiled and said, "I love everything about you."

Emily put her head against Michael's shoulder and drifted to sleep, but not nearly long enough. By the time they actually landed on Australian soil, she was exhausted. In Brisbane they were met by the pilot of a private plane that had been arranged to take them to Michael's home. As they flew, Michael pointed out the landscape and places of interest. Emily held his hand tightly, feeling more overwhelmed and in awe the farther she got from her own home. She drifted to sleep after a while and woke up when Michael nudged her, saying, "We're almost there."

Emily wiped the sleep out of her eyes and focused on the view out the window as the plane made a wide, sweeping circle, but she felt a little too dazed to realize what she was seeing. The pilot made a smooth landing on a dry, flat stretch of land. While they were getting the luggage out of the plane, she noticed a vehicle coming toward them on a dirt road, with a cloud of dust trailing behind. The Toyota Land Cruiser stopped beside them, and a rough-looking man got out. Michael introduced Murphy and added, "He's been working with us forever."

"At least," Murphy said. Then he tipped his hat toward her, saying, "A pleasure, Miss Ladd."

"The pleasure is mine," Emily said.

Once the luggage had been loaded, Murphy handed Michael the keys before he climbed into the back seat. Michael opened the passenger door of the Cruiser for Emily, although it took her a moment to figure out what he was doing before she climbed in. Michael sat in the driver's seat, and she commented, "The steering wheel is on the wrong side, Michael."

"That all depends on whether or not you're an Australian," he said with a little smirk.

Murphy asked Emily where she was from. She turned to tell him, and they began chatting comfortably. Michael interjected, "Murphy's great-grandfather worked in our stables when my great-grandfather was struggling to keep this land in the 1880s."

"How fascinating," Emily said, more to Murphy than to Michael.

The conversation ceased, allowing Emily to fully absorb her surroundings as they drove beneath an iron archway that read: Byrnehouse-Davies. The dirt road merged into a paved one, and they drove past the boys' home Michael had told her about. It was a beautiful building that looked like a combination of a hotel and a school. The road then wound through some trees and around a large, Victorian home that took Emily's breath away. As Michael parked the Cruiser, Emily turned to look the other way, and her gaze took in the stables and racing facilities. She felt suddenly as if a bucket of cold water had been thrown in her face. In an instant many little things she had known about Michael suddenly made perfect sense. It had crossed her mind more than once that his family was likely well off. The fact that he was attending college on a different continent and that he could afford to bring her home with him certainly indicated some measure of affluence. But seeing for herself the place where he had been raised brought everything together perfectly in her mind. She turned to him, eyes wide, noting that he looked somehow guilty. He'd been holding out on her and he knew it.

Emily didn't have a chance to say anything before Michael and Murphy unloaded the luggage and carried it toward the house. Emily picked up the smaller of her bags and followed. Before the men reached the door, a woman came running out and Michael immediately dropped the bags in order to hug her tightly. From pictures she had seen, Emily knew it was Michael's mother, but she was more vibrant and attractive than her pictures had portrayed. She drew back from the hug and took Michael's face into her hands, saying warmly, "You do look different since you got that degree; more educated or something."

Michael laughed and hugged his mother again. Once their greeting was finished, Michael turned toward Emily, saying with a broad smile, "Emily, this is the other lady in my life—my mother, LeNay Hamilton. Mother, this is Emily Ladd."

"I am so thrilled to finally meet you," LeNay said, stepping forward to hug Emily, letting out a delighted burst of laughter as she did. She took Emily's shoulders into her hands and said with a little wink, "I hope my son has been a gentleman."

"Oh, he has!" Emily said firmly.

"That's good then," LeNay said, and turned toward the house, putting her arm through Emily's. "We're going to have to make certain you have a wonderful time while you're here, then maybe you'll want to come back." LeNay looked back at Michael and winked again. He chuckled and picked up the luggage, following them inside.

Emily was stunned speechless as she stepped into the house and followed Michael up what LeNay called "the back stairs." On the landing Emily gave Michael a hard glare and she felt certain that he knew her thoughts by the way he shrugged sheepishly and led the way to one of what she realized were many guest rooms. LeNay pointed out certain features of the room, concluding in a quiet voice, "Much of the furnishings are original from when the house was built in the 1880s."

"It's beautiful," Emily said, meaning it. The house wasn't gaudy or excessive. She was simply having trouble accepting what it meant in relation to this man she had fallen in love with.

LeNay moved toward the door. "Well, I'll leave you to get settled in, Emily. Let me know if you need anything at all. Supper will be ready in another hour or so."

"Thank you, Mother," Michael said.

"It's good to have you home," she said, winking at him before leaving the room.

Once she was alone with Michael, Emily said firmly, "J. Michael Hamilton, you've been holding out on me."

"I don't know what you're talking about," he said with mock innocence.

"You know perfectly well what I'm talking about. I may be a simple farm girl, but I'm intelligent enough to recognize old money when I see it."

Michael sighed loudly and sat in a tapestried wingback chair, hanging his leg over the arm. "What did you expect me to do, Emily? I doubt you'd have thought much of me if I'd said, 'Let's go out again tomorrow. By the way, I'm rich.'"

Emily had to admit, "That's what most men would have done—if only indirectly."

"Exactly." He pointed a finger at her. "I really wasn't trying to hide it. I just didn't think it was necessary to bring it up formally. So now that you know, I would like you to know my stand on money."

"I'm listening," she said when he hesitated.

"I was raised to use it wisely, give it where it's needed, and to pretend I don't have it. As long as you didn't know I was rich, I didn't have to wonder if you were attracted to my money. Not that I would have anyway. You're not that kind of girl. But I've come across a few who were, and I just prefer to keep it to myself."

Emily looked at him deeply and had to admit, "I understand, Michael. I'm not angry, really, just . . . surprised."

"Maybe I should have told you sooner," he admitted.

"It's okay," she said, looking out the window at the view of the stable yard below. "Might I ask just how rich you are?"

Michael gave an embarrassed chuckle. "You want the truth?"

"Of course I want the truth," she said.

"When you become Mrs. Hamilton, I'll let you take over the checkbook," he said lightly. "I guess you should know the truth."

She turned and gave him a comical glare, which made him chuckle. But he still seemed embarrassed. "You don't have to tell me if you don't want to," she said.

"It's okay," he said more seriously. "Really, you should know. Our family has been very blessed this way, but it can bring on some unique challenges as well. If you're going to be a part of the family, you should know what you're getting into."

"You make it sound like I would be marrying into the mafia or something."

"It's not quite that bad," he said, seeming serious. She realized then that he really did see the money as more of a challenge than anything. "But . . . it's a secret. I don't want anybody to know."

"Okay, I understand."

"You see . . . in American money, Byrnehouse-Davies and Hamilton, which is in essence the family estate originating from Jess Davies and Alexa Byrnehouse, who were married in 1890, is presently worth somewhere in the neighborhood of . . ." He leaned forward and motioned for her to come closer. Even though they were the only ones in the room, he whispered an amount in her ear, as if he didn't want the walls to overhear. She made him repeat it, certain she'd heard him wrong. Then she had to admit that she'd never even stopped to comprehend such an amount of money.

"You're kidding," she said with a dubious chuckle.

"No," he replied almost guiltily.

"You're kidding." She laughed.

He shook his head and laughed with her. "Will you still marry me?" he asked as if he seriously wondered if she might not, now that she knew the truth.

"You haven't asked me; I'm a little old-fashioned that way."

He grinned, but his eyes became tender. "I'm going to do that one of these days."

"So, where did it come from?" she asked.

"What?"

"The money, silly."

"Oh, the money. Well, my great-grandfather, Jess Davies, was the son of a miner who came to Australia to make his fortune. He did well enough, steaded this land and built this home. Well . . . actually it wasn't *this* home. It was one that looked just like it. After he died, the house burned to the ground. Jess mortgaged the land to build another house . . . *this* house. For years he struggled to keep his land, betting everything on horse races and scraping by. As the story goes, he married Alexandra Byrnehouse, who was later declared to be one of the best horse trainers in Australia. Eventually they inherited everything her father owned. There's more to the story that I'll tell you eventually, but apparently Tyson Byrnehouse was extremely wealthy. He was not only the second son of an English Earl or something, but he had made some good investments here in Australia that had paid off well. So Jess and Alexa merged the name to Byrnehouse-Davies and built the boys' home, and they dove into the breeding and racing business. In essence the horses have kept the boys' home funded, and most of the time they cover the cost of running the station and—"

"The what?"

"The station . . . the . . ." He snapped his fingers in a way that was common while he tried to think of the American equivalent. "The . . . estate . . . the ranch."

"Ah." She nodded, enlightened.

"Anyway, very little money actually comes out of the original fortune, so it just keeps growing. My family, right back to Jess, has always had strong policies on giving away as much as we can manage without getting obtrusive. And the boys' home is a good way to use it up. My grandfather, Michael Hamilton the first, was brought to the boys' home at age eleven, and it was discovered later that he'd been beaten and tortured by his father. He grew up here and eventually ended up marrying Jess and Alexa's daughter, Emma, and Jess gave him a job as the administrator of the boys' home. The records prove that he worked miracles with the boys, and the tradition has carried on. Two of my cousins run the home now, for the most part, and my family oversees the horses. I'm not certain how it happened, but I inherited the house."

"This is yours?" She looked around, and he nodded sheepishly.

"Technically, yes. You see, I'm the only direct male descendant. But then, it's all really just part of the family estate when you look at the big picture. The home is still used as it was originally intended— as an extended family home. My sister's family will always live here as well, and my mother, of course."

"Incredible," Emily said. "And I thought I knew everything about you."

"Now you do." He leaned forward. "Do you still love me?"

"Forever," she said. "If nothing else, I don't feel so guilty about what it must have cost you to get me here."

"You shouldn't anyway," he said, coming to his feet. "Now, why don't you freshen up a bit, and we'll go eat something. I think we'll turn in early tonight and sleep off the jet lag. When you're feeling up to it, I'll give you the grand tour, and maybe I'll even take you riding."

"Roiding?" she said, mimicking his accent, and he growled at her, which made her laugh.

"My room is in the next hall, two doors down, if you need me. I'll come back in . . ." he glanced at his watch, "about forty minutes to get you for supper."

"Is it casual?"

"It's always casual," he said, and left her alone.

Chapter Three

Once Emily recovered from the jet lag, she began absorbing Michael's world as if she had flown to Neverland. LeNay Hamilton was kind and warm, and Emily felt completely comfortable with her. Emily was disappointed to realize that Michael's only sibling, his older sister, was out of the country with her husband's family and wouldn't be returning until after Emily went back to the States. His only other immediate family was his mother, since his father had passed away many years earlier.

Emily loved watching Michael mesh into his surroundings so perfectly, especially in the stables and around the horses. Watching him curry a fine stallion, she commented to him, "This is obviously a place where you feel very comfortable."

"This is home," he said, looking around serenely, then he set his gaze firmly on her. "With any luck it will be your home too." Emily smiled, and he added, "What would you think of making Australia your home, Emily?" She felt her eyes widen, and he added, "I mean . . . not right away. I want you to get your degree first and . . ."

"Is this a proposal?" she asked.

"Of course not." He smiled. "This is a speculation. Proposals come on bended knee in romantic settings, don't they?"

"I suppose that depends on who is doing the proposing."

"Well, when I propose, you'll know it."

"Is this . . . foreshadowing, then?" she asked impishly.

"Quite." He smiled slyly, then became serious. "Do you think you could be happy here, Emily?"

"If I said yes, we wouldn't have any reason to stay here a month, so ask me later."

"I'll do that," he said. "For now I think it's time I taught you to ride."

"I'll try to *ride*," she said, "but I'm not sure if I can *roid.*"

"Ah, shut up," he insisted lightly, kissing her.

Using what Michael called the family's age-old technique in teaching children to ride, he saddled one horse and helped Emily mount, then he quickly got into the saddle behind her, reaching around her to take the reins. She grabbed onto his legs when the horse danced slightly, and Michael chuckled. "It's alright, Emily," he said. "She's as gentle as a lamb, and I'm in full control. See, watch this." He demonstrated the movement of the reins and horse's reactions, then he walked the mare outside. They rode for the better part of the morning so she could get a feel for the basic skills without having to think about it. She laughed and held tightly to Michael when he took the horse through a long gallop, then they cantered back toward the corrals. Michael moved the reins into his right hand and pushed his arm around her waist with a warm embrace. She put her hand over his, and he said behind her ear, "I love you, Emily Ladd."

"I love you too, J. Michael Hamilton," she said.

Emily was almost disappointed when Michael dismounted. In spite of being somewhat saddle sore, she enjoyed being so close to him.

"What do you think so far?" he asked, taking hold of her waist to help her down.

"I think I like it," she said with enthusiasm.

"Good." He smiled. "Tomorrow we'll get you on a horse of your own."

Through the following days Emily took to riding with little trouble. When Michael challenged her to ride his prize stallion and she did it successfully, he rewarded her with a pair of black leather riding boots that she described as beautifully classic.

On quiet afternoons, Michael got out family history records and journals and photographs of all the people he'd told her stories about. They got into long conversations about genealogy, and Emily found an opportunity to tell him more about the purpose of temples. He seemed intrigued but said nothing about his feelings on the subject. Emily became thoroughly fascinated with Michael's family history, and she couldn't help feeling a desire to become a part of it.

Through her visit, Emily quickly became comfortable in Michael's home and with his lifestyle. She had long talks with LeNay and enjoyed helping her and Michael in the kitchen. Michael said more than once that she fit into his home and his life like a missing puzzle piece, and she couldn't deny feeling the same way.

As the time drew closer for Emily to return to the States, she felt a deep sadness envelop her. Two days before her scheduled departure, she and Michael sat on the veranda and talked all through the night. She realized that she'd never felt happier or more content. But when she thought of having to leave this place, sadness overtook her. She felt as if she belonged here, and leaving just didn't seem right.

The following day, after catching up on her sleep, Emily was struck with a reality she didn't know how to confront. Michael had alluded to marriage many times in their conversations, and she felt certain it was inevitable. Still, her feelings about marrying in the temple had not lessened. In analyzing her love for Michael, and how deeply comfortable she felt in his world, she had asked herself a thousand times if she should be willing to marry him under any circumstances, with the firm belief that eventually he would come around and embrace her beliefs. But the feeling remained strong inside of her that marrying in the temple was the right thing to do. She also felt strongly that Michael *would* come around, and she needed to be patient. She was willing to wait a reasonable amount of time for him to be ready for baptism. And she was willing to wait through the required time following baptism until he would be able to go to the temple. But with the time that had passed, she began to wonder if any amount of waiting would be futile. In spite of his unquestioning support of her beliefs, and his willingness to participate in any activity related to her religion, he had given no indication that joining the Church had ever entered his mind.

The night before they would be leaving to go back to the States, Emily felt downright depressed. She made great effort to keep a cheery façade, but she felt sure Michael could see through her efforts. He proved her right as they walked hand in hand around the house after supper. He broke the silence between them by asking, "What's wrong, Emily?"

"How do you know something's wrong?" she asked, not completely serious.

"Your efforts in being cheerful are admirable, Emily. But I know something's wrong."

"How perceptive you are," she said softly, putting her arm around his waist. He tightened his arm around her shoulders as they walked. She sighed deeply and leaned her head onto his shoulder. "I just don't want to go home, Michael. Everything just feels so . . . perfect here."

"Everything here feels better with you in the middle of it," he said, pressing a kiss into her hair. "With any luck it won't be long before you can make this home."

"That's a nice thought," she said, then sighed again.

Following a length of silence, Michael said in a tender voice, "I want you to know, Emily, how much I appreciate your acceptance of our differences."

Emily stopped walking and looked up at him. "What differences?" she asked.

"Well," he sounded subtly nervous, "beyond growing up on different continents, the only thing I can think of would be religious differences."

Emily looked down abruptly. While it was tempting to try and express how she *really* felt about that, her tongue felt swollen in her mouth, leaving her completely incapable of speaking.

Michael took her shoulders into his hands and looked into her eyes. "When we first met, I was so thoroughly stricken with you, and . . . my deepest fear was that you wouldn't even consider going out with me because I wasn't a member. But you did. You've never once let it come between us, and I want you to know that I'm grateful. One of the many things I love about our relationship is the way we can respect and support each other's beliefs, and in spite of our differences, we can be so thoroughly happy together."

Emily watched her view of Michael become blurred behind the rising tears in her eyes. She blinked and felt them fall down her face. He smiled and wiped them away before he bent to kiss her. It was obvious he believed her tears were evidence that she shared his sentiment. She couldn't bring herself to tell him the truth. She'd banked everything on his eventually joining the Church so that they could be married in the temple. She couldn't question the peace she'd felt when the Spirit had let her know that he would come around. As he drew her into his arms and kissed her again, she told herself that she simply had to continue being patient. Surely he *would* come around. She loved him so much! Everything felt so perfectly right with him—everything except this one thing. But this one thing meant more to her than anything else in the world. *He'll come around,* she told herself, becoming lost in his kiss. *Oh, how she loved him!*

Emily convinced herself that all would be well and felt certain that in leaving his beautiful home, she would soon return to live there permanently. The journey back to Utah was long and exhausting, without the anticipation she had experienced on her trip to Australia. But with Michael at her side, his hand in hers, it was still enjoyable.

Emily had barely recovered from the jet lag when she received news that her older sisters were both coming home to Idaho for a visit, and Emily decided it would be a good time for her to go home and spend some time catching up with her family. And with that trip, everything had changed.

* * *

Emily forced herself to the present as her memories became difficult, rather than tender. While she'd been daydreaming the sun had come up and the day was brilliant and warm. Realizing she was still in her bathrobe, she hurried upstairs to get dressed. Through the remainder of the day, Emily's mind kept straying to her memories of dating Michael. She felt a profound heartache in recalling how she had made the decision to marry another man, and it had been many years, following her first husband's death, before she and Michael had married. The heartache they had both endured during those years came back to her with clarity, and she had to find a place to be alone and have a good, long cry. Once she got the sadness out of her system, she reminded herself that she knew now, just as she'd known then, that marrying Ryan Hall had been the right thing to do. It had been a necessary step for her—and for

Michael. There had been much they'd needed to learn, and they'd learned most of it the hard way. But just as the Lord had promised her back in college, Michael *had* come around. He'd been baptized before she married him, and through the remainder of his life he had served faithfully in many callings in the Church. They had gone to the temple together, and they had served missions together. She had been truly blessed.

While Emily continued to be preoccupied with memories of her life with Michael—and even her years without him—she felt drawn to the computer where she began writing them down. She'd kept a journal through most of her life, sometimes more faithfully than others, but she'd never actually written any kind of a personal history. With too much time on her hands and too many thoughts in her head, she felt it was an appropriate project. Perhaps writing down her memories, and taking some time with them, would help her feel more prepared to move on to a new phase in her life. Her children made inquiries over what she was doing, and they seemed pleased. They even helped spur her memories along as they reminisced about years gone by. Referring to journals—both hers and Michael's—as well as photo albums, also helped bring her memories back to life. Emily was grateful to be using a computer, which allowed her to write her memories out of order and then move the text around and print it off in sections, which she put into a binder.

Days flew quickly as she engrossed herself in her project, and every once in a while Emily attempted to remove her wedding ring. It still wouldn't budge, and again she wondered if that was a sign. Perhaps she needed to find contentment with her life as it was and keep her wedding ring in place as a symbol of her eternal commitment to Michael.

A few weeks into her project, Emily reached a point where writing her memories came to an abrupt halt. She knew there was a great deal more to be written, but she just couldn't get the words to come. She attempted to update some photo albums and scrapbooks, but she couldn't seem to focus on anything that required thought. She felt as if she were wandering around in some kind of fog; as if she was supposed to figure something out or do something or change something—but she had no idea what.

For three days the fog continued while Emily prayed and pondered the situation, and she went without two meals, hoping a fast would bring her closer to the answers. After sharing supper with her family, and breaking her fast, Emily washed the pans in a sink full of soapy water, while Emma loaded the dishwasher, and Tamra cleared the table. Rhea sat at the table playing with the baby, while Scott and Jess took the other children outside to play on the lawn and release some of their energy before bedtime. Emily became pleasantly distracted listening to the warm chatter between Emma and Tamra. They were as close as if they had been born sisters, and Emily felt greatly blessed to have them living under her roof. Her attention then turned to Rhea, who was making the baby giggle. Her presence in the home was a blessing as well.

Emily gasped softly as a strange sensation took her off guard. She lifted her left hand out of the soapy water and gasped again to see her wedding ring absent.

"Are you okay?" Tamra asked, but she could only stare at her hand as if she'd never seen it before while her heart quickened unexpectedly.

"You didn't cut yourself, did you?" Emma asked, sounding concerned.

"No, I'm fine," Emily said, groping in the bottom of the sink for her ring. "I just lost my ring; it's in here somewhere."

"Oh, you mustn't lose that," Emma said lightly.

Emily found it in the bottom of the sink and picked it up to look at it, covered in suds. It looked different somehow, not on her finger. "No, I mustn't lose that," Emily said quietly and slipped it into the pocket of her jeans before she finished washing the pans. Once the kitchen was in order, Emily excused herself and went up to her room. She pulled the ring out of her pocket and sat on the edge of her bed, turning it over and over between her fingers. She contemplated what this might mean. If she had considered not being able to remove the ring as a sign, then what did it mean to have it suddenly fall off? She'd tried soapy water before—many times. If anything, the warmth of the water tended to make her fingers swell a bit. Emily pondered her left hand without the ring. A deep impression of paler skin made it evident that she'd worn it for many years. She set the ring in the palm of her hand and studied it closely, then she turned it over and did the same. And then she cried. She held it tightly in her fist and cried until her head pounded and her stomach hurt. She curled up on the bed, and the tears flowed on. In her heart she knew it was time to move on, to start over, to let go. And while aspects of such a decision were intriguing and offered some hope that she might get beyond this loneliness, she felt a deep heartache in letting go of Michael as the romantic figure in her life. One day they would be together again, but for now, she was lonely and tired of waiting.

Emily drifted to sleep encircled with heartache, praying that she could find peace with her decision. She awoke in the middle of the night with the lamp still on, and the ring still in her hand. She set the ring on the bedside table and changed into a nightgown before she crawled into the bed and went back to sleep. She woke just past dawn feeling an undeniable peace. Moving on was the right thing to do, and she knew it. After kneeling by the bed for a lengthy prayer, Emily picked up the ring from the bedside table. She pondered it with her fingers and shed a few stray tears, then she tucked it safely into the back of her jewelry box, muttering quietly, "One day, Michael, we will be together again. You know that I love you. I'll always love you." She felt certain he understood; in fact, she knew beyond any doubt that he would encourage her to take this step. Perhaps he was even surprised that she had waited so long to move forward. The problem came with her relative certainty that their children wouldn't necessarily agree. Still, she reminded herself that she was an adult and what they thought on the matter did not change where she stood.

With fresh resolve Emily took a long, hot bath and was in the kitchen fixing breakfast before any of her family showed up. Once the meal was over, she went to the computer. But rather than working on her personal history, she went directly to the Internet. She was grateful for the way her children had helped her keep up with technology. She enjoyed researching and reading about many topics, and she'd become very proficient at keeping in touch with family and friends via e-mail. And she was well aware that the Internet offered a number of options for getting to know people of the opposite sex. Within a few days, Emily had researched a number of singles sites and decided that the ones strictly for LDS people suited her better than the others she had looked into. She registered herself on a couple of sites and was even brave enough to put a photograph on the site along with her personal information and interests. And then the responses began coming in. There were so many that it was difficult to sift through them all. She prayed for discernment and at the same time reminded herself to relax and simply enjoy this new hobby she'd discovered. She found that it was relatively easy to pick up on certain things in people's letters that indicated problems she wanted to steer clear of. As she felt the Spirit guiding her, she was able to communicate with some people who helped fill the emptiness in her life.

Emily didn't try to hide her new interest from her children, but she couldn't deny being grateful that none of them had actually caught her looking through the profiles of older, single men. She knew that eventually they would find out what she was doing with her spare time, but she wasn't certain they would appreciate her endeavors. Sooner or later she knew the cat would be out of the bag, but she wasn't going to encourage it out any sooner than necessary.

More than two weeks after Emily had tucked away her wedding ring, she sat down at the breakfast table, holding little Laura on her lap. The meal proceeded as normal until Jess spouted with astonishment, "Mother? You're not wearing your ring!"

All eyes turned toward her, stunned. Rhea was quick to add, "You didn't lose it, did you?"

"No, I didn't lose it," Emily said quietly. Jess and Emma exchanged a concerned glance, as if they might have preferred a lost ring over the only other possible reason for its absence.

"You took it off?" Jess asked, sounding appalled.

"I did," Emily said, with no apology.

"But . . ." Jess said, "you always said that you still felt married."

"For a long time I did," Emily explained. "I don't feel that way anymore."

Following several grueling seconds of stark silence, Emma asked, "So, how is it that you feel, Mother?"

Emily took a deep breath. "To put it succinctly, I feel that your father is very busy on the other side of the veil, and it's time for me to move on with my life."

"Move on?" Jess echoed cautiously. "What exactly does that mean?"

"Well," Emily said, "I've been thinking that I'd like to get out more, start dating again."

Jess and Emma both looked so thoroughly stunned that Emily almost felt angry. "What?" she demanded.

"Nothing," Emma said. "It's just that . . ."

When she didn't finish, Jess added, "You're just so . . ."

"Old?" Emily guessed. "You were going to say old, weren't you?"

"No!" Jess insisted.

"Then what exactly were you going to say?" Jess said nothing and she added quickly, "You were going to say that I'm just so old; if you're too polite to say it, you were thinking it. So, you tell me, since you're so young, when exactly does a person become too old to enjoy life? When does one become too *old* to want the companionship of the opposite sex?" Neither answered, and she went on. "I'm not too old to care for your babies and chase your toddlers around. I'm not to old to drive six hours to visit a friend, or to walk five miles without getting winded. I'm not too old to cook for fifty people or keep a garden almost single-handedly. So, what exactly am I too old for?"

"I didn't say you were too old," Jess said firmly.

"No, but you were thinking it," Emily countered.

"Mother," Emma said in the same tone she would use to talk to one of the children, "as you pointed out, you are not too old to do anything you set out to do. You're fit and healthy and we are all grateful. I must confess that . . . it's not your age that concerns me."

Emily felt her eyes narrow on her youngest daughter. "What exactly *does* concern you?"

Emma cleared her throat and exchanged a cautious glance with Jess before she faced her mother again and said, "It's just that . . . well . . . I mean . . ."

"Just say it and get it over with," Emily said.

"It's just the idea, I guess; the principle. *Dating?* It feels like such a betrayal to Dad."

Emily made a scoffing noise. "Your father has been dead for six years, Emma. My first husband—the father of your sisters—had only been gone about three months when I started seeing your father.

Healing beyond the death of a loved one is relative. I've healed as far as it's possible. I miss him. We'll be together again someday, but for now . . . I'm lonely."

"How can you be lonely in a house full of people when . . ." Jess stopped when his mother glared at him.

Tamra said, "That's a really stupid question, Jess."

"Perhaps," Emily said, "but I'll answer it anyway. I'm lonely because you all have each other. The hours from bedtime to breakfast are torturous. Your father and I used to snuggle in bed and talk until we were exhausted, then we'd fall asleep holding hands. I'm lonely. He's been gone six years. *Six years.*"

Following another length of tense silence, Jess finally said, "Okay, it's been a long time, Mother, and I can understand how lonely you must be, but . . . isn't this kind of sudden? Maybe you should give it some thought, some time or—"

"Did you think I wouldn't have?" Emily asked, hating the defensiveness in her own voice. "You have absolutely no comprehension of the days and weeks I have prayed and stewed over this, trying to come to terms with letting go and moving on, when I love him more than life itself." Her voice broke. "I have fasted and cried and struggled with this. It's time for me to move on, and I don't have to justify anything or apologize to my own children." She got up and left the room, mostly wanting to be alone before the hovering tears burst out of her.

Jess watched his mother leave the room, wondering why he felt so completely disheartened—and concerned. The question inside of him deepened when Scott said, "Forgive me if I'm being obnoxious, but I think you guys need to lighten up."

"Yes, I agree with him," Tamra said. "Everything your mother said is true."

Rhea added firmly, "I'm certain she didn't come to this decision easily. If I know her, she's been bawling her eyes out when she's alone."

Tamra looked at her aunt and asked, "And what about you? You're alone, too."

"Ah, it's different for me," Rhea said. "Art was a good man and I miss him at times, but I'm content. We never shared what Emily shared with Michael. I don't really feel alone the way she does."

"And that's just the point," Scott said. "She's alone. She's living in a house full of noisy people, but I wonder how it must be for her to feel completely alone at the end of the day."

Emma sniffled and wiped a hand over her cheeks to dry them. "I'm sure you're right," she said, and Scott put his arm around her shoulders.

Jess swallowed carefully, fighting his own emotion over the situation in order to consider the obvious. "Yes," he said, "I'm sure you're right as well."

"But you still don't like it," Tamra said as if she could read his mind.

"No," Jess had to admit, "I still don't like it."

"Well, I don't like it either," Emma admitted. Jess was grateful to hear her express his own thoughts perfectly when she added, "It's just so difficult to imagine her with *anyone* but my father. And I must admit that I actually worry for her. I mean . . . how many years *has* it been since she went out on a date? It's a vicious world out there."

"I couldn't have said it better myself," Jess said.

"Okay," Tamra said gently, "your feelings are valid. She's your mother and the thought of romantic involvement with someone besides your father is difficult. We can all accept that. Anybody who has lost a parent could probably agree. And yes, it's a vicious world out there. But you're all forgetting one very important point. Emily is a wise and intelligent woman. She's lived through two marriages and lived on two continents. She's raised her children and seen them through more tragedies and challenges than we can count. And she is one of the most spiritual people I've ever known. I really think Emily can handle dating." She smiled and added, "It might be an adventure, but I think she can handle it."

Jess couldn't dispute what his wife was saying, but that didn't make his uneasiness go away. He concluded that his feelings were his problem, so he kept his mouth shut. Through the day as he went about his usual business, he couldn't force the situation from his mind. He finally came to the conclusion that he might not be able to counter his mother's choices with any kind of logic, but he was her only living son, and he had a right to be concerned for her. He also owed her an apology.

Praying that he could express his concerns appropriately, Jess left work a little early. He found his mother in the home office, sitting at the computer.

"Hello," he said, and she looked up, immediately showing a smile.

"Oh, hello," she said. "What a nice surprise. You're home early."

"Yes, I am," he said, taking a seat.

"Any reason in particular?" she asked, turning her chair to face him.

Jess looked directly at his mother and just said what he needed to say. "I owe you an apology, Mother." Her eyes showed surprise, but she said nothing so he hurried on, borrowing Tamra's words of earlier. "You are a wise, intelligent woman, and I know you're capable of making your own life's decisions. I apologize if anything I said was unfair or inappropriate."

"It's okay, Jess," she said, taking his hand. "I know this is a big step, and I know that my decisions do affect my family. I just ask you to trust my judgment."

"Okay," Jess said, and Emily leaned forward enough to give him a hug. Looking over her shoulder, his eye caught the computer screen, and the uneasiness he'd been trying to suppress heightened dramatically. As Emily drew away from their quick embrace, he leaned back in his chair, telling himself to stay calm and not say anything stupid to counter the apology he'd just given her. Doing his best to make the question sound like a polite inquiry, he asked, "So, what are you doing there?"

Emily glanced at the screen where the picture and profile of a man were clearly displayed. She reminded herself not to apologize or justify herself—and not to get defensive. She simply stated, "It's a site for older LDS singles."

"I see," Jess said, clearing his throat more loudly than he'd intended. He swallowed carefully and forced away any hint of disconcertment in his voice by covering it with a point of humor. "Did you say *older?* Come now, Mother. You're not old."

"I didn't say I was old," she chuckled. "Older is relative. I'm older than you, so that just makes me older than the average person in the dating market. So, I'm older, not old. In fact," she chuckled again, "I'm old enough to be your mother."

Jess sensed that her attempts at humor were for the same reason as his. But he just forced a smile and said, "So you are. But then, I'm practically a baby, so you can't be very old."

Emily watched Jess for a moment while she paused to gauge the tension between them. Deciding that she wasn't going to live with such tension, she knew the only other option was to take it head on. "Jess," she said gently, again taking his hand, "why don't you tell me what you're *really* thinking?"

Jess shifted abruptly in his chair and coughed. Caught off guard by the question, it took him a long moment to find a suitable answer that didn't sound childish or obnoxious. He finally managed to say, "It just feels a little . . . weird, I guess. I mean . . . you're my mother. And you're . . ." He motioned toward the computer screen. "It's like you're . . . shopping for a man, or something."

Emily laughed softly. "Well, that is kind of how it seems. That's just the way this Internet thing has affected the world, I suppose. But . . . in case you've not noticed, we live in the middle of nowhere. It's a great blessing to have something like this that gives me the opportunity to get to know other single people who are my peers."

Jess thought of a hundred things he wanted to say, but none of them were appropriate. He settled for saying, "Just be careful, okay? There are a lot of creeps out there."

"I'll be careful," she said. "I promise."

"Okay." He stood. "I guess I'll go find my wife. She would probably appreciate my showing up a little early to relieve her from the little ankle-biters."

"She probably would," Emily said, wishing there wasn't still this tension between them. She concluded that they might just have to agree that on this point, they disagreed. Still, she felt compelled to say one more thing. "Jess," she said, and he turned back. "Listen to me." She looked at him firmly. "I'm not certain what concerns you or bothers you most about this situation. But let me say . . . there will never be another man like Michael Hamilton. I'm not trying to replace him, Jess. I simply believe there might be someone out there who could bless my life—and perhaps I could bless his as well." She offered a tender smile. "A man does not have to fill your father's shoes in order to fill my loneliness."

Jess felt her words settle into his spirit, and he felt sure she was right. Trying to consider how all of this must feel from her perspective, he stepped back into the room and hugged his mother tightly. "You deserve to be happy, Emily Hamilton," he said. He took hold of her shoulders and looked into her eyes. "So stop worrying about me. I'm a big boy now, Mom. I'll get over it."

He left the room before he had a chance to say anything that might let on to his own belief that he wasn't so sure he'd get over it. He just missed his father so much. Michael Hamilton's absence still seemed all wrong, and the thought of his mother bringing another man into the household made it feel even more wrong. But this decision wasn't up to him. He felt sure there were many times in the past when his mother had not agreed with his behavior or his decisions, but she had always loved and accepted him unconditionally. If nothing else, he could return that favor. But it wasn't necessarily going to be easy.

* * *

Emily found a great deal of enjoyment in corresponding with people, both men and women, whom she had come in contact with through LDS Internet sites. With time passing, however, she began to feel that written correspondence just wasn't enough. She barely asked herself what she might do about it, and the answer became clearly obvious. She made a few phone calls and was pleased to see that her idea would work out well. She was also pleased to know that her other three children were not having nearly the problem with her dating that Emma, and especially Jess, seemed to be having. Allison was very supportive, even enthusiastic, about this step. It was nice to feel like she had an ally. Knowing Jess and Emma might not be very happy about her plans, she waited until all the arrangements had been made before she even brought it up.

"I'm going to Utah," Emily announced at the breakfast table once she'd finished eating.

"What for?" Emma asked, sounding concerned.

"I have a daughter who lives in Utah," Emily explained as if they didn't know, "and I thought I might stay with her for a while and get out of this rut that I'm in. I talked to Allison this morning, and she thinks it's a great idea."

"Okay," Jess said, "but . . . you have a daughter in California and one in Adelaide, too. Why Utah?"

"It's obvious, isn't it?" Tamra said with a little smile. "There's a high concentration of Latter-day Saints in Utah. Good place to find a date, eh?"

Emily smiled at Tamra then turned to look at the others, focusing mostly on Jess and Emma. "I would like the opportunity to have a social life. They have firesides and dances and—"

"You *are* going to Utah to find a date," Emma said as if it were criminal.

Emily swallowed the temptation to get angry. "Never mind my reasons for going," Emily said, rising from the table. "I'm a grown woman, and I'm running away from home. It's all arranged. I'll keep in touch."

Once she was packed and ready to leave, Emily took flowers to Michael's grave and lingered there a long while, contemplating the path her life was taking. She felt certain he was pleased with this course for her, and in her heart she knew it was right. She exchanged brief good-byes with her family and had Murphy fly her to Sydney where she caught a direct flight to Los Angeles. While she would miss her loved ones she was leaving behind, this was far from the first time she'd traveled alone to be with *other* loved ones. She felt better already with the change of scenery, and she also felt a definite excitement at the possibility of new adventures before her.

* * *

Jess kept telling himself that he should be happy to see his mother taking these steps in her life, but he just couldn't shake this ongoing uneasiness. Taking into account the time difference from Australia to Utah, he called Allison, hoping to get some validation of his feelings. Once they'd exchanged typical greetings, he asked, "Mom's on her way there, I hear."

"That's what I understand," Allison said.

"So . . . what's your take on this . . . dating thing she's doing?"

"I think it's great," Allison said with an enthusiasm that took Jess by surprise. "But I take it you don't."

"You've been talking to our mother," he said.

"Yes, I have. And all she said was that you were struggling with this. But I didn't have to know that—your voice tells me that you don't like it."

"Well, I *don't* like it," he said.

Allison urged him to talk through his feelings, much the way Tamra had done. He came to the same conclusions. There was no logical reason he shouldn't be able to accept this and be happy about it. But he wasn't, and that was nobody's problem but his own.

When Jess brought up the idea that this felt like such a betrayal to their father, Allison said, "Allow me to offer some perspective here, Jess. The first time I saw Michael Hamilton, he was standing in my house. He was there when I got home from school. My father had been dead three months."

"Whoa," Jess said, realizing he'd never stopped to look at his parents' history from this perspective before. "That must have been tough."

"Yes, it was. I didn't like it at all. But do you think if I had stomped my foot and thrown a fit that he would have gone away?"

"Not likely."

"Well, there were times when I didn't make it very easy for them, but then . . . I was nine. By the time I was ten I could clearly see that Michael Hamilton was the best thing that had ever happened to us. Obviously the circumstances vary between then and now, Jess. But we need to allow her to get on with her life and not cause stress for her. This can't be easy. If she had her choice, she would be living with Michael at her side."

"That would be my choice too," Jess said.

"And mine," Allison admitted. "But that choice is not an option at the moment. What our mother is doing is right and good, Jess."

"I know," he said, but he had trouble accepting it. They talked for a while more, and Allison encouraged him to make the issue a matter of prayer. And surely, with time, he would come to feel peace. He thanked her for her time and insight and ended the call with a determination to do as she'd suggested. And hopefully with time, and with

God's help, he could come to terms with this and accept it. But it wasn't going to be easy.

Chapter Four

Through the long flight, Emily couldn't help thinking of all the long hours she'd spent in the air with Michael at her side. They'd traveled back and forth to the States more times than she could count, mostly to visit their children who lived there. And they'd made many trips to Adelaide to see their daughter, Amee. Technically Amee and her two sisters were not Michael's daughters, but he'd come into their lives when Amee was little more than a baby, and he'd taken over being her father as quickly as she had taken to calling him Daddy. Never once had Emily ever felt that Michael treated her daughters any differently than the children they had brought into the world together. Amee looked more like her blood father than her sisters did, and it was more difficult for her to fit into the family by her physical appearance, but Michael had always told her how beautiful she was.

Emily's mind wandered to the day Amee had been married to Daniel in the Sydney Temple. While the family had waited in the celestial room for the sealing to begin, Emily turned to see Michael and Amee talking quietly, his hands on her shoulders. It was one of those moments that Emily had etched into her memory like a mental photograph. She didn't know what he was telling her, but she couldn't miss the tears Amee wiped from her face with a lacy, white handkerchief, and then she wiped at Michael's face, and it became evident he was crying, too. They hugged tightly, then Michael took her face into his hands and pressed a kiss to her brow. Amee then turned away and took hold of her fiancé's hand, while Michael watched them walk away. Emily nudged him, asking quietly, "What was that all about?"

He gave her a mischievous smile and whispered, "I told her if he ever made her unhappy, I would give him a bloody nose."

Emily smiled at him. "The conversation appeared a bit more tender than that."

Michael's expression sobered, and his voice softened further. "I told her she was amazing and incredible, and no father could be more proud or happy on this day. And I told her she deserved to be deliriously happy for the rest of forever."

"I love you, Michael Hamilton." He looked directly at her, seeming surprised, as if to question why she should say it with such intensity at that moment. She went on to share her thoughts. "Do you remember the first time you saw Amee?"

Michael's chin almost quivered as he said, "How could I ever forget? She was covered in pink yogurt from trying to feed it to Alexa. You washed her at the sink and set her down. She looked up at me and said, 'Who's 'at?'" He imitated her baby talk perfectly, then laughed softly. "After you told her my name, she said 'Mikow' then ran off. She had stitches on her forehead from running into something the day before."

Emily touched his face. "Funny, from the way you've always treated her, I would have thought the first time you saw her would have been in the delivery room at the hospital."

"No, I missed that," he said, looking toward Amee on the other side of the celestial room, dressed as a temple bride. "But I was there for the important stuff."

"So you were," Emily said, kissing him quickly before the family was called into the sealing room for the marriage to take place. Michael sat in one of the witness chairs, while Emily sat next to the bride until it was time for her to kneel at the altar. More than once through the ceremony, Emily met her husband's eyes across the room. She knew he shared her thoughts. Being in the temple together and seeing their daughter sealed was a tremendous blessing and privilege, but Michael and Emily had never been able to kneel together at the altar for their own sealing. They had done many proxies, but never their own. It was a technicality that could not be resolved as long as they were living. Because Emily had been married in the temple previously, and her husband was now dead, she could not be sealed to another man in this lifetime. They knew that once she and Michael were both dead, the sealing could be done by proxy on their behalf, and they both felt confident that they were indeed meant to be together forever. And they would be, as they lived for those blessings. Still, it was difficult for both of them. Nevertheless, Michael gave her a warm smile and a little wink as the sealer finalized the marriage, speaking of time and all eternity. Oh, how she loved him!

* * *

Emily leaned back against the seat and looked out the plane window, coming back to the present only long enough for her mind to wander to the day Amee had called home, less than two years later. Emily was just about to fix some breakfast when she heard the phone ring, and Michael had hollered from the other room, "I'll get it." Half a minute later he peeked into the kitchen and said, "Pick up the extension. It's Amee; she wants to talk to both of us."

Emily could see from the look on his face that it wasn't likely good news, but the way he shrugged his shoulders made it evident he had no idea what the problem might be. Michael went back down the hall to use the phone he'd answered, and Emily picked up the phone in the kitchen and sat down. "Hi, honey," Emily said, "what's up?"

"Are you there, Dad?" Amee asked.

"I'm here," Michael said.

"I . . . don't know where to start," Amee said, her voice trembling.

"Just say what you need to say," Michael said tenderly. "We're not going to think any less of you, no matter what you have to tell us."

Emily was amazed at how he'd come so close to her concerns when she tearfully responded, "But . . . I've been such a fool, and . . . I feel like I . . . failed you, both of you . . . and myself. I kept thinking that . . . it would get better, somehow; that I . . . could fix it."

"Fix what, honey?" Emily asked.

Amee cried for a full minute before she could get control of her emotions enough to speak. Emily put a hand over her mouth while tears spilled down her own face. Whatever was wrong, the heartache she felt on her daughter's behalf was indescribable.

"It's okay, Amee," Michael said gently through the phone. "Whatever it is, we'll get through it together."

Amee sniffled and struggled for her composure. "Well, I'll just get to the point. I'm kicking him out. I'm not going to live like this any longer. I'm sorry if you're disappointed in me, but—"

"Now why do you think we would be disappointed?" Michael interrupted firmly.

"My marriage failed. I've—"

"Tell us what you did wrong, Amee," Michael said, and Emily was grateful for his ability to speak. She was so lost in a torrent of memories and emotions that she could only hold her hand over her mouth and listen. "Did you lie to him, cheat on him?"

"No, of course not!" Amee insisted.

"Is there some normal obligation of being a wife and mother that you've severely neglected?" Michael asked.

Amee's tears came again. "All I ever wanted was to be a good wife and mother; I'm not perfect, but . . . I just don't understand what went wrong. It was like . . . right from the start, he just . . . expected me to read his mind or something, then became angry when I didn't. It's like once the honeymoon was over I suddenly became a second-rate person; I could never make him happy. What I did was never good enough."

Emily's distress increased for reasons she had trouble comprehending. For a moment she almost wished that Amee was prone to exaggeration or stretching the truth. But they both knew her well, and she'd always been completely honest. If anything she might be prone to minimizing a problem. Emily was relieved when Michael asked what she wanted to ask herself but was incapable of doing so. "Did he hurt you, Amee?" She said nothing, and he added, "I want you to be completely honest with us. Did he ever hurt you or the baby? Ever? Even a little?"

"No," she said firmly. "I mean . . . not physically, ever. But he gets so . . . angry, and . . ." Her tears turned to sobbing.

"What, Amee?" Michael pressed gently.

"He's just said some . . . awful things, and . . . I finally reached a point where I couldn't take it anymore. I talked to the bishop about it. He said that if Daniel was willing to get some counseling with me and work on the problems, then I should give the marriage all I've got, but . . ."

"He won't go?" Michael guessed.

"You got it," Amee said. "I've pleaded and begged, and I finally gave him an ultimatum. I told him if he ever talked to me that way again, he was out of here. He laughed at me, told me I could never do it, that he'd never let me kick him out. But . . . but . . . last night he got so horribly angry, worse than he ever has. In the middle of the night it hit me that if I let him get away with that . . . if I don't follow through on my threat . . . then . . ." She sobbed.

"What?" Michael asked.

"Then . . . it will never end . . . he'll never change. If he wants to share his life with his wife and son, he's going to have to earn that right."

"That's my girl," Michael said.

"But I'm scared, Dad. Am I doing the right thing? This marriage was supposed to be forever."

"Forever takes hard work and commitment from both sides, Amee. Men who belittle and scream at their wives will never be allowed to be with them forever. If he was willing to change and work it out, that would be different. But you're right; you can't bluff. If you told him he's out, then he's out. Maybe being separated will prompt him to agree to some counseling. But you can't get to step two until you take step one."

"Okay, but . . . I'm scared, Dad. He just left for work, but . . . what do I do when he comes home? I know I could leave, but . . . I'm afraid if I leave the house, he'll take it over or . . . oh, I don't know. I'm just . . . scared and confused, and . . . I'm sorry I didn't tell you things were bad before now. I just—"

"It's okay, kid. We understand, truly. And your mother and I can be there before supper . . . if that's what you want."

Amee became too emotional to speak; she finally managed to say, "You're like a walking miracle, Dad. You'd really do that?"

"You'd better believe it. We're on our way. Why don't you go shopping or something, and then you can pick us up at the airport."

Amee quickly got off the phone, not wanting to use up any more time that they could use in getting there. As soon as Emily hung up, she knew she should hurry upstairs and pack a few things, but all she could do was press her face into her hands and cry. She became oblivious to everything but her own sadness until she felt Michael's hands on her shoulders, then his arms came around her, urging her to her feet and into his embrace. "It's going to be alright, darlin'," he muttered near her ear. "I know it's hard, but we're going to take good care of her."

"I know," she said, sniffling loudly. "It's just that . . . when I think of her suffering in silence all this time, and . . ." She sobbed quietly and Michael grabbed a clean dish towel to wipe her tears. "Oh, Michael. It all came back to me. I know *exactly* how she feels."

"I know you do," he said gently, looking into her eyes. "It all came back to me too. I will never forget how I felt when you told me how unhappy you had been all those years."

"You were furious."

"Yes, I was. I wanted to kill him. Well . . . I would have liked to give him a black eye."

"But when you came face-to-face with him, you didn't."

"No, I didn't."

"He changed after that, you know. After you told him you would steal me away if he didn't treat me right."

"I don't think I put it exactly like that."

"No, but . . . he changed after that; things were much better for us, for what little time we had left."

"Yes, I know," Michael said, but he said it sadly, and she couldn't help thinking of how difficult the entire situation had been for him.

"Perhaps Daniel will change too, if she makes it clear that she's serious."

"Perhaps," Michael said. "In the meantime, our daughter needs us."

Michael flew the private plane to the airport nearest Amee's home. Long stretches of silence were interspersed between bouts of conversation as they attempted to digest this new twist in their daughter's life. Emily had expressed some concerns before Amee had even married Daniel, and they had seen some little clues that things were not as they should be in the marriage. Still, neither of them would have guessed that it was as bad as Amee had told them. Emily's mind kept being drawn to the past, into the years that she had endured a difficult marriage prior to her first husband's death. One thought kept coming to her over and over, until she had to voice it.

"Michael," she said, and he glanced toward her while he kept the plane in control. "How could she marry someone so much like her father, when she doesn't even remember him?"

"Most likely for the same reasons you did."

"What reasons would you be referring to?" she asked.

"You told me that you knew it was the right thing to do, that it was necessary for your growth—and mine—and Ryan's as well. Maybe Amee just needed this experience. And whether Daniel comes around or not, he will have to face God one day with the knowledge that he was given a fair chance with a good woman."

"She is a good woman, Michael. I mean . . . she's not perfect. We know she can be a bit willful at times, but . . . I believe her when she says she's been a good wife and mother."

"Yes, so do I. She is a good woman . . . like her mother." Michael reached for her hand and squeezed it, and the remainder of the journey passed mostly in silence.

Amee met them at the airport, looking drawn and tired. She hugged them each tightly, then Michael asked, "Where's the baby?"

"I left him with Lottie, a friend of mine in the ward."

They shared small talk as they went to the car, then made the drive to Lottie's neighborhood. A few minutes from her friend's home, Amee became emotional as she said, "I can't believe you're both really here. When I called I was hoping for some advice, but . . . you're just the best parents in the world. Your being here is more than an answer to prayers—it's a miracle."

"It's not the first time your father has been the means for a miracle to take place," Emily said.

Michael gave Emily a comical scowl that made her laugh, then he said, "I think it's the other way around." He then turned to Amee and asked, "What do you want us to do? We don't want to overstep our bounds here; we just want to help as far as it's appropriate."

Amee pulled the car up in front of an unfamiliar house where she went in and came out a few minutes later with her nine-month-old son. Michael and Emily both made a fuss over him as he was put into his car seat. As she drove to her home, Amee said, "I told Daniel last night that he needed to leave. He just said some awful things and basically told me I was dreaming. I slept on the couch and didn't see him before he left for work this morning. When he comes home, I just want to tell him that he needs to leave. He's got friends he can stay with, or he can afford a motel if he has to. He's also got a brother who lives alone and has plenty of space; it's not like I'm throwing him out in the cold. I've got everything he needs already packed." Amee became visibly nervous. "But . . . how can I tell him without . . . having him get horribly angry, and . . ."

"Do you think he'll behave that way with us there?" Emily asked.

"I honestly don't know, but . . . in a way I wish he would, just so you could tell me I'm not crazy."

Through the remainder of the drive they discussed the best way to handle the situation, and arrived at the house less than twenty minutes before Daniel was due to arrive home. Michael put his son-in-law's luggage near the front door, then the three of them knelt together to pray. Michael offered the prayer at Amee's request. He asked for divine protection and guidance in this difficult situation. He asked that Daniel's heart might be softened toward his wife and son, and that this separation might compel him to do the right thing and be willing to learn how to be more appropriate toward his wife and to manage his anger. After the amen was spoken, Amee hugged her father tightly, then her mother, then she went into the bathroom to freshen up and compose herself before Daniel came home.

Emily and Michael made themselves comfortable in the dining room, playing with the baby in an area where they could remain out of sight but hear what was going on in the front room and entry hall. Emily reached for Michael's hand when they heard the front door open, knowing that Amee was waiting for Daniel in the hall.

"Hello," they heard Daniel say cheerfully, as if nothing in the world was wrong.

"Hello," Amee said gravely.

"Something wrong?" Daniel asked.

"Yes, something is terribly wrong. I told you last night that you needed to leave. Apparently you didn't believe me."

He made a scoffing noise. "Was I supposed to? You can't just kick me out of my own house."

"It's my house too, and I deserve to live here in peace. We can get some counseling and work this through, if that's what you want. But I will not live in fear of your temper."

Emily's stomach tightened painfully as Daniel immediately blew into a tirade, using a string of profanity that made her skin crawl. The baby began to cry, obviously upset by the shouting in the other room, but Daniel paid no attention to his son. Emily met Michael's eyes and saw his astonishment—and his anger. As he rose to his feet, she touched his arm and whispered, "Stay calm."

"Oh, I'm calm," he whispered back, but she wasn't so sure. Holding the baby close, she followed him, hoping she might be able to help keep this from getting out of hand. Michael stood in the doorway of the front room for a full minute, his feet braced apart, his hands behind his back, while Daniel continued to shout at Amee, and the baby continued to cry.

Michael finally cleared his throat, and Daniel turned toward him, startled. His embarrassment was immediately evident, but it quickly turned again to anger as he snarled at Amee, "Why didn't you tell me we weren't alone?"

"I wasn't aware," Amee said coolly, "that there were different rules for how a man should treat his wife when alone as opposed to being in the presence of her family."

Daniel scowled at her, then turned to Michael and said as if nothing were wrong, "I'm sorry you had to hear that." The baby finally quieted down in Emily's arms.

"So am I," Michael said. "But now that I have, you can be sure I'm not going to stand by and let you speak that way to my daughter—ever again. You'd do well to take your things and go."

Michael motioned toward the luggage. Daniel's eyes followed, then widened in angry astonishment as he glared at Amee. "You *can't* be serious," he muttered hotly.

"Quite serious," Amee said. "I packed everything you would need. You can come back and get the rest on the weekend, but you'd better call first; I'll be changing the locks."

"This is insane!" Daniel shouted. "You cannot throw me out of my own home!" At his shouting the baby started screaming again. Amee just stared at him. He turned to Michael and shouted, "You have no right to come into my home and tell me what to do!"

Michael said with an even voice, "Now you listen to me, young man, and listen carefully. I was a witness when you exchanged vows with my daughter. I signed my name to a document stating that you agreed to cherish this woman in every respect. You're not keeping your end of the bargain. When you learn to treat her the way she deserves to be treated, you are welcome to come back. But if you can't lower your pride enough to fix the problem, you have no rights as far as my daughter is concerned."

"And what makes you so sure the problems are all mine?" Daniel barked.

Amee answered with perfect confidence. "I would be more than happy to meet with you and a decent counselor and work out whatever problems I might be contributing to this marriage. While we are separated we can work things out, if that's what you want. You've lost your right to live under the same roof with us. You're going to have to earn it back."

Daniel made an angry noise. "This is unbelievable!"

"That's what I was thinking," Michael said.

"Just go," Amee said, and she hurried to take the baby from her mother.

Daniel turned angrily toward Michael. "You've got a lot of nerve coming in here, talking about rights. She's my wife, but she's not even your daughter."

Emily and Amee both gasped as Michael crossed the room in a flash and took Daniel by the collar, pushing him up against the wall. "She *is* my daughter, and I will see that she is safe and well in every respect. I earned the right to be her father because I *love* her! And I respect her, and I took care of her. What you have earned is the right to leave while the leaving is good."

"Are you threatening me?"

"You bet I am. If you *ever* do her or that baby harm in any way, you will regret ever coming against this family."

Emily wondered if he would question Michael on that; surely Daniel knew, as did anyone who knew Michael well, that he would never do anything violent or unethical. But Daniel either believed he'd make good on his threat, or he'd endured enough humiliation for one day. He pushed Michael away, picked up his luggage, and glared at Amee. "You'll be hearing from my attorney."

"We'll look forward to it," Michael said, opening the door for him. Once he was gone, Michael closed the door and locked it. Amee handed the baby back to her mother and eagerly melted in Michael's embrace. She sobbed helplessly for a few minutes, then Michael wiped her tears and told her everything was going to be all right.

Michael and Emily stayed for another week, long enough to see that all the locks were changed, that the proper legal steps had been taken, and to be present when Daniel came to get the rest of his things. Daniel made no effort to resolve the problems or make amends. He simply jumped headlong into legal battles that created a great deal of hardship for Amee.

It took nearly two years for the dust to settle over Amee's divorce. She phoned home nearly every day, usually in tears over something horrible Daniel had said to her, or something he'd threatened to do to bring more difficulty into her life. She came home for an occasional visit and even debated whether or not to move home temporarily. But she had prayerfully come to the conclusion that her own home was where she needed to be. She lived in a good neighborhood and had the support of friends and ward members. She knew it was where she belonged, and she had to stand her ground. Eventually Daniel realized that he was not going to ruffle Amee or intimidate her. His attempts to see his son soon diminished when he met another woman and married her. Life gradually evened out for Amee, and everything became better when she met Randy. He was everything that she had once hoped Daniel would be. Emily felt a deep gratification to see Amee and Randy so happy. She and Michael had helped carry her through the nightmare of divorce, and they were able to fully appreciate her joy in making a good life with the right man. Michael and Randy hit it off rather well, even though they had little in common beyond their love for the same woman.

* * *

Emily sighed and shifted in her seat while the low hum of jet engines brought her fully back to the present. She thought of how difficult Michael's death had been for Amee, but Michael himself had helped her deal with his passing by giving her a priesthood blessing only hours before he died.

Emily drifted to sleep and didn't wake up until just a short while before the flight landed in Los Angeles. From there she flew into Salt

Lake City, where Allison met her at the airport. Allison's children were in school, and the two of them had a good visit through the drive to Allison's home. Over the next few days Emily got settled into a comfortable routine that wasn't unfamiliar. She'd stayed with her daughter's family many times and had always felt at home with them.

On an afternoon when Allison was busy at home, Emily borrowed her car and took a long drive through nearby areas that had once been so familiar to her. She drove around the BYU campus, amazed at how some things had changed so drastically, and some things looked so much the same. She wandered into the neighborhood in Orem where she had lived with her first husband, when Allison, Amee, and Alexa had been young children. The house she'd once lived in was beyond recognition, with new siding, a new fence, much larger trees, and completely different landscaping. She thought of how her first husband had been killed while they'd lived in this home, and this was where Michael Hamilton had found her not many months later.

Noting the house next door, she thought of her friend Penny, who had lived there, and of all they had shared through their lives. Emily had kept in touch with Penny, who was now living in South Dakota with one of her children since her husband had also passed away.

Emily drove deeper into the same neighborhood, searching for the house where she and Michael had lived when Jess and James had been young, before Emma had been born. They'd come back to Utah so that Emily could get her degree at BYU, and Michael had found a home near her dear friend, Penny. Emily was shocked to see, instead of the house, a fourplex of apartments. Concluding that she couldn't expect things to stay the same, she drove to Sean and Tara's home and spent the remainder of the day visiting with them. Sean was almost like one of her own children, and she enjoyed reminiscing with him and his sweet wife. She felt some validation from him as he encouraged her to pursue her current quest. He told her it was a wise, healthy decision—and his being a professional psychologist didn't hurt any.

Over the next few days, Emily found herself once again obsessed with memories that had been spurred by seeing once-familiar places. She used a laptop computer she'd brought with her to record some additional memories from her life that were then inserted into her personal history. Still preoccupied with the past, she went to church with Allison's family and thoroughly enjoyed the meetings. She'd attended this ward many times through the years and she'd become acquainted with some of the women in Relief Society, so she felt right at home. It was announced that a senior couple who had been serving a mission had returned early, due to the sister's health problem. They asked for prayers on behalf of this sister, and Emily wrote the sister's name in her planner so that she would be able to pray for her by name.

Through the remainder of the day, Emily's thoughts remained with this couple, and how their mission was being cut short. How could she ever forget when, with little warning, she and Michael had needed to return home from serving in the Philippines. Lying in bed that night, she became preoccupied with one of the most difficult events of her life. If she closed her eyes and concentrated, she could almost feel Michael's hand in hers, just as it had been through the torturous days and nights that had followed their being called into the mission president's office.

* * *

"Is there a problem?" Michael asked once he and Emily were seated across the desk from him.

"Yes, I'm afraid there is," the president said with a solemnity that made Emily's heart pound. She reached for Michael's hand and knew from the way he squeezed it that he shared her fear. "I received a call from your stake president in Australia," the president continued. "There's been an accident."

Emily couldn't recall his exact words, but she had no trouble remembering the message that came through, or the way she melted into a heap of sorrow at the news. Her son and daughter-in-law had been killed, their infant daughter was in the care of her other children, and Jess—who had been driving the car—was in critical condition, not expected to pull through. His closest friend, Byron, who was almost like another son to Michael and Emily, had also been killed. The shock and grief were indescribable, and her most conscious realization was the fact that Michael was at her side, holding her, sustaining her, sharing her every emotion. No one but Michael could fully understand the loss. No one but Michael could fully share this grief. They were his children too. They were in it together.

Emily remembered little of their hurried efforts to pack up their things and return home. The travel time felt torturously long when there was nothing to do but sit and wonder how it had happened, and how they were going to cope. Amidst her disbelief that this was happening at all, her most fervent prayers were for Jess—that he *would* pull through. If she couldn't fathom accepting the death of one son, how could she possibly bear losing them both? While she and Michael talked but little, she knew that his thoughts were much in the same vein. But there was only so much to say, and once it had been said three or four times, they just sat side by side in silence, counting the minutes as they drew closer to home. And always his hand was in hers, or his arm was securely around her. *They were in it together.*

Michael and Emily arrived at the hospital to find their daughters all gathered in the waiting room of the intensive care unit. They'd all been notified immediately of the accident and had flown in as quickly as possible. When Emily saw their red faces and swollen eyes, the reality began to descend that this was not just some horrible misunderstanding. It truly had happened. She wondered how she would ever give her daughters the comfort they needed when she felt herself crumbling inside. But Michael squeezed her hand, and she knew she didn't have to do it alone. After sharing several rounds of tearful embraces, they all sat together and Emily was told more details of what had happened, while knots tightened in her stomach. Funeral arrangements were well underway for James, Krista, and Byron, but that in itself took a backseat to the reality that Jess was hooked to life support, barely clinging to this world.

When it seemed there was nothing more to say, Emily and Michael were shown to Jess's room by a compassionate nurse. Since only two visitors were allowed at a time, the girls remained in the waiting room. The nurse briefly summarized his numerous injuries and what to expect when they saw him, but Emily still felt as if she'd hyperventilate when they entered the room to see their son bruised and battered beyond recognition, with more medical paraphernalia

attached to him than she could count. She was grateful for his unconscious state when she became so upset that she could hardly breathe.
Michael held her close while he cried his own tears. If nothing else,
she was grateful to know that she did not have to face this alone.

Emily quickly lost count of the hours that she and Michael spent
at Jess's side, leaving only occasionally when one of his sisters was
sitting with him. In spite of his comatose state, they talked to him on
and on, expressing their love for him and their hope for his recovery.
The only time that Jess was left without a family member in his room
was during the viewings and funerals of those who had been in the
accident with him. Once the dust had settled from the funerals, the
girls had no choice but to return to their lives. They had school, families, and jobs to attend to. But Emily and Michael continued practically living at the hospital.

When Jess finally came out of the coma, Emily felt ecstatic. But
the news they had to share with him began a whole new cycle of grief
when Jess had to face what they had barely begun to accept. From
that point on, Jess's healing was slow but steady. Michael and Emily
spent every waking hour focusing on their son, helping him get
through the ordeal of having his body put back together. Seventeen
weeks beyond the accident, he finally went home from the hospital,
but it was long after that before his body returned to normal. And it
was years before his spirt healed from this tremendous loss.

For Emily, that accident and its repercussions had likely been the
worst thing she'd ever endured. Her first husband had been killed in
an accident, and she'd nearly died in one herself. She'd lost an infant
to death, and there had been many other struggles in her life. But that
accident had taken more from her than anything else ever had. Still,
the memories were filled with peace and hope. She'd come to know
that it had indeed been time for James and Krista to go, just as it had
been for Byron. Observing Jess's heartache for years after the accident
had been at least as difficult, as well as the grief of his sisters—a grief
that was difficult to console when she struggled with it so much
herself. They had all come through brilliantly in the long run. Jess
was now happy and healthy and a great strength to her. To see him in
the present, it was difficult to comprehend how difficult that time
had been. But through it all, Michael had been at her side. He'd

struggled with his own grief and heartache over the incident, but he was always there with a shoulder to cry on, a listening ear, a warm embrace, and he was always willing, even eager, to use the priesthood to give comfort and strength to his loved ones. Even through his own struggle with cancer, years later, he remained a stalwart to his family—right until the end.

Emily finally drifted to sleep with her memories of Michael clear in her mind. She felt a deep gratitude for the life she had shared with Michael and for all he had done to strengthen her through their years together. She reminded herself that this separation of death was only temporary and held him close to her heart as she slept.

Emily woke up determined to stop wallowing in the past and get on with her life. Again feeling like the personal history she'd been writing was completed for the moment, she began focusing more on expanding her social circle. She quickly learned what worked for her and what didn't. Some experiences were enjoyable, others a disaster. But at least she wasn't in a rut, she concluded. And she did her best to simply make the most of what life had given her.

Chapter Five

Jess couldn't believe how much he missed having his mother around. Maybe he wouldn't have been so conscious of her absence if he weren't so preoccupied with what she might be doing. Through Emily's regular phone calls and e-mails, Jess and the rest of the family were kept informed of the many social events their mother was attending and the people she had become acquainted with. She made a couple of very good friends, women who were divorced and near the same age. She'd said many times that most of the other women she'd gotten to know who were in the same age range were simply too old for her taste. She said they acted old and they made her feel old. But Emily enjoyed doing things with Jennifer and Sandra because they shared Emily's youthful spirit. The three of them had taken a road trip to southern California, going through Las Vegas, and visiting children and grandchildren en route. Emily included a trip to her daughter Alexa's home and had a wonderful time. Jess liked the idea of his mother getting out and doing such things with other women, even though he missed having her under their roof. But her interest in men was something he still struggled with. He had listened politely and said very little through their conversations as she'd told him the challenges and positive points regarding Internet dating. She had learned to be able to tell a great deal about a person through their e-mail letters back and forth, but not enough to discern that a gentleman named Lucas was no gentleman at all. When she'd finally agreed to meet him at a fireside, it quickly became evident that Lucas had the delusion of believing he was much younger and thinner than he'd claimed to be in his e-mails. The age and weight didn't bother

Emily, but the fact that he'd lied about himself bothered her very much.

As Emily reported home about her other adventures with older, single men, Jess began to feel hopeful that she simply would never find anyone to meet her high standards. She had talked of meeting many kind gentlemen who seemed decent and good, but they simply held no interest for her. However, at one of the dances she'd attended, she'd met a man who truly believed he was a secret agent, something akin to James Bond. But he seemed relatively normal in contrast to the man who had told Emily, quite seriously, of his experiences traveling through time.

"No wonder they're on their own," Emily said. "No wonder their wives divorced them and no one else wants them. I wonder if there are any decent men my age out there at all."

"I wonder," Jess said, unwilling to admit that he secretly hoped not.

"Actually, there are some decent men," Emily countered as if to dash Jess's hopes, "but that doesn't necessarily mean I have anything in common with any of them."

Jess kept to himself his wish that she might be right.

Emily's discouragement deepened when she actually became intrigued with a man named Joshua, until she found out he was unemployed and living in his car—and had been for more than two years. She told her family adventures related to several men with equally colorful circumstances. Some she had actually been intrigued with enough to go out on a date, but more than half of those quickly made it clear they had dishonorable intentions—a fact that made Jess's blood boil. But he felt most angry over the man who had proposed plural marriage to his mother. He already had a wife at home, but he was out looking for another one.

"I guess he missed that declaration," Emily told Jess over the phone.

"What declaration?" he asked.

"That the Church doesn't condone plural marriage anymore."

"That declaration was made a long time before this guy was ever born," Jess pointed out, grateful he wasn't on the same continent, which made it easier to resist the temptation to find the guy and give him a bloody nose.

A few weeks later, Emily had nearly given up—something Jess kept hoping she would do—when she e-mailed home about Rick. She'd met him at a singles conference, where they had both attended a workshop on gardening. He was a retired dentist who had lost his wife to cancer a few years earlier. They had found much to talk about, and Emily appreciated having someone who truly understood what it was like to lose a spouse to such a horrible disease. Rick asked Emily out to dinner, and one date had turned into five. Emily reported that, as of yet, she'd not been able to find anything wrong with him, and she was very much enjoying his company.

Feeling something close to panic, Jess called Allison to get her side of the story. All she had to say was that she'd met Rick, and he seemed very nice, even though he was very different from either of the men Emily had once been married to. Emily spent very little time at home; she was spending a great deal of time with Rick.

Jess noticed over the following weeks that his mother's calls and e-mails became very sparse. She said little beyond that she was doing well and having fun, and she hoped all was well with her loved ones. Jess tried to tell himself every day that this was okay, that his mother had every right in the world to be seeing this man. But he felt decidedly uneasy. He couldn't decide if his uneasiness was over his mother dating in general, or if something wasn't right. Tamra suggested that it wasn't up to him to make decisions in regard to his mother, and therefore he would not be receiving inspiration on her behalf, and he needed to let it go. Maybe she was right; maybe she wasn't. Either way, he couldn't do anything about it, so he tried very hard to follow her advice and let it go, praying that his mother wouldn't come home with a new husband.

* * *

After many days of not hearing from Emily, the phone rang just as Jess was getting ready to crawl into bed. Jess answered and felt relieved to hear his mother's voice.

"Hello, Jess," she said, sounding tired.

"Mother. You *are* alive."

"Funny," she said, obviously not thinking it was.

"It's good to hear from you. How are you?"

"I'm fine," she said. "Are you busy tomorrow?"

"Nothing unusual, why?"

"Could you pick me up in Sydney?"

"I could!" he said, unable to hide his enthusiasm. He'd missed her greatly and the very idea of having her come home made him feel happier than he'd felt for days. She told him when her flight would be arriving and got off the phone. Only then did it occur to Jess that maybe she wasn't coming home alone. Would she bring someone with her and not give them any warning? He didn't think so, but the idea still concerned him.

The following day when Jess saw his mother at the airport, he was relieved to see her alone, then concerned when he observed her countenance. She smiled when she saw him, but there was a heaviness in her eyes that worried him. They embraced tightly, then he took her shoulders into his hands. "You okay?" he asked.

Emily looked deeply at her son, freshly amazed at his resemblance to Michael. She wanted to scream and shout and tell him that she wasn't okay, that she ached for the company of her dear, sweet husband, that she longed to be with him again, to be spared the nonsense and cruelty of this world. But she simply smiled and said, "I'm much better now. Take me home; we'll talk on the way."

Jess was relieved to hear her say they would talk. He put his arm around her shoulders as they walked together to claim her baggage. She said little as they shared a quick meal at the airport, and they were soon on their way home in the private plane that Jess was flying. An hour into the flight they had shared nothing but small talk, and Jess finally said, "So, are you going to tell me what's wrong?" She gave him a mild glare, and he added, "Don't try to convince me nothing is wrong."

"I wasn't going to. I just don't want to talk about it."

"That's your option, but . . ."

"But I should; I know," she said, remaining silent while Jess wondered if she would go on. She finally asked, "When you were dating, did you have trouble with . . ."

"What?" he asked when she hesitated.

"The money," she said, and he inhaled deeply, if only to sustain the immediate anger he felt upon hearing what seemed to be a clue as to what was troubling his mother.

"I did some, yes. I'm sure I told you about it at the time."

"Tell me again. I'm getting old; my memory's going, I believe."

"Old? Oh, no. You're not old, Emily Hamilton."

"Now you're patronizing me."

"I'm just accepting what you taught me before you went to Utah. You're not old."

"Well, I feel old."

"Well, I feel old at times. Challenges have a way of making us feel older than our years, I believe."

"I'm sure you're right," she said. "So, tell me . . . about your problems with dating and money."

"As I recall, it seems there are two general opinions about money. When girls found out I came from an affluent family, they either treated me like I had the plague because—"

"Because a camel could go through the eye of a needle easier than a rich man could go to heaven," she provided. "Yes, I now recall your father talking about that from his dating years."

"See, your memory is just fine." She made a noncommittal noise and motioned for him to go on. "Or," he said, "their interest peaks incredibly, because—as some people say—it's just as easy to fall in love with a rich man as a poor man."

"Or woman," she said.

"What happened?" he asked.

"Well, to put it succinctly," she said, an edge to her voice, "Rick apparently had a great deal of interest in falling in love with a rich woman."

"Oh, I see," Jess said, trying to sound compassionate, even though he felt relieved to know the relationship hadn't worked out. Immediate guilt overtook him for such thoughts when his mother started to cry. Seeing her tears, he had to admit, "I'm truly sorry, Mother."

He reached for her hand to squeeze it just as she said, "I suppose it simply wasn't meant to be."

"*What* wasn't meant to be?" he asked.

Staring out the window, she said, "Rick and I were going to be married."

Jess swallowed carefully and counted to ten. "I see. When were you going to let us in on the news?"

"I was just about to do that when I started to pick up on the problem."

"And I assume the problem came up when he realized you were a *wealthy* widow?"

"Actually . . . I never tried to hide the fact. I never came out and said anything about the money, but I suppose it's evident. I mostly talk about my family, which naturally brings up the vacations we've taken, the family businesses. And of course, I showed him pictures of my family. It had never occurred to me that those pictures also include the stables, the house, the planes—all in the background. But . . . as we got talking about getting married, he'd make little comments. After a few such comments I began to feel uneasy. Then I really started paying attention. Turns out he has practically nothing—a fact that in itself wouldn't necessarily bother me, but . . . I began to wonder *why* he had nothing. He's a retired dentist, apparently did well with his career. As far as I can figure, he's done poorly managing his money, and I can't begin to guess where much of it's gone. When I questioned him directly, he got awfully defensive. He doesn't even have a home; he's renting a condo."

"I see," Jess said again. "So . . . are you saying he was simply wanting to marry for money?"

"Oh . . . I believe he was fond of me, but . . . I'm certain the money was a great incentive. Once I started questioning his theories about money, we sure began arguing a lot." She sighed loudly. "It really doesn't matter anymore. It's over and done. I guess I can chalk it up to experience."

"I'm truly sorry, Mother," Jess said but he wasn't sure that she believed him. "So, what now?" he asked.

"Now," she said, inhaling deeply, "I am going to enjoy my family and be content with what I've got. Maybe I just needed to see for myself that there is no man in this world who can truly take your father's place."

"No, but as you once pointed out, a man doesn't have to fill his shoes in order to fill your loneliness."

Emily sighed again. She sounded sad as she said, "There are worse things than being lonely, like being married to the wrong person. I've lived through a challenging marriage before; I don't want to do it again." She blew out a long, slow breath. "I'm tired of this quest for companionship. I made some good friends and had some good experiences. I'm glad to be going home. I missed you—all of you."

"Well, we missed you too," Jess said. "It's just not right without you."

"Don't get too comfortable with me around," she said. "I'm not going to be here forever."

"You're going back to Utah?" he asked.

"A visit here and there, I suspect," she said, laughing softly. She seemed more relaxed now that she'd spilled her confession. "But what I meant is that I'm not going to live forever."

Jess chuckled. "If you're not too old to walk five miles without getting winded, I'm not terribly worried about your dying on us."

She smiled at him and said, "Well, when I do go, I'll sure be glad to be with your father again."

"You miss him."

"More than I could ever tell you," she said, her voice cracking with emotion. Again Jess squeezed her hand. "It's just like . . . everything inside of me feels like we're supposed to be together, and this separation feels all wrong. Still, I'm not going to waste what's left of my life by wishing he were here—or that I was there. I'm going to be grateful for what I've got and enjoy every moment."

"Sounds like a good plan."

"But when I *do* go, I don't want you waiting a minute longer than necessary before you have me sealed to your father."

Jess looked at her deeply. "Of course," he said, knowing they'd talked about this many times. He wondered why it now seemed so important to her.

"And there's some notes on what I want for my funeral in the back of my journal," she added.

"Mother!" he said, clearly appalled. He didn't like the course of this conversation at all. "Just stick around, okay?"

"Okay," she said, smiling at him.

When they finally arrived at the station, everyone was so glad to see Emily that the negative aspects of their conversation slipped away. Later, when all of the children were in bed, Emily repeated to Emma, Scott, Tamra, and Rhea the news she had told Jess on the plane, although she told them more quickly and with less emotion, leaving the room before anyone could respond.

The next morning everything was quickly back to normal. Emily integrated herself into their routine as if she'd never been gone. Through the weeks that followed, she seemed perfectly content and happy, but Jess sensed an underlying loneliness in her, and his heart ached on her behalf. He thought of how dearly he loved Tamra, and he wondered how he could live without her as long as his parents had been separated by the veil between this life and the next.

Jess had completely forgotten about his mother's talk of death until Tamra commented to him one morning about the projects his mother had been keeping busy with. Feeling somewhat concerned, he left the boys' home late morning to check in on his mother. He found her typing at the home office computer, with a number of odds and ends, including a couple of empty boxes, spread around the room.

"What are you up to?" he asked.

She turned toward him and smiled. "What a nice surprise. Shouldn't you be looking out for those boys?"

"They're all doing just fine. How are you?" He sauntered into the room and sat down.

"I'm fine."

"But you didn't answer my question," he said lightly, stretching out his legs and crossing them at the ankles. "What are you up to?"

"Oh, just finishing up some projects that have always nagged at me."

"Such as?" he prodded.

"Well . . . I finally got my personal history all organized and typed up. After I'm dead you can print it off and make certain each of my children get a copy."

"Why don't you print it off and give us each a copy now. If we wait until you're dead, we'll all be too senile to enjoy it."

Emily laughed softly. "Don't be so sure."

Jess debated whether or not to admit to what he was feeling and decided to go for it. "You know, Mother, I have a hard time hearing you talk like that."

"Like what?" She looked astonished, as if she had no idea she'd said anything disconcerting.

"About dying. It's been hard enough to learn to live without Dad; don't be thinking we're ready to live without you."

"Would you ever be ready?" she asked, increasing his uneasiness.

"I'll be a lot more ready when you're old and frail and need a full-time nurse."

Emily made a scoffing noise. "Heaven forbid that I would live that long; I pray it never comes to that."

Jess couldn't blame her for that. Still, he felt he had to say, "I want you to be around a good, long time."

"And I likely will be," she said matter-of-factly. "But you know what? It's not up to you or me when I go, so just stop worrying about it. When it's time for me to go, I'll be going. It's out of our hands. We both know that well enough."

"Yes, we certainly do," he said, unable to disagree. "But . . . why all this energy you're putting into finishing up . . . projects?"

"I'll just feel better knowing they're done. I got the scrapbooks and personal histories all up to date; of course Emma and Tamra help keep me up on that. But no one could write my history but me."

"That's true. And now it's done."

"Well . . . provided nothing else exciting happens in my life."

"There's always that possibility."

"I think I've had enough excitement for three lifetimes," she said. Her voice betrayed that by excitement, she really meant trials. And yes, she'd certainly had her fair share.

Jess remained quiet for a few minutes while she continued to type. He looked around the room and asked what he considered an obvious question. "So, what are you doing now?"

"Well . . . I just wanted to organize all these boxes of keepsakes. Most of them are just silly things, but they have meaning to me in one way or another."

"Like this?" he asked, picking up an old, worn pacifier.

"Yes, like that," she chuckled. "That was Allison's; it was a part of her anatomy until she was three."

He pointed at a well-worn pair of boots. "And I'll bet that's your first pair of riding boots."

"They are, indeed," she said. "Your father gave them to me when I came here during college."

"A tradition, I believe."

"What's that?"

"Hamilton men giving the women they love their first pair of riding boots."

Emily gave a nostalgic sigh. "So it would seem."

A minute later, Jess asked, "So what are you typing there?"

"I'm making notes to go with these things, so that my children will know what they are and what they mean when I'm not around to explain."

Jess took a sharp breath. "There you go again."

"What?"

"Making implications that you're leaving."

"Whether I leave next week or in twenty years, I want to have these things done. I think you're paranoid."

"Maybe I am," Jess admitted. "I must confess that I'm spoiled. How many men get to live with a wife, a sister, and a mother all under the same roof?"

Emily chuckled. "Most men would find that torturous."

"Maybe most men don't have such a fine mother and sister."

"Maybe," she said, smiling at him. "But then, most mothers don't have such a fine son looking out for their every need."

"I was under the impression that you pretty much took care of yourself."

"For the moment. Just wait until I'm old and frail and need a full-time nurse."

"I'd love to," he said, then laughed.

Emily turned to look at her son, cherishing his laughter. *Oh, how he laughed like his father!*

A few days later the adults all ended up on the veranda after the children had been put to bed. It was a common scene that Emily dearly loved, to just have this portion of her family around her, visiting and laughing together. Her recent adventures in the States came up, and they asked more questions about some of the things she'd done there. She told them more about the women she'd gotten to know and the friendships she'd gained. There were a few women that she was keeping in touch with through e-mail, and she shared with her family how much these women had inspired her.

"How is that?" Tamra asked.

"Well," Emily said, "because they've been through so much, and they've still kept their testimonies intact, most of them, anyway."

"You've been through a great deal, yourself," Tamra said.

"I suppose." Emily shrugged. "But . . . it was different for many of the single women I met." She went on to share some of the tragic stories she'd encountered from women who had survived divorces due to many different causes. Emily felt freshly stunned to think of the heartache that tore marriages apart due to affairs, pornography, and many types of abuse. She told her children how she'd come to believe that widowed people were lonely, but many divorced people had survived having their souls ripped in half. She had been inspired by many of these women who had survived such horrors with their testimonies of the gospel still strong and true. And while some hadn't survived spiritually, she still considered them amazing because of what they had been through, and they were still striving to move forward and become stronger.

"Well, I think you're pretty amazing, too," Scott said. "It can't be easy living without the children you've lost—and your husband."

Emily gracefully changed the subject, not certain why Scott's comment struck her so deeply. She finally excused herself when she feared she wouldn't be able to keep her emotion under control much longer. She went up to her room and had a good cry before she went to sleep, convincing herself that she could be content until she could be with Michael again.

* * *

Over the next few weeks, Emily kept busy with her projects until she reached a point where she truly felt like everything was as much in order as it possibly could be. Her personal history was completed up to the present. She would continue to keep a journal and occasionally update what she'd written on the computer if she felt the desire. She felt good about the record of her life that she was leaving behind for her loved ones, and knowing that her affairs and possessions were in order. There was only one thing that she felt had to be addressed. She knew it wouldn't go over very well, but something inside of her just had to say it and get it over with. The next time all of the adults were gathered, she simply announced, "There's something I need to say. I'm not implying anything. I just feel like it needs to be said. When I die, there are some—"

"Mother!" Emma said. "How can you say such a thing when—"

"Hear me out," Emily said firmly. "I'm not telling you I've had any premonitions, or anything. I simply . . . want to know that everything is in order. I want you to know there is a list in the back of my journal of some things I would like for my funeral. Whether it's next year, or in twenty years, that list will be in my current journal. Everything else is in order. There. That's all I have to say, except for . . ."

"What?" Jess insisted when she hesitated.

Looking directly at him, Emily said, "I know you already know this, and it likely goes without saying, but I just need to say it once more. Promise me . . . as soon as the waiting period has passed, that you will make certain your father and I are sealed. Promise me."

"I promise," Jess said, and Emily left the room. Again she went to her room and had a good cry. The next morning she made up her mind that with her projects completed she needed to find something more to do with herself. She went to church with a prayer in her heart and was pleased when an answer presented itself. Later that day, near the end of Sunday dinner, she announced, "Oh, by the way, I've signed up to volunteer at a care center tomorrow. I'll be leaving about nine in the morning."

"Okay," Jess said. "Do you need a ride or—"

"I'm perfectly capable of driving into town," Emily said. "Thank you anyway, but I'll be fine. I've actually signed up to go every Monday for a month."

"That's nice," Emma said. "You ought to brighten the place up a bit."

Emily laughed softly. "I don't know about that, but it could be an adventure."

"Is that the new retirement place that was built just a year or two ago?" Rhea asked.

"I believe so," Emily said. "Apparently it has a care facility in one section with a nursing staff, and the other section is retirement apartments."

"Do you know what you'll be doing?" Scott asked.

"Not exactly. They just said they needed volunteers to help out through a temporary staff shortage."

"We'll expect a full report tomorrow evening at supper," Scott said with a smile.

The following morning Emily set out early, liking the sense of purpose she felt already in meeting this appointment. Pondering her destination and what might be expected of her there, she was grateful for her experience serving in the Relief Society, where she'd had many opportunities to help elderly sisters with a number of different challenges. Still, she felt a little nervous, not quite knowing what to expect.

She arrived at the facility to find it much larger and finer than she'd anticipated. It resembled a fine hotel more than a care center. At the front desk she was greeted warmly by a middle-aged woman who guided her to a room where she was met by a woman named Chloe, who was the geriatric director.

"So, what would you like me to do?" Emily asked. "I don't know that I have much experience, but I'm willing to try just about anything."

"I like your attitude, Mrs. Hamilton," Chloe said.

"Oh, please. Call me Emily."

"Okay, Emily. I'm thinking your time could be most beneficial right now with Esther. She's needing more care since her last stroke, but she might be kind of ornery. She still hasn't adjusted to not being able to take care of herself."

"I'll do what I can," Emily said.

Chloe took Emily to a lovely room where Esther was sitting in a rocking chair next to the bed. Emily introduced herself and spent the rest of the morning helping Esther get dressed, then fixing her hair and makeup. Esther's stroke had mostly paralyzed one side of her body. Her cantankerous attitude slowly melted with Emily's gentle efforts to communicate and help her feel attractive. She managed to communicate to Emily that she'd not worn makeup since her stroke, and she was enjoying the extra attention. In spite of Emily's awkwardness in dealing with a challenging situation, she gradually began to relax and enjoy her time with Esther.

Lunch for two was brought into the room, and Emily helped Esther eat between taking bites of her own meal. When the lunch trays were taken away, they were informed that there would be singing time in the activity area in a short while. Emily asked Esther if she would like to go for a walk before activities began, and she eagerly agreed. Emily pushed the wheelchair out into a beautiful garden area where they strolled and paused occasionally to admire one thing or another. They arrived at the activity area a few minutes before singing time began. Emily situated Esther's wheelchair next to a chair where she could sit. Seeing several other elderly people in the room, she suddenly felt very young and healthy. Some were walking on their own and seemed rather spry, others were dealing with varying degrees of disability. She couldn't help pondering the tragedy of old age and disease, and a part of her longed to pass into the next life before she ever had to be subjected to the horrors of a deteriorating body.

Emily found singing time rather humorous. The song leader was a plump, lively woman who led the music with the enthusiasm of a ringmaster at a circus. With recorded music on a tape player nearby, the group haphazardly sang songs that had been popular when most of these people would have been in college. Everyone appeared to be enjoying themselves, except for a tiny, little lady who seemed disoriented and upset. She was not in a wheelchair, and she was the only patient in the room not dressed in clothes for lounging. She wore a lavender dress and quite a bit of jewelry. And sitting beside her, gently attempting to keep her calm and ease her anxiety, was a man. Emily couldn't help discreetly observing them. By the way this man gently interacted with this woman, she felt sure he must be her son. She was touched by the tender way he held her hand and rubbed soothing fingers on her arm. He kept whispering in her ear and smiling gently at her, and gradually she became more calm and focused on the music.

When singing time was over, a nurse told Emily that she would stay with Esther now, and she was free to leave. Emily spoke to Esther for a few minutes first, telling her how she'd enjoyed their visit, and she would be back next week to spend some more time with her. After Esther was wheeled away, Emily noticed that the woman in the lavender dress was crying, and the man sitting beside her was drying her tears. Emily told herself she should just leave and not intrude, but something compelled her to approach them.

"Excuse me," she said, and they both looked up. "I don't want to intrude, but . . ." she focused on the woman, "I couldn't help noticing how lovely you look."

"Why, thank you," the woman said, beaming as she took Emily's hand between both of hers. Emily glanced at the man seated beside her, noting that he too was pleased. "What's your name, dear?"

"Emily," she said. "And yours?"

"Just call me Bertie," the woman said. She turned to the man sitting beside her and added, "And this is . . ." She hesitated as if she didn't know, and Emily wondered if she had an illness that affected her memory.

"Samuel," the man said with a deep voice and a ring of laughter.

"Is this your son?" Emily asked Bertie.

"Oh, no," Samuel said, his laughter deepening. "We only just met this morning."

Emily turned to meet Samuel's eyes and couldn't help but feel impressed with his warmth and tenderness toward this woman who was a complete stranger to him. Emily's own awkwardness in dealing with Esther came back to her, and she felt certain this man had a gift. She was kept from commenting when a nurse came to take Bertie to her room. Samuel told the older woman tenderly that he would be back in a few days to see her again. Emily said good-bye to Bertie as well, telling her what a pleasure it had been to meet her.

"I'll stop by and see you next time I come," Emily promised, squeezing Bertie's hand.

As the nurse and Bertie walked away, Emily realized she was standing beside Samuel, feeling suddenly more awkward than she'd felt with Esther. She hurried to say, "Bertie seems more calm now."

"She'll be alright once she gets settled in. She just arrived last night, and with Alzheimer's taking hold, she's a bit disoriented, naturally. But they'll take good care of her."

Emily turned to face him. "You spend a lot of time here, I take it," she said.

"I do," he said, and laughter rang through the words in a way that she now realized was common for him. While Emily was wondering what to say next, he held out a hand and said, "Samuel Reid."

"Emily Hamilton," she said, shaking his hand.

"You're not Australian," he said. "I detect something foreign in that accent. No, don't tell me. Let me guess. You're American. But you've lived here for many years."

Emily couldn't hold back a little laugh. "That's very good, Mr. Reid."

"Please, call me Samuel," he said, motioning toward a sofa on the far side of the room. "Are you in a hurry?" he asked.

"Not particularly," Emily said, glancing around to realize the room had completely emptied except for the two of them. She watched this man discreetly as he moved toward the sofa. He wore jeans and a T-shirt, making it clearly evident that he was lean and fit. She guessed him to be a little younger than she was, though not by much. Still, she'd learned that age could be difficult to gauge at this time of life. What little hair he had was gray and cut close to his head; his features were firm and strong. Overall, she couldn't help thinking he was attractive. Recalling his tenderness with Bertie heightened his appeal in her eyes. She had to assume he was single due to the absence of a wedding ring, but even more so by his attentive body language as he sat down beside her and turned to offer a smile.

"So, what brings you here, Emily Hamilton?"

"I heard at church yesterday that they were in need of some volunteers, so I took Mondays for a month to start with. We'll see where life is by then." She smiled. "And what about you, Samuel Reid?"

"I live close by," he said. "I'm retired, too much time on my hands. I enjoy being here." He chuckled. "I feel very young and healthy when I come here."

Emily laughed softly. "I was thinking *exactly* the same thing."

He chuckled again in response to her statement, then a tense silence descended between them. Emily was thinking it might be best to just excuse herself when she glanced toward him to find him staring at her. When their eyes met he glanced away quickly, seeming subtly embarrassed. The implication made Emily's heart quicken. In the breadth of a single moment she asked herself two simple questions and got two very obvious answers. Was she attracted to this man? Yes. Was he attracted to her? Yes. She asked herself a third question. Was this good or not? Well, it certainly wasn't bad, but it would take time to know for certain if he was as decent a human being as he seemed.

She was just wondering how to open some conversation to ease the tension when he said, "If I'm being too bold or nosy, just say so, but . . . I can't think of anything else to say, so . . ."

"Go on," she urged, thinking if nothing else that hearing his bold, nosy question might give her some insight into his character.

"How long has it been?" he asked gently.

"How long has *what* been?"

"Since he died."

Emily gave him a startled glance. "Next you're going to tell me you're psychic."

"Not even close," he said, glancing down humbly. "Let's just say I've always had a certain fascination with the human experience. I've always been a people watcher, so to speak. And you just have a certain . . . look about you, an aura, perhaps."

"You can tell I'm on my own," she stated.

"Yes."

"How do you know I'm not divorced?"

"Just a hunch, perhaps. Or maybe . . . it's a certain something in a person's eyes that's difficult to describe. In my experience, losing a spouse to death is heartbreaking. Losing a spouse to divorce is like having your soul ripped out and run over with a truck." Emily found herself looking directly at him as he spoke, intrigued with concepts that made so much sense, theories she had seen evidence of herself through her association with other single adults. He smiled and added, "You have more of broken-heart look, as opposed to . . ."

"Having my soul run over by a truck," she said.

"Yes, that's it."

"And what about you?" she asked. "Which category do you fall into, Mr. Reid?"

"You tell me, Mrs. Hamilton."

Emily took a deep breath, feeling warmed for some reason by the way he'd called her *Mrs.* Hamilton. She looked into his unyielding gaze and said, "You have more of a broken-heart look."

"Very good," he said with laughter in his words.

"How long?" she asked gently.

"Twenty-seven years and four months," he said.

"Good heavens," she muttered. "Has there been no one in all those years?"

"Oh, I've dated quite a bit—off and on. But I've never found anyone that could even buffer a degree of the ache I feel for Arlene." He sighed. "And what about you, Mrs. Hamilton?"

Emily sighed as well. "Michael has been gone just over six years."

"You had many years together, then," he said.

"Yes, we did."

"That must be difficult then, to let go of something that was the center of your life for so long."

Emily absorbed his genuine empathy then countered, "Yes, but . . . it doesn't take years for someone to become the center of your life."

"No," he said, "that can happen in a matter of hours . . . or minutes."

Emily wondered by the intensity of his gaze if he was implying something. Then she realized that she truly hoped so. Not through all her many weeks of dating Rick had she ever felt this comfortable, this validated. Samuel Reid looked nothing like Michael Hamilton. But for the first time since Michael's death, she felt completely comfortable and somehow secure in the presence of a man who was her peer. She had to wonder if this was what she'd been searching for all these months. She certainly hoped so, but cautioned herself against moving too quickly. She felt both relieved and disappointed when he said that he needed to be going.

"Perhaps I'll see you again next Monday?" he asked with a hopeful lilt that was touching.

"I'll look forward to it," Emily said, and watched him walk away.

Chapter Six

Emily said nothing to her family about Samuel Reid, but through the following week she found herself thinking of him a great deal. Her anticipation for returning to the care center on Monday made her feel as silly as a teenager. Once Monday arrived, she enjoyed her time with Esther and felt much more relaxed than the previous week. With Esther in her wheelchair they went for a walk and located Bertie's room, where they had a nice visit. But she saw no sign of Samuel Reid. When lunch was over they gathered once again in the activity area, and Emily felt almost giddy to see Samuel there, moving around the room and greeting many of the elderly residents. She was pleased when he caught her eye and smiled widely. When singing time was over and the residents were put into the care of other people, Emily once again found herself alone in the room with Samuel. They exchanged greetings and small talk for a short while before Emily began probing him with questions about himself. She learned that he'd made his living as an architect until his retirement. He loved to golf and go fishing, which he described as very quiet, unhurried hobbies. He'd lived in the area for many years and had for most of those years spent much time with a small group of close friends. But all of them had now either passed away or had moved elsewhere upon retirement.

When Samuel declared he'd said enough about himself, Emily felt compelled to say, "So, tell me about Arlene. I would love to know more about her."

Samuel sighed, then his countenance became pleasant. "We met in college," he said. "It was like . . . one look and I had to know her better. One date and I couldn't fathom ever being without her. It was as if our spirits just needed to be together." He looked at her and added, "You know what I'm talking about, don't you." It was not a question.

"Yes, I do," she said. "Please . . . go on."

"Well, we got married and spent some years just . . . traveling and playing in between getting our education. Then Trent came along, and everything that was good between us became better. He was such a joy—still is."

"Where is he now?"

"Happily married, three kids, living in England. Works for a great company that has branches all over the world. I don't see him nearly often enough, but he's a great kid."

"Are there any others?"

Samuel glanced down abruptly. "No, he's the only one. Arlene died in childbirth with the second one. It was a girl, but neither of them made it through."

"I'm so sorry," Emily said, putting a hand on his arm.

Samuel glanced to where her hand was resting, then he looked up at her face. "You're very sweet. It was by far the most difficult thing I've ever lived through. But as you can see, I *did* live through it. If not for Trent, I might easily have gone off the deep end. But I wanted to be a good father . . . for Arlene, if not for Trent. There were times when I felt sure she was close by, guiding me in raising him."

"Yes, I know what you mean," Emily said. "I mean . . . by the time I lost Michael, the children were all raised, but . . . when challenges came up, I often felt as if Michael was beside me, sustaining me, somehow."

Their eyes met, and he smiled. Silence fell for a few moments until he said, "Tell me, Mrs. Hamilton, if you—"

"Please . . . call me Emily."

"It would be an honor," he said. "If I call you Emily, does that mean we're friends now?"

"I would think so," she said, amazed at how thoroughly comfortable she felt.

"Very well, Emily my friend, tell me . . . if you could—"

"Is this a test?"

"No, I don't believe so. Truthfully, this is the question I ask nearly everyone I meet when I can't think of anything to say. It's just . . . perhaps a way of getting to know a person better."

"Okay," Emily laughed, "I'm ready."

"If you could have anything in the world, what would it be?"

Emily only had to think for about twenty seconds before she said, "I have everything I want." Samuel looked surprised, perhaps taken off guard. She asked, "Is that the wrong answer?"

"No, of course not. There's no wrong answer. It's just that . . . I've never heard anyone say that before. I just think . . . that's amazing . . . to have everything you want."

"Is it?" Emily laughed softly. "Well . . . I mean, life isn't perfect, but it's very good, and I have much to be grateful for." She felt a bit unnerved by the overt fascination in his eyes and had to look away. "What about you?" she asked.

"Well, there's only one thing I want," he said.

"What is that?"

"I would give everything I have to just know that I could be with Arlene again, to know that this separation is not the end. Is there truly life after death? Can we be with our loved ones again?"

Emily was completely unprepared for the tears that burned into her eyes. Through her life she'd heard countless tales of Latter-day Saints being asked such golden questions, and of the marvelous things that occurred as a result. But she'd never imagined such an opportunity presenting itself to her. She'd had some great experiences through the missions she had served with Michael, and she'd gone out of her way dozens of times to share the gospel with people she came in contact with. A few of those encounters had resulted in someone coming into the fold. But never had she been asked such a sincere, heartfelt question—a question to which she knew the answer.

While she was attempting to come up with the right words, and to get control of her emotions, Samuel reached for a box of tissues on a table nearby and handed it to her. "Thank you," she said, dabbing her eyes, but she still didn't know what to say. Her mind was completely blank. She offered a quick, silent prayer for guidance. But still her mind was blank, and before she could come up with an answer they were interrupted by a nurse coming into the room to ask

Samuel if he would be willing to help with a patient whose volunteer hadn't shown up. He eagerly agreed and told Emily he would see her next week. Emily asked the nurse if there was anything more she could do, but it was evident that everything was under control for the moment, so she went home.

Again Emily anticipated her time at the care center, and the week dragged while she pondered her conversations with Samuel and the way she'd felt in his presence. Logically she reminded herself not to let some silly infatuation cloud her judgment and set her up for more hurt. She prayed daily that she would have discernment and guidance in this matter, and she found only positive feelings in her thoughts of Samuel. She also pondered the golden question he had asked and prayed that she might have the opportunity to open that conversation again. For many reasons she greatly looked forward to seeing Samuel again. Still, she said nothing to her family, but she found herself counting the days—and then the hours.

On Monday the routine repeated itself once again, except that no interruptions came to deter an especially long conversation with Samuel that carried them through the bulk of the afternoon. Just when she was beginning to think that perhaps she should excuse herself and not monopolize him too much, he said, "Hey, would you consider letting me take you out to dinner?"

Emily looked up at him, startled. "Are you asking me on a date?"

"That depends," he chuckled. "If you have some policy against going on dates, then no, it's not a date. On the other hand, if you would consider going out with me, then yes, it's most definitely a date."

"Well then," she said, coming to her feet. "It's a date."

He grinned as he stood beside her, then he let out a little laugh and Emily joined him. She could never explain how much she was enjoying his company—but it was evident that he felt the same way. Just the way he looked at her filled something deep inside. Oh, how she had missed being looked at that way!

"So, what are you in the mood for?" he asked, moving into the hallway.

"Anything, really," she said. "I'm not terribly difficult to please."

They stepped outside, and she glanced at her watch, glad to see that they were early enough to miss the usual dinner rush, and she had plenty of time before she would feel the need to get home. Still, she had to say, "I'm just going to take a minute and call home, so they won't be worried."

He seemed surprised and amused. "They?" he asked while she was dialing the number on her mobile phone.

"My family. I'll tell you in a minute." She held up a finger as the phone was answered. "Hello, Scott," she said.

"Mother! What are you up to?"

"Well, I'm not coming home for a while yet. I didn't want anyone to worry."

"Okay," he said. "Does this mean you're missing supper?"

"Yes, as a matter of fact. Are you cooking?"

"No, Emma is. I've got baby duty."

"Good for you," Emily said. "Anyway, I'm actually going out to eat, so don't wait for me."

"Sounds fun. Did you run into an old friend?"

"No, a new one, actually. I'm going on a date." She smiled at Samuel as she said it, and he smiled back.

"Ooh, a date," Scott said. "I can't wait to tell Jess."

"Well, you can tell Jess, but remind him when you do that I'm not a teenager."

"I'll do that," Scott said. "Have a marvelous time."

"Thank you. I believe I will. I'll call when I'm starting home," she said, which was standard family protocol since the drive was long and over deserted roads.

Emily finished her call and stuck the phone in her purse. "Okay," she said, "let's go."

Samuel motioned her toward his car, a mid-sized red convertible. He opened the door for her and asked, "Would you prefer the top up or down?"

"Oh, down," she said eagerly, "unless you can't handle what the wind will do to my hair."

"Oh I love the windblown effect," he said, walking around the car to get in on his side. He turned the ignition, then lowered the top while Emily found a scrunchie in her purse and pulled her hair into a ponytail.

As he began to drive and the wind whipped through Emily's hair, she said to Samuel, "I like what the wind does to *your* hair."

He laughed deeply, and she laughed with him as he quickly rubbed a hand over his nearly bald head. Impulsively she added, "Michael wore his hair like that before he died."

Samuel's expression became quickly sober. He glanced toward her then back to the road. "Cancer?" he asked gently.

"Yes," she said, and looked the opposite direction.

"I'm so sorry," he said and she was surprised to feel him take her hand. He squeezed gently and she squeezed back, amazed at how right it felt to be holding his hand. She was relieved when he didn't let go. "I'm a cancer survivor," he said, and Emily looked at him abruptly. "About eight, nine years ago. I had a tumor in one lung, even though I never smoked. I went through some pretty hefty chemo. My hair never looked quite the same when it grew back, so I just went with the Captain Picard look."

"I like it," she said with a smile. "It suits you."

"Why thank you, Mrs. Hamilton," he said.

Emily lifted her face to the wind and closed her eyes, wondering why she felt happier than she had in months, maybe longer. When they arrived at the restaurant, a steakhouse that was one of her favorites, he opened the car door for her, then held her hand as they went inside.

"I assume," he said, "that since we're on a date it's okay if I hold your hand."

"Of course," she said, smiling.

Once they were seated and had ordered, Samuel took her hand across the table and said, "So, tell me about your family. Tell me about Scott . . . and Jess." It took her a moment to recall that he'd heard her use the names in her phone conversation. While she was thinking where to begin, he said, "Scott is thrilled that you have a date, but Jess won't be. Your sons?"

"Jess is my son," Emily said. "Scott, my son-in-law."

"And who exactly is it that you live with?"

"All of them," she said, laughing softly when his eyes widened. "Well, let me explain. We live in a very old family home. It was built in the Victorian era and it's huge. It's also in the middle of nowhere. We have two family businesses that have also been handed down along with the house. One is a boys' home, the other is horses. Scott oversees the horses, Jess oversees the boys' home. I live with both of their families in a house so large that we only crowd each other in the kitchen."

After Emily said it she had to wonder if she was divulging too much information. Would Samuel pick up on the hints of her wealth the way Rick had? Was he the kind of man to seek out money in a relationship? She prayed that she would be discerning and told herself that she wasn't going to hide anything or play games.

"How delightful," he said.

"It is, actually. I have my own space and privacy when I need it, but it's wonderful having them under the same roof."

"So, Scott is married to your daughter."

"That's right. Emma. She is my youngest."

"Are Jess and Emma your only children?"

Emily laughed softly. "Now you're asking questions that don't have simple answers."

"I'm not in any hurry," he said, and she couldn't miss the genuine interest and yes—adoration—glowing in his eyes.

"Well, just like you and Arlene, Michael and I met at college."

"In the States?"

"That's right. And yes, we fell quickly in love and everything was wonderful, except that . . . for reasons I'll get into another time, I ended up marrying someone else."

"Really?" He sounded both distressed and amazed.

"Really. It was a decision that brought many challenges into my life, as well as Michael's. But I know it was the right thing to do. We had much to learn—both of us. Anyway, I had three daughters with Ryan, and then he was killed. Michael came back into my life in a way that is nothing less than miraculous. He brought me to Australia, married me, took my girls on like they were his own, and we had four more children."

"Good heavens," he chuckled. "Seven children? That's incredible. If I knew nothing more about you, I would be amazed just to know that you raised seven children."

"Raised six, actually," she said. "One of the twins died right after birth."

"Oh, I'm sorry," he said. "Twins?"

"That's right. Emma and Tyson. As I mentioned, Emma is my youngest. Her twin brother was born with a heart problem and didn't live long."

"And where are the other children now?"

"Well, Allison is the oldest. She lives in Utah with her husband and children. The next is Amee; she's in Adelaide with her family. Alexa is the third, and she lives in California."

"They're all married?"

"They are," Emily said. "Amee went through a divorce, but she's happily married now."

"That's wonderful," he said. "Who comes next?"

"Well, Jess. I already told you about him. Jess and Tamra live with me and have five children. And Emma and Scott have a baby girl."

"That's quite a houseful," he said with a chuckle. "But you forgot one. I was counting. You only told me about six children."

"Oh . . . well . . . James and his wife were killed in an accident."

Samuel let out a soft gasp and squeezed her hand gently. "You've lived through some tough times, Emily Hamilton."

Emily looked into his eyes, reminded of the way Michael had once called her Emily Ladd. But rather than missing Michael, she felt touched. "And so have you," she said, returning the squeeze of his hand.

A tension descended between them that was both exciting and unnerving. Emily broke it by saying, "I have a picture, if you're interested."

"Oh, very much," he said.

Emily reached into her purse. Rather than carrying around a pile of pictures of everyone in the family, she had taken to carrying a four-by-six copy of the family portrait that had been taken the Christmas following Scott and Emma's marriage. The entire family was on the lawn in front of the house, all wearing white. The picture was in a plastic sleeve to protect it from the hazards of her purse. She pulled it out and handed it to Samuel. She watched his eyes widen and nearly sparkle with genuine intrigue. "What a beautiful family," he said.

"Thank you," she said. "They are my pride and joy. We've had a couple of babies since then." She turned it over to show him the little photos of the newest additions, tucked into the other side of the plastic sleeve.

"Adorable," he said, and Emily put the pictures back in her purse.

Their meal was brought to the table, and they shared small talk as they proceeded to eat. Filling in a brief lull, Samuel said, "So, you're a religious woman."

"Is this another of your psychic assessments?"

"No," Samuel chuckled. "You told me you went to church; that's how you learned they needed help at the care center."

"So I did," she said. "Yes, I'm religious. And you?"

"No, not really," he said. "And since your children are going to drill you about this man you went on a date with, I'll tell you what you can tell them."

"Okay," she said, intrigued with the idea.

"You tell them he's not a religious man, but he had a Christian upbringing, and he believes in God. He's not perfect, but he tries to be a good man. He doesn't sleep around, and he's never been drunk." He took a bite of his steak and added, "Of course, you haven't known me long enough to know if I'm a man of integrity, so you'll just have to assume I'm telling you the truth."

Emily just smiled and took a drink of water. She knew he was telling the truth. She could never explain to him how she knew; she just knew. "And what will you tell Trent about me?" she asked. When he said nothing she asked, "Is that so difficult to answer?"

"Perhaps," he said, saying nothing more until he added earnestly, "Emily, there's so much I want to say, but . . . I . . . I'm almost afraid to say anything at all for fear that . . ."

"What?" she asked.

"All the things that keep coming to mind sound so much like placating sweet talk—like something a man would say just to have his way with a beautiful woman."

"I'm flattered—as any woman my age would be, but I have to tell you I don't believe in intimacy outside of marriage."

"How refreshing that is!" he said with dreamy eyes.

"Is it?"

"Oh, yes!"

Following a minute of silence, Emily couldn't resist saying, "I'm ready."

"For what?"

"To hear what you want to say—the words you fear will sound like placating sweet talk. I heard an implication that you might think I'm beautiful. Michael thought I was beautiful, but then . . . he fell in love with me when I was in college. I think he would have loved me no matter what I looked like."

"You are beautiful, Emily. And while you are lovely to look at, sitting there across the table, that's not why I want to sit here with you for the rest of my life."

"They might shove us out before then," Emily said, and he laughed softly.

"Here, the parking lot, anywhere you might want to go or be. I want to be with you, Emily, because . . ."

"Yes?"

"Because you're funny, you're wise, you're humble, and tender, and you make me feel like whatever might be left of my life could actually be worth living. I know we've not known each other long, but since I first laid eyes on you, I've had difficulty thinking of anything else."

Emily felt suddenly overcome by his words and glanced down, attempting to discern whether or not they were as genuine as they seemed. She felt somewhat comforted to hear that he'd been thinking of her as she'd been thinking of him. Attempting to ease the tension, she said, "That *does* sound like placating sweet talk."

"Does it?"

"A bit, yes . . . but . . ."

"But?"

She looked directly at him. "It doesn't *feel* that way." He smiled, and she was grateful to have found a thought to ease the thickening tension, "So, what will you tell Trent?"

"I'll tell him that for the first time since his mother died, I'm getting to know a woman who actually stirs me."

Emily felt stunned, unable to speak. The problem being that he stirred her too. She tried to tell herself that it had only been two weeks since she'd first laid eyes on him. But since when had she lived her life according to logic? Or at the very least, she wasn't one to allow logic to override her feelings. She wondered for a moment if she was being foolish, but he wasn't asking her to marry him on the spot. She could take all the time in the world to get to know him, enjoy his company, and just bask in the light he'd brought into her life. Again she felt the need to ease the tension. She smiled and said, "Now *that* does sound like sweet talk."

"Not placating?"

"Just sweet," she said.

"And why is that?"

"Because I believe you're telling me the truth."

"How can you be sure?" he asked.

"I don't think I can be completely sure without the test of time."

"Oh, the test of time. I think I like that."

"You do?" she asked.

"Oh yes. I'm hoping that means we will be spending a great deal of time together."

"How delightful," she said. "And perhaps with enough time you can be sure that I'm telling the truth, as well."

"About what?"

"About what I'm going to tell you."

"And what is that?" he asked with that laughter ringing through his voice that she had already grown to love.

"That for the first time since I lost Michael, I've met a man who actually stirs *me*."

Samuel brought her hand to his lips and placed a tender kiss there. "I do believe you mean that."

"I do," she said, then they both started laughing at the same time before she even managed to add, "No pun intended."

They finished their meal with conversation that was anything but small talk. Long after they'd finished eating, they sat facing each other over an empty table, sharing experiences from their lives, both joyous and tragic. When they finally left the restaurant, Samuel put his arm around Emily's shoulders as he walked her to the car. How good it felt to lean against a strong, masculine shoulder and to smell the subtle aroma of this morning's aftershave lotion. In the car he said, "So, has there been anyone at all since Michael?"

"I've tried a number of first dates," she said, and he laughed, as if he understood completely. "Beyond that there was a man named Rick. I enjoyed his company and we spent a great deal of time together, but . . ."

"But?"

Emily wanted to say that it had never felt anything like this with Rick. She settled for saying, "It kind of fell apart in a hurry when I asked him some questions about money, and a series of arguments followed."

"Ooh," he said. "Maybe we should wait until a second date to talk about money. Unless of course you want to just get it out of the way."

"Okay," she said, "tell me your theory on money."

"My theory?" he asked. "I'm not sure I have a theory. I just . . . have enough to meet my needs. What else matters?"

Her mind wandered with the thought until he said, "What about you, Mrs. Hamilton? What's your theory on money?"

Emily took a deep breath. "I believe that having too much or too little only creates a problem when your priorities are screwed up. Having money only enhances who and what you really are. If you're stingy and selfish, then money will make you more stingy and selfish. If you are generous and gracious, then money will make you more so. If you're unhappy without money, you're going to be more unhappy with it."

"I've never looked at it that way, but I do believe you're right."

"So, we might as well just cut to the chase," Emily said. "It won't take you long to figure it out anyway, psychic as you are."

He laughed. "Figure what out?" he asked. She hesitated, and he said, "That you're so happy and generous and gracious because you were already that way before you married a very wealthy Michael Hamilton?" Emily felt her eyes widen as she attempted to gauge whether or not she should feel defensive. "No, I'm not psychic," he said. "But I have lived in this area for many years. You don't live around here without knowing about Byrnehouse-Davies & Hamilton. When you told me about the boys' home, the horses . . . well, it's not so difficult to figure out." He looked at her hard and said, "You seem . . . upset? Offended?"

"Forgive me," she said, taking a deep breath. "Rick's theory on money was that it was just as easy to fall in love with a rich woman as it was a poor one. To be quite honest, the experience made me a little leery."

"It's okay, Emily. I told you, I have sufficient for my needs."

Emily smiled and decided to leave it at that. She reminded herself that with time she would come to know for certain if her instincts were being honest with her.

"What about you?" she asked as he drove. "Has there been anyone else since Arlene?"

"No one worth mentioning," he said. "I was actually engaged once, but I quickly realized that I was wanting to marry her for the wrong reasons. She would have been a good mother to Trent, but I didn't love her enough to be a good husband. She has remained a good friend, and, indirectly, she was a good mother to Trent. She eventually married and is quite happy, as far as I know."

Samuel glanced at his watch and said, "Hey, do you have time to go for a little walk before you start home?"

Emily glanced at her own watch. She had no desire whatsoever to say good night to this man. "Sure, why not? It's not even dark yet."

He pulled the car over near the care center, and she realized there were even more lovely gardens surrounding the building than she'd realized when she'd been visiting with Esther. They walked slowly, hand in hand, until he put his arm around her, and she wondered how she had ever coped at all without a man in her life. Then she had to ask herself if Samuel Reid could be considered in her life when she'd known him so short a time. A comfortable silence fell over them and Emily's mind began to wander through all that had happened since she'd first laid eyes on Samuel Reid. She felt a little quivery inside to realize how everything had changed. *Everything.* Then her heart quickened as she recalled his comment about wanting to be with Arlene again. She wondered if this might be the right time to bring that up again; and she couldn't think of any reason not to.

They sat together on a little iron bench beneath a tree where they could see the sun sinking toward the horizon, but the silence persisted. Emily took a deep breath and said quietly, "Samuel, there's something I feel I have to say."

"Okay," he said, looking directly at her.

"I can answer your question," she said.

"What question?"

"That thing you want more than anything in the world," she said, and he turned toward her abruptly.

"Really?" he asked, sounding skeptical.

"Yes, but I must clarify something. You said that being with Arlene again was what you wanted more than anything in this world. But it's really a heavenly issue, isn't it?"

"I suppose it is," he said, his skepticism deepening.

Emily felt nervous and prayed that she would be guided in her words, that his spirit would be touched, his heart softened, his mind opened.

"And you say you have the answer?" he asked, almost sounding rude.

"I do," she said in a gentle voice that she hoped would keep the proper spirit to this conversation. "The answer is deep and complicated, Samuel, and yet it's very simple. I feel like there are a dozen or more steps to explain the answer and get to the point, and it could take hours. But I'm just going to skip to the point, and then we can talk more another time, and if you're interested, I can give you the long version."

He gave her a smile that erased his skeptical mood as he said, "I think I'd like to hear the long version, if only so I could spend more time with you."

Emily laughed softly. "I think that could be arranged."

"So get to the point, then," he said more seriously.

Emily turned to look directly at him. "Marriage can be eternal, Samuel, if it's done in the proper way, by the proper authority."

"What are you saying?" he asked in a growl of a whisper.

"That death doesn't have to be the end; it can be the beginning."

"But she's already dead," he said with a resignation that was heartbreaking.

"It can be done by proxy for those who have already died."

Samuel stared at her for more than a minute, and Emily just stared back, allowing him the time to digest what he'd heard. He finally said, "This is a religious thing then."

"It is," she said.

"And you really believe it's possible . . . to be together . . . in the next life?"

"No, Samuel. I *know* it's possible. I know it beyond any shadow of a doubt."

She watched his brow furrow and his eyes narrow. He looked away abruptly and coughed. When he pressed a thumb and forefinger over his eyes, she realized he was fighting tears. She allowed him time to digest what she'd said—and whatever it might be that he was feeling. He finally turned to face her, and with a tender voice and curiosity sparkling in his eyes, he said, "I think that I actually believe you. But I'm assuming that to make such a thing happen could be a long and difficult path."

"Not necessarily. It all depends on a person's attitude, I suppose."

"I think I should very much like to hear the long version."

"And I'll look forward to sharing it. However, I am old enough to be a grandmother, you know. And I have an hour's drive."

"Would you like me to drive you home—"

"And then what? Drive back alone?"

"It would be worth it."

"You're very sweet," she said. "But I can manage fine, thank you."

"Will you call me when you get home, so that I know you're safe?"

Emily inhaled deeply. How good it felt to have a man concerned for her safety! He was so like Michael in so many ways. "I will if you'll give me your phone number."

"I'll give you mine if you'll give me yours," he said, and she laughed.

They exchanged numbers, and he walked her to her car. For a moment she feared he might try to kiss her, and then she feared that he wouldn't. The way she felt in his presence battled momentarily with the logic of this being their first date. Of course, they'd talked more than many people might in ten dates. Still, he settled the problem perfectly when he pressed a lingering kiss to her cheek.

"Good night, Emily. It's been an unfathomable pleasure."

"Good night, Samuel," she said. "Thank you for a wonderful evening. I'll call as soon as I'm home."

"I'll be counting the minutes," he said, and she got into the car.

Emily was grateful for the long drive and the time it gave her to ponder the amazing events of this day, combined with her previous encounters with Samuel the last couple of weeks. At first she felt elated and as giddy as a schoolgirl, then doubts began to fill her mind, telling her it was too good to be true, that surely he had some hidden faults that were destined to bring grief into her life. She began to pray for guidance and discernment, and she continued to pray through the remainder of the drive. Pulling the car up beside the house, she turned it off and sat there, just savoring the silence, attempting to decipher what she was feeling. She gasped as a familiar presence seemed to surround her. She closed her eyes to hold the sensation closer. "Michael," she whispered, unable to recall the last time she had felt his spirit close to her. But rarely had the sensation been so overt; it had more often been subtle and barely definable—yet undeniable nevertheless.

For a moment she wondered if he would be jealous or frustrated with her attention to another man. But she'd barely entertained the idea when a thought appeared as clearly in her mind as if he had whispered the words in her ear. *Samuel is a good man, Emily. He will bless your life, as you will bless his.*

Emily gasped again as she absorbed what this meant. She had been the recipient of communication through the ministering of angels before, but it had never come to her more clearly than this. She felt tangible evidence of Michael's love surrounding her, filling her, giving her hope that one day they *would* be together again. And then he was gone. She cried for several minutes, feeling a combination of sorrow and joy. Then she got out of the car and walked toward the house.

"Thank you, Michael," she whispered into the night air before she opened the door. "I love you too." Then she went inside, ready to move into a new phase of her life, and confident that she was on the right path.

Emily was met at the top of the stairs by Jess, wearing pajama pants and a T-shirt. "I'm glad you're home safe," he said.

"What is this?" she asked with a little laugh. "Is this role reversal? You're going to be my parent and see that I come home on time?"

He chuckled and put his arms around her. "I just want to know that you're safe because I love you."

"And I'm grateful," she said, looking up at him.

"What is this?" he asked, taking hold of her chin. Emily glanced down when she realized that she couldn't stop smiling. He lifted her face and chuckled again. "Maybe you should tell me about this date."

"I met a man at the care center, and—"

"One of the residents?" he teased.

"No." Emily laughed. "The residents make me feel very young, indeed."

"You are very young."

"You're flattering me again."

"So you met him at the care center."

"That's right. He was helping out as well. He's retired and likes to spend time there quite frequently. We've been talking . . . while I've been there the last couple of weeks. He took me to dinner, then we went for a walk."

"And you're grinning like a Cheshire cat."

"Well," she laughed softly, "it was a really nice date." She kissed Jess's cheek. "Now, if you'll excuse me . . . he wanted me to call and let him know I got home safely."

"Ooh, this is serious," Jess said. He said it lightly, but Emily sensed that he was struggling with this. He was saying all the right things to be supportive, but his teasing didn't fool her. She knew this would be difficult for him. But she felt certain he would adjust with time. And they all had plenty of time.

Chapter Seven

Emily hurried to brush her teeth and get ready for bed so that she could sit in bed to call Samuel. She had a hunch that they wouldn't get off the phone quickly, and she was completely relaxed before they finally said good night with the promise that they would talk in the morning.

Emily slept deeply and peacefully and woke up feeling happier than she had since she'd lost Michael. Pondering the miracles of the previous day, she had a feeling that more miracles were underfoot. She also knew that miracles didn't happen without opposition. Still, she knew in her heart what was right, and she would press forward.

At the breakfast table Emily endured some teasing about her date, then Scott said, "Seriously, Mom. Tell us about him."

Emily repeated, almost word for word, the statement Samuel had told her to tell her family. She told them about the golden question he had asked her and the answer she'd been able to give him. She said nothing about the depth of her feelings for this man, nor Samuel's apparent feelings for her. And she kept to herself the incredible, sacred moment she'd shared with Michael that had let her know she was on the right path.

"He's not a member of the Church," Jess pointed out, as if she might not have noticed.

"And neither was your father when I met him," Emily said. No one had a comeback for that.

Jess watched his mother talking about this man she had met and wondered how he should feel. He couldn't deny how happy she seemed. She was positively glowing. But what if this guy turned out to be like Rick? What if he broke her heart? What if he was after her money? And what if he turned out to be a decent guy, and he moved in and started sleeping in Michael Hamilton's bed? Jess reminded himself, as he had a hundred times before, that his mother was a wise, intelligent woman with a strong spirit, and she had the right to date—and even marry—if she chose to. His feelings were his own problem, and he was going to have to let them go.

Breakfast was barely over when the phone rang. Jess was closest and quickly picked it up. "Hello," he said, startled to hear a man say, "Hello, I'm looking for Emily Hamilton."

Jess smirked at his mother and said, "Then you're looking in the right place."

The man on the other end of the phone gave a deep chuckle and asked, "Would I be speaking to Jess or Scott? No, wait, it must be Jess."

"How can you be sure?" Jess asked.

"Scott is American."

"That's true," Jess said. "So, you've got it right."

"Well, it's nice to meet you, Jess—relatively speaking. Samuel Reid speaking."

"Hello, Mr. Reid," he said, and his mother faintly blushed.

"May I speak to your mother?" Samuel asked.

"She's right here," Jess said, handing Emily the phone.

Jess, Tamra, Scott, and Emma all stood and watched Emily while the glow in her face brightened as she talked. She turned her back to them, making them all chuckle softly. Her side of the conversation was nothing more than a series of words like "yes," and "okay," and an occasional "that sounds great." She finished with a firm, "I'll see you soon, then."

She hung up the phone and said smugly, "I'm going to town for the day."

"Ooh," Scott said, "and what will you be doing?"

"He said it was a surprise," Emily said, giving them each a quick hug. "You all have a marvelous day, and I'll see you later."

"When?" Jess asked.

"I don't know—later," she said as she hurried up the stairs.

Once she was gone, Tamra said, "You're acting like her father or something."

Jess just changed the subject and tried not to think about what this could mean.

Emily rushed into her bathroom where she checked her appearance. She grabbed her purse, checked its contents, and added a couple of things before she went back downstairs and out to the car. After saying a little prayer, as she always did before driving anywhere, she headed into town, unable to keep from laughing spontaneously just to keep the happiness from exploding.

Emily found Samuel at the care center, visiting with Bertie. He rose when she entered the room and pressed a kiss to her cheek. She was so glad to see him that it took great willpower not to just hug him the same way she'd hugged her children after breakfast. Emily sat and visited with Samuel and Bertie for a short while before they said good-bye to Bertie and went out to Samuel's car. Once on the road, he said, "Now, I must confess I'm not very good at this dating thing. So, this might not be very original, but if you're up to it, I'd like to cook lunch for you."

"You cook?" she asked.

"I've been on my own for twenty-seven years," he said. "I manage fairly well in the kitchen. Is that good or bad?"

"It's great," she said. "It's just that . . . Michael loved to cook. I guess you could say I like having a man who can find his way around in the kitchen." Samuel smiled, then she added, "I'm sorry."

"For what?"

"I shouldn't compare you to Michael like that."

"I don't know how you could help it. You lived a lifetime with him, and it hasn't been so many years."

"Yes, but . . . it's not really right, is it?"

"As long as you don't start pointing out my inadequacies in contrast to Michael, I'm okay with it." He took her hand and added, "I'm not going to try to replace him, Emily. But maybe I can help fill in the hole he left in your life—and maybe you can do the same for me."

Emily smiled at him but couldn't speak due to the knot in her throat. He asked, "Did I say something wrong?"

"No, of course not. It's just that . . . I appreciate your attitude, and I believe you're right. When I first told my children I was ready to start dating, some of them had a hard time with it. I think Jess is still struggling with it, especially. But . . . I told him that a man didn't need to fill his father's shoes, in order to fill my loneliness." She squeezed his hand and smiled at him. "I just want you to know that works both ways. I could never replace Arlene or what you felt for her—still feel for her. But maybe I can fill a hole."

"Maybe," he said, his smile widening. Then he chuckled.

"What's funny?" she asked.

"We've barely known each other a couple of weeks, and listen to us."

"Well . . . I wouldn't expect either of us to do anything too rash or impulsive, however . . . I don't know about you, but . . . if something feels right, then it feels right."

She sensed that the ensuing silence was due to Samuel fighting his feelings. She was glad to know that he had tender feelings. "Yes, I agree," he said, his voice breaking. Emily kissed his cheek, and he squeezed her hand.

Together they went grocery shopping, which he said was mandatory for them to do together in order to learn each other's tastes, and also to make the cooking-lunch date complete. Emily was beginning to think that the way they agreed on the items to be purchased was almost eerie until he asked what kind of wine she preferred. "I'm sorry," she said, "but I don't drink."

"Not at all?" he asked, sounding more intrigued than astonished.

"Not at all," she said. "Water would be fine for me, thank you. You're welcome to drink whatever you like."

"Okay," he said, and he bought a bottle of expensive red wine.

A similar conversation came up over coffee, but they quickly moved on with their shopping. With the groceries loaded into the backseat of the car, Emily was surprised when he returned to the care center, but parked on the other side of the building.

"You live here?" she asked.

"I do," he said, offering a brief explanation before he got out of the car. "I got tired of keeping up the yard and a home once Trent was long gone. So I sold the house and got an apartment here. It's nice because the residents are all retired people, and we have a great time. When I get too decrepit to take care of myself, they can just move me to the other side." He smiled. "So you see, my future is all worked out."

"Sounds like a good plan," she said, liking the way he had a plan that suited a man with no family close by. But she couldn't help pondering the idea of what it might be like if marriage actually ended up a part of their future. She reminded herself to give such an idea some time. They had plenty of time.

Emily helped him carry the groceries to his apartment on the second floor. She was impressed with the comfort and spaciousness of the place, and also by how tidy it was. He showed her pictures of Trent and Trent's wife, Julia, and their children. He showed her pictures of Arlene and of himself when he was younger. She felt certain she would have liked Arlene and wondered if one day they might be good friends. Emily helped Samuel in the kitchen, where it took a ridiculous amount of time to put together a pasta dish that Samuel declared was his specialty. When they sat down to eat at a beautifully set table, Emily said, "Do you mind if we bless it?"

"Of course not; please . . . feel free." He motioned toward her, and she bowed her head, offering a brief but sincere blessing on the food, and in the prayer she expressed gratitude for the friendship they had gained and were able to share. Samuel said amen, then offered her a warm smile before they started eating. She complimented his cooking in the midst of small talk, then he said, "There's something about your relationship with Michael that I haven't been able to stop thinking about. Perhaps you could help me understand. If you met him in college, and the two of you were so smitten with each other . . . why did you marry someone else?"

Emily sighed deeply and leaned back in her chair. She realized that in light of the present situation, this was not an easy question to answer. Still, the answer was simple, and he had a right to know. She cleared her throat gently and just said it. "Michael was not a member of the church that I belonged to, and I felt very strongly about marrying within the Church."

Emily saw the implication settle into Samuel's mind before he said, "I see." He took a sip of wine and asked, "And was that difference resolved?"

"It was," she said. "He became a member without my knowledge around the time my first husband was killed. However, when I told Michael I would marry him, I didn't know that he'd joined the Church."

"So . . . what changed?"

"Well . . . the simple version is that I knew in my heart it was right to marry Michael at that time, when it hadn't been right before. In both cases, I just did what I felt was right."

"A woman who trusts her instincts . . . and follows them."

Emily wanted to explain how the guidance of the Spirit worked in her life, but she didn't feel it was the right time to bring up anything more to do with religion—until he said, "So, what faith do you belong to, exactly?"

Emily said with perfect confidence, "It's The Church of Jesus Christ of Latter-day Saints, more commonly known as the Mormons."

His surprise was evident. And then he laughed. When he said nothing, Emily said, "You're laughing at me."

"Not at you, no," he said, chuckling again. "I'm just . . . surprised. You're a Mormon?"

"I am."

"You are not what I would have expected a Mormon to be."

"Well, truthfully we are one of the most misunderstood religions in the world. We're not living like the Amish people, and we don't practice polygamy. As you can see I'm just a rather ordinary woman."

"Oh, no," he shook his head, "not ordinary. Normal, perhaps, but never ordinary." She smiled, and he added, "Beyond your abstinence from liquor and coffee."

"There are many people who choose not to indulge in either, simply because they're not good for you. It's not so unusual, really."

"I suppose not," he said.

The conversation moved steadily on as they finished their meal and worked together to clean up the kitchen. They moved into the lounge room and sat close together on the sofa while they continued to talk. Emily felt embarrassed when she began to feel sleepy, until she realized that Samuel was feeling the same. When she commented, he said, "We didn't have this problem when we were dating in college."

"No, we certainly didn't."

He stood up and urged her to lie down. "Here," he said, "you take this sofa, and I'll take that one. After a good nap we'll decide what to do with the rest of our day."

Emily smiled up at him, then made herself comfortable and quickly drifted off to sleep. She woke once to hear Samuel snoring softly from the other couch. She rolled over and drifted back to sleep until she heard some noise in the kitchen. After a quick trip to the bathroom, she found Samuel in the kitchen with a glass of wine.

"Hello," he said, smiling brightly. "Did you rest?"

"Very well, thank you. And you?"

"Oh, yes." He took a sip of wine and said, "You looked so beautiful sleeping that I confess I couldn't resist just watching you."

Emily gave a self-conscious chuckle. "I don't know whether to feel embarrassed or flattered."

"Neither," he said, holding up his glass. "I'd offer you some, but . . ."

"It's alright." She got a glass out of the cabinet. "I know where to get a drink of water, thank you." She got some ice out of the freezer and poured water over it from a water filter near the tap.

"What should we do now?" he asked, and she glanced at the clock.

"Good heavens." She checked her watch to be certain it showed the same time. "I slept longer than I thought I had."

"Did you need to get home or—"

"Not necessarily, but . . ." She was struck with an idea and added cautiously, "Come home with me for dinner."

He chuckled, then said, "You're serious."

"Of course I'm serious."

"You're ready for me to meet the family?"

"I am."

"You know they'll probably be suspicious."

"Not necessarily," she said, while she couldn't help wondering how Jess might react.

"Well, I'm not a Mormon."

"I'm certain they can handle that," Emily said with a little laugh. "Come on, what do you say?"

"I'd love to," he said. "Why don't I just follow you out, so that you don't have to drive me home?"

"Okay, I won't argue with that," she said, grateful for an opportunity to call home on her mobile phone and pave the way a little in order to make this go as smoothly as possible. "Before I start home, however, I should call and see if we need anything picked up in town."

Samuel motioned toward the phone on the wall. "Feel free. I'll just freshen up a bit."

Emily dialed home while Samuel went into the other room and closed the door. Tamra answered the phone.

"Hello, dear," Emily said. "How is everything?"

"Fine? How are you?"

"I'm great," Emily said.

Tamra giggled. "I can't wait to hear all about this man you've met."

"And I can't wait to tell you, but . . . how about if you just meet him?"

"Really?" she said. "Are you bringing him out, then?"

"I've invited him. Who's cooking supper? I don't want to cause any stress."

"I am," she said, "but Rhea's helping me. We're doing chicken enchiladas. Is that all right?"

"It's great. We don't need to make a big deal out of it. We don't have anything to hide. If he can't handle dinner with the family as we really are, then . . . too bad."

"That's the spirit," Tamra said.

"So, are you okay with that? Or do you want me to bring home Chinese or something?"

"I'm fine with it. And you know Rhea can handle anything. You're not going to stress us out over a dinner guest."

"That's my girl," Emily said. "Now, do we need anything in town? Groceries? Anything?"

Tamra thought for a moment then said, "Not that I can think of. Nothing we can't do without for a day or two."

"Okay then, we'll be on our way in a few minutes. You might give the others a fair warning."

"I'll do that," Tamra said. "But . . ."

"But?"

"Maybe you should call Jess yourself."

"I intend to," Emily said.

"I don't understand why this is so difficult for him," Tamra said. "We've talked about it a great deal, but . . . it's just hard for him."

"I know," Emily said. "I'll talk to him. Thank you, Tamra."

Emily ended her call just before Samuel came out of the bedroom wearing the same jeans but a navy blue, button-up shirt. Her heart quickened at the sight of him.

"All ready?" she asked.

"I am." He picked up his keys and opened the door. He walked her to her car where they exchanged mobile phone numbers in case there was a reason to communicate while driving. Once in the car, Emily secured her hands-free cord into the phone and called the boys' home. As she pulled out onto the road, with Samuel's car in her rearview mirror, the secretary at the boys' home told her that Jess was on the phone, but she'd have him call back as soon as he was finished. A couple of minutes later the phone rang, and Emily pushed the button to turn it on.

"What's up?" Jess asked.

"I'm bringing Samuel home for supper."

"I see," Jess said.

"You will be civil, won't you?" Emily asked.

"Of course I will."

"Okay," Emily said, "I know you'll be civil, but . . . I guess what I'm asking is . . . will you give him a fair chance? He's a good man, Jess."

"And how can you know that in so short a time?"

"I just know," she said.

Following half a minute of silence where it became evident that Jess didn't know what to say, he finally asked, "So what did you do today?"

"We went grocery shopping and cooked lunch at his apartment."

"He lives in an apartment?" Jess asked, as if it were somehow a crime.

"Yes, a very fine one. It's in a retirement facility. Then we took a nap and—"

"A *nap?*" he echoed, sounding appalled.

"Yes, a nap, Jess. I fell asleep on one sofa, and he fell asleep on the other. We're *old* you know, and we were tired. He snores. Is there anything else you want to know?"

"If you're bringing him home with you, then . . . you must really like him."

"I really do," Emily said. "I truly believe that we can bless his life, and the other way around. I know this is difficult for you, but please . . . be gracious."

"I'm sorry I've been so ratty, Mother. I know it's not fair to you. Logically there is no reason I should have a problem with any of this. I know you're an intelligent woman, and you got along just fine without me for years. I know I should be happy to see you having a social life, and I know it's perfectly appropriate. It's just . . . hard."

"Why, Jess? Tell me why. Let's talk about it."

"If I knew, I would love to tell you. I can't explain it; I just know it's hard. So . . . forgive me for being a brat. I will be gracious; I promise."

"Thank you, and . . . apology accepted. You're a good man, Jess. And I love you."

"I love you too, Mom. Drive carefully, okay?"

"I will. See you in a while."

Emily ended the call and put more attention into watching Samuel in her rearview mirror. There was too much dust trailing behind her to actually see him, but she knew he was there. And that alone gave her an underlying peace that was difficult to define. When she passed under the iron archway just before the boys' home, the road became paved and she was able to actually see Samuel's face in the mirror. She felt a quiver in her stomach at the sight of him. And when she thought of how quickly he had come into her life and filled a hole there, she couldn't hold back a little burst of laughter.

Emily drove around the house and parked the car where the drive ended, between the house and the stables. Samuel pulled up behind her just as she got out of the car. For a moment Emily wondered if he might be appraising the physical evidence of the family's assets. But his smile was focused completely on her as he got out of his car and closed the door.

"Now you know where to find me," she said, taking his hand.

"How delightful," he said, glancing around. "What a beautiful place to raise a family."

"Yes, it certainly is," Emily said. "Shall we go inside? I think it's almost time for supper."

"Of course," he said, chuckling tensely. "I confess I'm a bit nervous. I haven't been faced with meeting a girl's family since I was dating Arlene in college."

Emily laughed. "I'm hardly a girl, and we do have several advantages."

"Like what?"

"Well, you don't have to convince anyone that you'll be a good provider or good at raising children."

"No, I certainly don't," he chuckled.

They walked together into the house and immediately heard Tamra call from the kitchen, "Is that you, Mom?"

"It's me," Emily said and led Samuel into the kitchen where they found Tamra wiping her hands on her apron and Rhea stirring something at the stove. "Hello, Tamra. This is Samuel Reid. Samuel, my daughter-in-law, Tamra Hamilton."

"A pleasure to meet you," Samuel said, reaching out his free hand to shake Tamra's.

"Oh, the pleasure is all mine," Tamra said.

"You're American," Samuel said.

"Originally," Tamra said with a smile. "Australian-American, really. Just like Emily." The women shared a smile.

"And this is Tamra's Aunt Rhea," Emily said, motioning toward her. "She lives with us."

"A pleasure to meet you, Rhea," Samuel said.

"Indeed," Rhea said, winking at Emily, which made everyone in the room chuckle.

"So, what brought you to Australia?" Samuel asked Tamra.

Tamra shrugged and said, "It's kind of a long story, but . . . well . . . Rhea came here before I did, but in the long run . . . God just led me here."

"A lovely place to be led," Samuel said, looking at Emily.

"It is indeed," Tamra said. "Just make yourself at home. We can eat shortly. It's nothing fancy."

"No worries," Samuel said. "If I—"

He was interrupted by the clatter of children coming up the long hall. Emily turned toward the door just as five children ran into the kitchen, all excited to see their grandmother. She heard Samuel chuckle a couple of times as she took a minute to greet them all properly. Emma came behind them with Laura in her arms. Emily introduced Samuel to Emma and the children, and a moment later Scott came in from the stables. He kissed Emma in greeting, took the baby from her, then eagerly introduced himself to Samuel.

"It is such a pleasure to meet you, Mr. Reid," Scott said. "I suspect you're the reason Emily was glowing at breakfast."

Emily blushed slightly, making Scott chuckle. "And I thought I was the one glowing," Samuel said. He then said to Scott, "So, you're another American member of the family."

"Getting more Australian by the year," Scott said with pride.

"And what brought you to Australia?" Samuel asked, as if he was genuinely interested in each member of Emily's family.

Scott shrugged and chuckled. "I think God just sort of . . . led me here."

Samuel turned to look at Emily, seeming surprised. Emily and Tamra both chuckled before Emily said, "They didn't collaborate on that answer, honest."

"What answer?" Scott asked.

"Well, Tamra answered that question pretty much the same way," Emily explained. She then said to Samuel, "Have a seat; make yourself at home. Mealtime here can be fairly entertaining."

"I hope you survive," Emma said, pulling dishes out of a cupboard.

"Oh, it's far too quiet at my place," Samuel said.

"You won't get quiet here," Tamra said, helping Emma set the table. "Well, the kids do go to bed eventually, and fortunately it's a pretty big house; otherwise we'd drive each other crazy."

While Scott sat near Samuel and entertained the baby, the women worked together to get the meal on and get the children washed up and in their places at the table, except for Claire, who was put into a highchair. Emily noticed that Samuel seemed comfortable, even though a bit amazed. He'd probably never even imagined such a noisy scene at a dinner table. But he appeared to be enjoying himself, and Emily couldn't help thinking how he seemed to fit in so well.

* * *

Jess purposely waited until the last possible moment to leave his office at the boys' home and go into the house for supper. He had to keep reminding himself that it was okay for his mother to be bringing a man home and that he'd promised her he would be civil and appropriate. Still, repeating it over and over didn't dispel his deep instinct that she belonged with his father—and only with his father.

Approaching the kitchen, he heard the typical noise of his children combined with the laughter of adults. He took a deep breath and entered the room, grateful to get a solid glimpse of this man, who was sitting next to Scott, before anyone noticed him there. He didn't know what he'd expected, but already he felt surprised. There was something about the way he seemed so comfortable sitting among the family in the kitchen that made Jess think perhaps this wouldn't be so bad after all.

"Oh hi," Tamra said, noticing Jess there.

He became distracted by his wife as she crossed the room and greeted him with a kiss. He was then assaulted by Evelyn, Michael, Joshua, and Tyson all running to get a hug. He laughed and returned their affection while Claire wiggled impatiently in her highchair, reaching toward him, saying, "Daddy, Daddy! Hug me! Hug me!"

He set the twins down and picked Claire up, laughing as she gave him a loud smooch. He got Claire settled again into her high chair while Tamra put the enchiladas on the table. He actually forgot there was someone beyond family in the room until he turned around and heard his mother say, "And that's Jess."

Jess watched this man come to his feet and step forward, his hand outstretched. "A pleasure to meet you, Jess," he said as Jess shook his hand.

"Jess, this is Samuel Reid," Emily added.

"Good to meet you," Jess said.

Samuel smiled and said, "So, I hear you're the spitting image of your father."

"That's what they tell me," Jess said, unable to deny how the statement made this easier somehow. Just the fact that this man acknowledged his father seemed a positive point.

"I understand he was an amazing man, and you're reputed to take after him in many respects."

Jess chuckled and glanced down, feeling mildly embarrassed. "I won't dispute my father being an amazing man. As for anything else you've heard, you might do well to get a second opinion."

Samuel chuckled, then Tamra declared that they could sit down and begin. Jess asked Evelyn to offer the blessing. She said a fairly eloquent prayer, in it asking that Grandma's new friend would have a good time while he was here.

"Thank you," Jess said to her with a smile after the amen was spoken.

"You have a beautiful daughter there," Samuel said to Jess as the meal proceeded.

"Yes, I do," Jess said with pride, winking at Evelyn. "Although, I must confess that I can't take any credit for that."

"How is that?" Samuel asked, seeming intrigued.

Jess and Evelyn exchanged a tender smile as he said, "Why don't you tell him how it works, sweetie."

Evelyn looked directly at Samuel and said, "My birth parents were killed in a car accident when I was just a baby. I don't remember them, but we have lots of pictures so I know what they look like. Jess used to be my uncle, until he married Tamra, and then they decided they wanted to be my parents here on this earth until I could be with my real parents again. So they adopted me, but my last name was still Hamilton."

Emily watched Samuel's expression as Evelyn gave her explanation. His smile made it clear he was impressed with this child. The interest in his eyes made Emily suspect that he'd picked up on the underlying message—the same message Emily had shared with him last night. The conversation moved on and Emily was pleased to see that even Jess appeared to be comfortable and relaxed. Perhaps his heart was finally softening to the idea of his mother having a man in her life.

At a lull in the conversation, Scott said, "So, tell us about your family, Samuel."

"I have only one son," Samuel said. "Trent is his name. He lives with his wife and children in England."

"You must miss them terribly," Tamra said.

"I do, yes," Samuel said. "But they're great at keeping in touch. We e-mail nearly every day, and they send lots of digital pictures. They're coming next month for a visit."

"Oh, how delightful," Emily said, hoping she would get to meet them. On the other hand she could well imagine that Samuel would be very occupied while they were here, and she might not be able to spend as much time with him herself. She was amazed at how the thought was difficult when they'd only been dating for a couple of days.

"If you have only one child," Emma said, "then this must seem like a circus." Just as she said it, the twins started fighting over who had taken the most bites, and Claire threw her cup on the floor. The adults responded with laughter while Jess broke up the fight and Tamra took care of the cup.

"It's very entertaining," Samuel said with that ring of laughter in his words that Emily liked so well.

"You should see it when they're *all* here," Emily said.

"Now *that* is a circus," Jess said. "When they're *all* here, I try to stay in hiding."

"It sounds delightful," Samuel said, and Jess made a comical noise of disbelief.

"Forgive me if I'm being nosy," Emma said to Samuel, "but I can't help wondering about Trent's mother. Is she—"

"You're welcome to ask anything you like," he said easily. "My wife passed away when Trent was three. It's pretty much been just me and Trent since then."

"How difficult that must have been!" Emma said.

"Yes, it certainly was," Samuel said, but he said it with a smile and a glow of serenity in his eyes. "But I have much to be grateful for."

Another ruckus from the children halted the conversation. When supper was over, Samuel offered to help with the dishes, but Tamra and Emma insisted that Emily take him on a walk around the grounds. Jess and Scott took the children upstairs, and Emily took Samuel by the hand, leading him outside. They wandered idly around the house while she told him the history of the home and the land. They walked into the stables and chatted comfortably with a couple of the hands who were finishing up the evening shift of caring for the animals. They ended up sitting on the veranda where Emily told him about the first time she'd come here during college, and about the many memories she had of sitting in this very spot.

While they were sitting there, Scott and Emma came out, holding hands. "Would we be intruding?" Emma asked.

"Not at all," Samuel said. "But you're missing that beautiful baby."

"She's down for the night," Scott said, "well most of it anyway . . . we hope." He set a baby monitor on the table nearby.

Scott and Emma sat down, and Samuel asked each of them questions about themselves. The conversation became lively and animated, and Emily was pleased to see how well they were getting along. Jess and Tamra eventually arrived and joined the conversation, once their children were all tucked into bed. Samuel reluctantly declared that he needed to get home, saying that he was too old to stay out too late, which brought a round of teasing, mostly aimed at Emily about all the things she wasn't too old to do. Emily walked Samuel to his car, well aware that her children had a clear view of the way Samuel kissed her cheek before he got into the car and drove away. She stood on the lawn and waved him off before she ambled back up to the veranda, where she was met with more teasing.

"He's quite a gentleman, Mother," Scott said. "When's the wedding?"

"Our first date was only yesterday," Emily said, but she couldn't keep from smiling.

Emma chuckled as she commented, "I haven't seen you smile like that since . . . well . . . when *did* she smile like that?"

"I can't recall," Tamra said, then more to Emily, "He really is quite charming. I just have to ask if . . . well, how are *you* feeling about this?"

Emily scanned the faces of her children. All were pleasantly inquisitive, except for Jess who looked cautious, perhaps concerned. But this was an opportunity for her to communicate what she was feeling. "Truthfully," she said, "Samuel is an amazing man. After what happened with Rick, I never dreamed there might actually be someone out there who could be so warm and compassionate, so . . . real and down to earth. I feel so completely comfortable with him that . . . I can't believe how short a time we've known each other. He fills the emptiness in me so thoroughly that I almost can't imagine how I was managing without him."

"That's incredible," Tamra said, seeming almost stunned.

"It's good to see you with that permanent grin on your face," Scott added.

"I can't argue with that," Emma said.

But Jess said nothing.

"So, where do you think this is headed?" Scott asked.

"I don't know," Emily said with a little laugh. "In truth, we hardly know each other. I just . . . want to enjoy his company, take it one day at a time, and see what happens."

"Sounds delightful," Tamra said.

"That's one of the advantages of being retired," Scott said. "The two of you don't have to work or go to school or even worry about a curfew."

"No, I suppose we don't," Emily said. "Although, I'm a bit too old to be staying up all hours the way I used to when I was young and dating. It is a little strange . . . to be dating and actually enjoying it. I realize now that with Rick it was . . ."

"What?" Emma prodded.

"Well . . . it was a diversion. My time with him wasn't miserable or anything. But looking back now, and comparing him to Samuel, I realize that there really wasn't any chemistry between us."

"But there is with Samuel?" Tamra asked as if Emily were telling a fairy tale.

"Need you ask?" Scott said. "That grin on her face is evidence enough of the chemistry, and the way she keeps blushing and giggling like a school girl."

For all her efforts, Emily couldn't keep herself from doing just that, then she felt especially embarrassed when they all laughed. Except Jess.

Emily decided to take it head on. "So, what do you think, Jess?" she asked. "You haven't said much."

"I was gracious and polite," Jess said.

"Yes, you were," Emily said.

"And I must admit he's a very nice man."

"Yes, he is."

"But this is all a bit . . . odd, isn't it?"

"It's certainly an adjustment," Emma said, as if to validate his feelings on the matter.

"He's not a member of the Church," Jess pointed out as if it had never come up before.

Emily sighed. "I consider that more of an opportunity than a detriment. The issue of finding an eternal companion and raising my family in the gospel is really irrelevant here, don't you think?"

She looked at Jess as she said it. His eyes widened as he asked, "What do you mean?"

"I mean that I already have an eternal companion, Jess. No matter what turns my life might take from here on, I will do everything in my power to be with your father forever. *He* is my eternal companion. I know it with all my heart and soul, and I'm not going to do anything to jeopardize the opportunity to receive that blessing when all is said and done. In the meantime, Samuel is a good man, and we have the opportunity to bring some good things into his life."

Emily felt certain she saw the glimmer of tears in Jess's eyes before he turned abruptly away. She asked if he was okay. He said that he was just tired and hurried into the house. Silence was left in the wake of his leaving until Tamra said gently, "He'll be alright. Eventually he'll see that this is a good thing."

"I hope so," Emily said. "Because I really believe that it is . . . a good thing."

Emily said good night and went up to bed. She slept with a prayer in her heart for Jess, and also prayed that her budding relationship with Samuel Reid might be all that it now seemed.

Chapter Eight

Emily slept well and got up early enough to be cooking breakfast before anyone else made it to the kitchen. Jess seemed fine at breakfast, and before he left for work he hugged her and kissed her brow, saying gently, "I love you, Mom."

"I love you too, Jess. I couldn't ask for a better son."

"I don't know about that," he said with a chuckle. "But I'll try to stay out of trouble."

A few minutes later Emily was loading the dishwasher when the phone rang. Emma answered it, then smirked as she handed it to Emily, whispering, "It's your boyfriend."

"Hello," Emily said, and felt herself go warm from the inside out to hear Samuel's voice, sounding as glad to be talking to her as she was to him.

"Hey," he said once the greetings had been finished, "I'm going to be helping at the care center for a few hours, and then I wondered if I would be imposing to come out and see you for a while this afternoon."

"Not at all," she said. "I would love to see you. In fact, you should just plan on staying for supper again."

"I don't want to wear out my welcome or—"

"I wouldn't have invited you if that was remotely a problem," she said.

"Well then, I'll look forward to it."

"So will I," Emily said.

"Emily," he added, sounding more serious, "there is something specific I want to talk to you about."

"Okay," she said cautiously.

"You told me something the other day that I must confess has stuck in my head; you said I could get the long version later. So I'm wondering if I could possibly get the long version."

"I would be honored to give you the long version," she said, and a warm tingle encompassed her every nerve.

After Emily had hung up the phone, she found Emma and Tamra both gazing at her with pleasant curiosity on their faces. It was Emma who asked, "The long version of what?"

Tamra added, "Whatever it is, it must really be something, judging by that look on your face."

"Well," Emily said, "it's not any great secret, or anything, but I trust if I tell you that you will handle it discreetly."

"Of course," they said together.

"Well," Emily said, "the other day he told me if he could have one wish it would be to know that he could be with Arlene again someday."

"His wife?" Emma asked.

"That's right."

"Oh, how sweet," Tamra said.

"So, I told him that I knew it was possible, and I gave him a one-minute explanation. I said I'd give him the long version later if he was interested. He just asked if he could come out this afternoon and get the long version."

"Oh my gosh! That is so neat!" Emma said.

"And I invited him to supper again," Emily added.

"And it's *your* turn to cook," Tamra said to Emma, who gave her a comical scowl.

Emily took advantage of the morning to catch up on a few odds and ends, including writing in her journal about the happenings of the past few days. By the time Samuel arrived, she felt anxious for his company and couldn't hold back a little laugh to see him get out of the car. She walked out to meet him and without even thinking about it, hugged him tightly. He returned her embrace with fervor and a delighted laugh, then he kissed her cheek.

"Hello, my dear," he said, taking both her hands into his. "Have I told you how you have brightened up a very dull life?"

Emily laughed again. "You hadn't put it quite that way."

"Well, you have," he said.

"I thought it was the other way around."

"Dull?" he said with mock astonishment. "With all the people who live in this house, how could your life be dull?"

"Well, lonely then," she said.

"Lonely?" he laughed. "With all the people who—"

"Yes," she said, nudging him playfully with her elbow, "you know very well what I'm talking about."

"Yes, I do," he said more seriously. "Jess has Tamra; Emma has Scott."

"Yes, and while Rhea is more my peer, and I am completely comfortable with her, we really don't have much in common. She's content with her life—loves to read and watch television. She's a good woman but has no interest in spiritual matters."

"Which are very important to you," Samuel observed with respect.

"Yes," she agreed.

"And while you have a houseful of children, they are not really yours *or* your responsibility."

"That's right," she said. "And while I know the family loves me and they appreciate what I do to help here and there, I know they could get by without me."

"I'm not sure I could," he said, kissing her hand.

"And I'm not sure what to think when you say such things."

"You can think that you've made a new friend who very much enjoys your company."

"The feeling is mutual," she said.

Samuel pointed to an area surrounded by a wrought-iron fence and said, "I'm assuming that would be a family cemetery."

"The headstones kind of give it away," Emily said.

"Would you mind if we take a closer look?"

"I'd love to show it to you." Emily led the way, keeping his hand in hers. Opening the squeaky gate, she said, "It is rather quaint, actually. Although it can be a bit eerie to think of actually having dead bodies buried in the yard."

"You don't seem the type to be ruffled by such a thing."

"Not ruffled, no. It's just . . . a strange feeling sometimes to think about it."

"Most specifically, Michael?" he asked, and she looked at him abruptly. "I mean . . . I'm guessing that it's most strange to think of Michael being buried in the yard."

"Yes, I suppose that's true. But I know well enough that his spirit lives on elsewhere, and this is not where the real Michael is residing." She sighed and felt good about adding, "There were many times when I felt his spirit close to me. Did you ever feel that way with Arlene?"

"A couple of times, yes. But that was a long, long time ago."

"So you believe in life after death?" Emily asked.

"I do, yes . . . but as I mentioned on the phone, I would very much like to hear more of your theories on such things."

Emily smiled and said, "We'll get to that."

Their attention turned once more to the graves. Emily started the tour with the oldest graves. "Benjamin and Emma were the first to live on this land. Ben built the original house, which was destroyed by fire. His son, Jess, rebuilt an exact replica of the house, which is where we live today."

"How fascinating," Samuel said, pressing a hand over the aging granite stone where their names were carved.

"And here is Richard Wilhite," she said, "who was an overseer here. He was briefly married to Alexandra Byrnehouse, and buried next to him is their infant daughter. Alexandra—or Alexa as we more commonly know her—later married Jess Davies, and they are buried together here."

"And he is the son of Benjamin and Emma," he observed.

"That's right," she said, "although I believe there's somewhat of a scandalous twist in there somewhere. I'd have to go look it up in their journals. I do know that when Jess and Alexa were married, they joined their names to form Byrnehouse-Davies, and soon afterward they inherited a fortune through the Byrnehouse line. And that's when they started the boys' home."

"Really?" he said, thoroughly intrigued. "I didn't realize it had been here for so many years."

"Oh yes. Jess and Alexa only had two children—a set of twins. Emma and Tyson. Emma ended up marrying a man—Michael Hamilton the first, in fact—who had come to the boys' home after being pulled off the streets at the age of eleven. He grew up here, stayed on to work, and eventually married Emma. But first he went to prison for a while and actually kidnapped Emma for ransom."

"Really?" he said again, laughing.

"Really," she said. "It's all recorded in family journals, and in fact Michael's grandparents told him the story when he was a child. His grandparents being Michael and Emma. Michael the first became the administrator of the boys' home and was said to have worked many miracles there. He's a legend around here." She laughed softly. "And somewhat of a rogue."

"How delightful," Samuel said.

Emily moved to another set of graves. "This is Emma's twin brother, Tyson, and his wife, Lacey. She was actually raised along with the twins, since she had been abandoned as a child." Moving on she said, "This is Richard Byrnehouse-Davies. He was the son of Tyson and Lacey, killed in World War II. And this is Jesse Michael Hamilton, my husband's father; and his mother, LeNay. I never met Jesse; he died when Michael was a child. But I knew LeNay well, an amazing woman, to say the least."

"And here is Michael," Samuel said solemnly, looking down at the newest headstone.

"Yes, this is Michael," she said, squatting down to touch the name. *Jess Michael Hamilton III.*

"And your name is already on the stone beside his," Samuel said, stating the obvious. "Does that feel a little eerie?"

"No, not really. When it's time for me to go, it only seems right that I should be buried here."

Samuel smiled. "I'm glad to hear you say that. I did the same when Arlene died. There's a plot waiting for me so that I can be right beside her. Even though it's been all these years, it just seems like the right thing to do."

Emily observed, "After all these years, you don't love her any less."

"No, I don't," he said. "I only miss her more. I've grown accustomed to her absence, but I will never feel completely right without her."

Emily felt sure she'd never get a better opportunity than that to open up *the longer version.* "And that's why you want to be with her forever."

"Yes, I do," he said. "And you believe that's possible."

Emily headed toward the gate. "I know a nice quiet place in the house where it will be much cooler than out here, and we can talk to our hearts' content."

"How delightful," he said, and walked with her around to the front of the house and through a door that was rarely used.

Once they were settled in the lounge room with the door closed, Emily said, "I actually grew up in the LDS faith."

"More commonly known as Mormon," he said.

"That's right. But I want you to know that I reached a point—as every member of the Church should—where I knew for myself that the things I had been taught were true. You see, the Holy Ghost can witness to a person whether or not the things they are reading, or hearing, or even saying, are true. I actually had a rather profound experience prior to leaving home for college, where I knew beyond any doubt that it was true. Through the years I've had many similar experiences that have repeatedly manifested the truth to me. I guess my point is that . . . you don't have to take my word on anything I might tell you. With time, and study, and prayer, you can know for yourself if what I'm telling you is true."

"Okay," he said, motioning for her to go on. She noted that his expression seemed more intrigued than skeptical. She hoped that some degree of his interest was truly for the message she had to share and not simply his attraction to her.

"Before I actually get to the part about eternal marriage, I want to tell you briefly about our religion."

"I'm listening," he said eagerly.

"Well, in a nutshell . . . in the years following Christ's death and resurrection, the church that he had established during his ministry gradually died out and faded away. A great apostasy occurred for many centuries. Of course many forms of Christianity existed on the earth, but there was no place that all of the truth, or the proper authority, could be found. In the early nineteenth century, God the Father and Jesus Christ appeared to a young man, who became the instrument to gradually restore the true gospel upon the earth with all of the keys and authority necessary to perform all of the ordinances required to return to live with the Father again. Are you with me?"

"I believe so," he said, looking a bit perplexed.

"You can stop me any time and ask questions," she said.

"Maybe later—go on."

"The Church now has a membership of many millions, all over the world. Everything we believe in is centered around Jesus Christ. In actuality, what people call Mormonism is Christianity in its truest form. And one of the most marvelous blessings that God has given us is the possibility of being united eternally as families. When two people are sealed in the temple, their marriage does not end at death. Children born into that marriage are automatically sealed to their parents. Sealings can be done following a civil marriage after a period of time has passed, and they can also be done for the dead by proxy."

Emily allowed him a few minutes to absorb what she had said. He looked deeply thoughtful, then turned to her and said, "So . . . if I come to know for myself that these things are true . . . then I can be . . . *sealed* . . . in the temple . . . to Arlene. And then we would be together . . . for eternity."

"That's right."

"It sounds too simple."

"Well . . . it is simple, in a way. But it's not necessarily easy. The temple is the final step in a progression of ordinances and requirements. First you must be baptized and become a member of the Church, and then there is a waiting period. Only worthy members of the Church can enter the temple."

"I see," he said, seeming a bit skeptical. "And . . . there is a temple around here?"

"There are more than a hundred temples all over the world; there are five in Australia."

"Really." He sounded impressed.

"They're in . . . let's see if I can get this right. Perth, Adelaide, Melbourne, Sydney, and the newest—and closest—is in Brisbane." Again there was silence until she said, "It probably sounds very overwhelming, but . . . if you're willing, I would like to ask you to read a book that is the basis for our beliefs, and there is a great website that could tell you more. Of course, I'm available to answer any questions you might have. And if you're interested, we could set up an appointment with some local missionaries who would probably do better than I in answering your questions." She added firmly, "And if you're not interested, all you have to do is say so. I'm sharing my beliefs, not trying to sell you something."

"Fair enough," he said. "Why don't you let me have a look at this book, and we'll start there."

"Fair enough," she echoed, then stood up to retrieve a spare copy of the Book of Mormon. She sat beside him and gave him a brief history of the book. She pointed out a few particular places that were especially important, including Moroni's promise at the end of the book. He thanked her and said he'd look forward to reading it, and then the subject was changed. They talked freely until supper, where Samuel seemed so at home that Emily might have thought he'd been coming to supper for weeks now. The family seemed relaxed and at ease; even Jess seemed to be doing better. But she had to wonder if he was just working hard at putting up a gracious front in Samuel's presence. Still, she felt certain that Jess couldn't keep spending time with Samuel and not grow to like him. After supper Emily and Samuel wandered out to the veranda and sat holding hands, visiting comfortably until he declared that he should likely start for home.

"I want to leave some time for reading before I pass out from old-age exhaustion," he said.

"I know what you mean," Emily agreed. "I don't know how old women like me can date younger men."

"And vice versa," he said. "It's nice to hang around with someone who has the same body clock."

They laughed together as they stood and moved toward the steps.

"Emily, wait," he said, taking hold of her arm. "One more thing."

"What?" she said, and he took her shoulders into his hands. Her heart quickened as their eyes met.

"I was going to kiss you . . . unless you have an objection."

Emily had to admit, "I can't think of one." He smiled, and her stomach fluttered as he bent to touch his lips to hers. She felt startled by how familiar it seemed, when she had come to believe that kissing a different man would feel entirely different. Samuel's kiss was meek and tender, but it was also lengthy and stirring. She took hold of his upper arms to keep herself steady as the fluttering in her stomach intensified and her knees went weak. When he drew back just far enough to give her a warm smile, she muttered quietly, "Oh, my. I think I'm too old to handle such . . . exhilaration."

"Never," he said, then kissed her again. "Was it, then?" he asked, his lips close to her ear.

"What?"

"Was it exhilarating?"

"Oh, yes!" she murmured, and he laughed softly, sending a shiver through her ear and down her spine.

Samuel looked into her eyes and touched her face with the back of his fingers. "It's nice to have a friend in my life."

"Yes, it is," she agreed. "But . . ."

"But what?"

"You're speaking of being friends when you've just kissed me?"

"Well . . . kissing friends, then," he said.

"Yes," she said, touching his face as well, "it's nice to have a kissing friend in my life."

Emily walked him to the car, feeling as if she might float away. Before he drove away he said, "I'll call first thing in the morning. Maybe we can figure out something to do."

"I'll look forward to it," she said, waving as he drove away.

The following morning Emily expected a call before breakfast was over, but two hours later she still hadn't heard from him. She hesitated calling him, not wanting to be too forward. Then she started to worry and dialed his number. It rang several times before he finally answered, sounding groggy.

"Are you okay?" she asked.

"Emily. Good heavens, I . . . What time is it?"

"Nearly eleven," she said.

"Oh my." He gave an embarrassed chuckle. "I'm so sorry." He sounded more coherent now. "It seems I must have . . . . well, I must have fallen asleep reading and didn't get the alarm set. I don't know what to say."

"It's okay. I'm just glad to know you're alright."

"Just . . . half asleep and . . . well, a bit embarrassed, but . . . okay otherwise. Good thing I didn't have a job to get to or I'd be out of work."

"There are advantages to being retired."

"Yes, there certainly are," he said. "So . . . in spite of getting a late start, would you like to do something today?"

"Sure, if you're up to it," she said. "Unless you have something else in mind, what would you think of a picnic?"

"Sounds marvelous," he said with enthusiasm.

"Well, I know the perfect spot. So if you're willing to come here, I'll have everything we need."

"Sounds marvelous," he repeated. "Are you sure I can't bring something?"

"Just yourself," she said, then ended the call.

Samuel arrived less than two hours later. Emily had everything packed into one of the family's Toyota Land Cruisers. He gave her a quick kiss in greeting, and they got into the Cruiser, with Emily driving. She winked at him and said, "We might need the four-wheel drive."

"Ooh, an adventure," he said.

"This is a favorite spot. Picnics have likely been taking place here for generations. If I was a little more agile, we could take horses, but . . . I don't have the confidence in that regard that I once had."

Samuel chuckled. "Well, I'm relieved to hear that because I haven't been on a horse in years, and even then my experience is terribly minimal."

As they moved into the foothills, Samuel said, "You seem to do great handling rugged terrain."

"I've had a little practice," she said with a smile. "You're welcome to drive, however, if you'd like to."

"Oh no. You're doing great."

Samuel was impressed when they arrived at the appointed spot. They spread out a blanket, and Samuel laughed when Emily produced some cushions for them to sit on. "I don't know about you," she said, "but my old bones don't do so well with sitting on the ground."

"Agreed," he said, and he helped her spread out the food she'd brought. They shared their meal with much laughter and conversation, then they both got sleepy at the same time and stretched out and fell asleep.

Emily woke to find Samuel sitting close by, reading from the Book of Mormon.

"Where were you hiding that?" she asked.

"Knapsack," he said, pointing to it near his side.

"Of course," she said, realizing now he'd had it with him when he'd arrived, but she'd not given it any thought.

"Did you rest well?" he asked.

"I did. You?"

"Not for long," he said. "I confess that I'm having trouble relaxing."

"Why?" she asked, feeling concerned. He tipped the book toward her, and she took notice of how far he was into it. "Good heavens," she said with a little laugh. "Have you read straight through, or have you been jumping around?"

"Straight through," he said.

"Is that why you didn't get to sleep last night?"

Samuel chuckled, seeming somewhat embarrassed. "I was just going to have a look through before I went to sleep. Next thing I knew, you were calling to wake me."

"So, what do you think so far?" she asked, sitting beside him.

He shook his head and chuckled again. "To say I'm engrossed would be a tremendous understatement. In a word . . . it's profound."

Emily couldn't keep from smiling as Samuel went on to discuss his perception of the stories and principles he'd read. They talked for another hour then headed home, still talking about the Book of Mormon. While their discussion remained more intellectual than spiritual, she couldn't help but notice his genuine enthusiasm as he spoke. She felt certain it was only a matter of time before he would come to know for himself that the book was true.

Emily didn't see Samuel the following day since he told her he had some things to catch up on. When she did see him, he'd finished reading the Book of Mormon and was full of questions and a desire to read it again. He agreed to go to church with the family on Sunday and to meet with the missionaries on Sunday evening. When Sunday arrived, Emily felt a childlike excitement to see Samuel, and beneath it she felt a deep joy and fulfillment that was difficult to describe. Her joy deepened walking into sacrament meeting with him. She enjoyed introducing him to many friends and ward members, who greeted him warmly. Even more, she enjoyed just holding his hand through the meeting. She liked the way he had come to seem so at home among her family. He even took little Claire out to the foyer when she started fussing. He came back twenty minutes later with her sleeping in his arms. As he sat down between Emily and Jess, she heard Jess whisper, "You must share your secret."

"Maybe I scared her into submission," Samuel whispered back.

Emily whispered to Samuel, "You must have a magic touch . . . Grandpa."

The remainder of the meetings went well, then Emily rode back to the house with Samuel instead of with the family. The full-time missionaries rode with Scott and Emma, since they had more space in their vehicle.

Through the entire drive Samuel asked Emily questions about the lessons he'd heard in Sunday School and priesthood meeting. He was fascinated with the concept of personal revelation, and Emily read to him from Doctrine and Covenants, section nine, while he drove. Once she'd read it, pointing out her personal take on some particular verses, Samuel was quiet for several minutes before he said, "So . . . I can know for myself . . . if a decision is right or not."

"That's right," she said. "Did you have any particular decision in mind?"

He looked at her intently before he turned back to the road. "Like whether or not I should be joining this church of yours."

"Well, it's not *my* church," Emily said, feeling her heart quicken to hear him say such a thing.

"This church you belong to, then," he clarified.

"The only reason you *should* join is if you know beyond any doubt that it's true and that it's right for you. I don't want you to do it for me, or for any other reason."

Samuel smiled and reached for her hand. "You're an amazing woman, Emily Hamilton."

"I'm just the messenger," she said as he kissed her hand.

"A very beautiful messenger," he said, "with a very profound message."

Sunday dinner was thoroughly enjoyable with the missionaries present. Jess, Emma, and Tamra all shared some of their own mission experiences, and Samuel was intrigued to learn more about the missionary program. Everyone pitched in to clean the kitchen and wash the dishes before the family gathered with the young elders, and they effectively answered Samuel's questions. They were pleased to know that he'd read the Book of Mormon, and they challenged him to specifically pray for an answer as to whether or not it was true. Samuel seemed a little taken aback by the challenge, but he agreed to it. They continued their discussion until the elders declared that they needed to return home. Samuel offered to give them a ride since he had to go that direction anyway.

The following morning Emily drove into town to keep her commitment at the care center. She enjoyed helping and visiting with Esther, and she also spent some time with Bertie. But most of all she enjoyed seeing Samuel there. She was amazed at how comfortable he seemed here, and his tenderness with the residents of the center touched her anew. She couldn't believe how deeply she had grown to care for him—and how much she had grown to respect and admire him. They left the care center together late in the afternoon. Walking outside, Emily said, "You should come to family home evening."

He gave a familiar laugh. "I think I heard such a thing mentioned at church yesterday, but you're going to have to explain."

"As members of the Church we are advised to have a weekly family gathering, and it's most commonly on Monday evenings. At our house we alternate weeks. Every other week, the two families meet separately, and occasionally I join one or the other, or less often I've gone to a family home evening group composed of older, single people."

"Older?" he echoed facetiously. "Not you."

"Okay," she chuckled, "more mature people."

"That's better."

"Anyway," she said, "on the alternating weeks, we all meet together and take turns being in charge. Tonight is one of those all-together nights. You should join us."

"I feel like I must surely be wearing out my welcome."

"I can assure you that's not the case," she said.

"And if it were, would you tell me?" he asked.

"Yes, actually I would . . . very tactfully, of course."

"Of course," he chuckled. "Well, I would love to come. Thank you. There are a couple of things I need to take care of at the moment. What time should I be there?"

"Seven would be great," Emily said. "Or come earlier if you get finished."

He kissed her quickly and walked her to her car. Through the drive home Emily felt deeply happy and content. She found herself talking out loud to Michael, something she did on occasion. Whether he was available to listen at the moment or not, it made her feel better to sort her thoughts out loud. She felt a deepening of conviction that Michael strongly approved of her relationship with Samuel and that pursuing a future with him was the right thing to do.

When she arrived home, she impulsively stopped at the boys' home, thinking Jess would likely still be at work. After chatting with the secretary for a few minutes, she determined that Jess was still in his office but on the phone. As soon as he was finished with his call, Emily knocked on his door. He smiled to see her and came to his feet. "What a pleasant surprise," he said, coming around the desk to embrace her. "How are you today, Mother?"

"I'm great. How are you?"

"I'm great too, if you must know."

"Are you really?" she asked as they were both seated. "I mean . . . what I'm really asking is . . . well, you seem to be okay with my dating Samuel and having him around so much, but . . . I want to know if you're *really* okay with it."

"You know what, Mom, even if I weren't it wouldn't matter. You have the right to—"

"I know all of that, Jess. And I'm not saying that I need your approval to do what I'm doing. We both established that a long time ago, but . . . I still want to know how you feel."

"Truthfully, I'm fine, Mom. Really."

"Really?" she asked gently, with hope.

"Really," he repeated with a little chuckle, then he leaned toward her and his expression sobered. "Do you want to know what made the biggest difference?"

"Yes, I do," she said.

"Well . . . I didn't realize what the problem was until I heard the words that solved it. And then it was like . . . wow. If that's the case, then I'm really okay with this."

"What? I'm lost."

"It was when you said that you already had an eternal companion, that you would be with my father forever. I suppose, at some deep, subconscious level, I was afraid you would end up spending many years with some other man and change your mind about who you wanted to be with forever. And I want you to be with my dad forever—selfish, perhaps . . . but that's the way I feel."

"You feel that way because it's right, Jess. But in this case, it's important to separate the here and now from eternity. It's right for your father and I to be together forever. It's right for me to be with Samuel now."

Jess nodded, and a moment later he asked, "Do you love him, Mother?"

Emily glanced down, feeling herself turn warm. "It sounds ridiculous after so short a time, but . . ." She looked up at him. "Yes, I do. Whatever little there might be left of my life, I want to spend it with him."

Jess smiled widely. "You deserve to be deliriously happy, Mother dear. But you've got twenty years at least before I'm going to let you leave us."

"Well, in that case, we'll hope that Samuel will be agreeable to moving in with me—once we're married, of course."

"Of course," Jess said.

They went on to talk for a short while about Samuel's zealous interest in the gospel, and Emily felt Jess's heart soften further with the growing evidence that Samuel was a good man with his heart in the right place.

Emily arrived at the house in time to help put supper on the table. The meal was enjoyable, but she missed Samuel. She couldn't help thinking that he should be here for every meal. She was pleased when other family members mentioned his absence, saying that it didn't seem right without him.

Samuel arrived while Emily was helping with the dishes. She offered him something to eat but he said he'd gotten something just before he'd left home. Family home evening was a great success, even though there were a few challenging antics from the children.

"This is when we call it family home screaming," Jess said to Samuel as he escorted one of the twins from the room for some time out.

Through the remainder of the evening, Emily discreetly watched Samuel, attempting to gauge her feelings accurately. She recalled telling Jess that she loved him, but now she had to ask herself if she truly did or if she was simply infatuated. It had been so many years since any such issue had come up in her life that she wondered if she knew the difference. She had believed she'd loved Rick, but looking back, she knew she really hadn't. But now, asking herself a few simple questions, she came up with the right answers. She *did* love Samuel. She felt genuinely concerned for his welfare, and she wanted nothing more than for him to be completely happy.

During the next couple of weeks Emily saw Samuel nearly every day. He came to the house as regularly as Emily went into town so that they could be together as much as possible. They put in time together at the care center, explored museums and went shopping, cooked together, and went to movies. They talked and laughed, studied and read, and Emily couldn't imagine ever being without him. He continued to meet with the missionaries, and Emily felt certain that he would inevitably choose to be baptized. He'd admitted that there was nothing in him that argued against becoming a member, but he hadn't felt that undeniable witness that he believed was necessary to take such a huge step. Emily encouraged him to keep praying and with time he would surely know beyond any doubt. Three weeks beyond their first date, Samuel came to the house for family home evening as usual. When the meeting broke up and the children were being put to bed, Emily walked Samuel to his car, feeling almost as if there was something she needed to do or say, but she didn't know what it was. Dismissing the thought as silly, she kissed him good night as usual and watched him drive away, grateful to have him in her life.

Chapter Nine

Later that night, Emily lay staring into the darkness, contemplating her relationship with Samuel. She felt frustrated with the travel time back and forth between his apartment and her home. She felt impatient to have him be a part of her life. These lonely late-night and early-morning hours had grown old years ago. She wanted someone to talk to in bed and wanted to wake up holding hands. She felt certain that marriage was inevitable, and she was surprised to realize that it had never actually come up between them. She fell asleep reminding herself to be patient and enjoy the journey life was taking her on. There was plenty of time to enjoy Samuel in her life and no need to hurry the pace. She woke up feeling anything but patient. For an hour she prayed and contemplated her feelings and finally came to one firm conclusion. There *wasn't* plenty of time. She didn't know why; she only knew that it was important to move forward. Following a hasty breakfast, she called Samuel and asked if she could talk to him. He eagerly agreed, and through the drive into town she continued to pray that the Spirit would guide her words, that she wouldn't end up making a fool of herself, or worse, offending this man she had grown to care for.

Emily uttered one more quick prayer and took a deep breath as she knocked at his apartment door. He opened it wearing a smile and greeted her with a warm kiss.

"Come in," he said and closed the door. "Are you hungry? Do you want something cold to drink or—"

"No, I'm fine. Thank you," she said.

"Have a seat then," he said, and she did. When they were seated, facing each other, he said, "So what's on your mind? I got the impression it was something specific."

"It is," she said, "but it's based on some feelings that are difficult to put into words, so I hope you'll be patient with me."

"Of course," he said, leaning back comfortably and motioning with his hand for her to continue.

Emily sighed deeply. "The thing is this . . . well, I've grown to care very much for you, Samuel, in a very short time."

"Yes, I know," he said, and his face darkened. "You're not trying to tell me you can't see me anymore, are you?"

"Of course not!" she said, grateful for the clear relief that showed on his face.

"Okay," he said, again motioning with his hand. "Go on."

Emily attempted to recapture her train of thought. Wanting to affirm that he felt the same for her, she was relieved to hear him say, "Perhaps I should have made more of a point to tell you how I feel, Emily . . . because I love you. I think I fell for you the first time we talked, but I've grown to love you more each day."

Emily savored his words, feeling a deep, absolute comfort. She felt tempted to analyze her feelings, or his, and to attempt putting all her thoughts into words. Instead she simply replied, "I love you too, Samuel."

He smiled and moved his chair closer so that he could take her hand. "Is this what you came to tell me?"

"Partly," she said. "The thing is . . . everything in my life just feels better and more right when you're in it, and when you're not there everything is just darker . . . and not so right. It seems so silly for us to be living an hour away from each other when we feel the way we do. I went to sleep last night telling myself to be patient, that there was plenty of time for our relationship to evolve and that we should simply enjoy this journey." She took a deep breath and cleared her throat gently. "All I can say is that I woke up feeling . . . an urgency . . . that perhaps we don't have all that much time, and . . . that perhaps we should be making the most of every minute we have together."

Emily watched him closely, waiting for a reaction, wondering why his eyes were suddenly clouded. He looked away and said nothing. She gave him some time to digest what she'd said, until she couldn't bear the silence. "Did I say something . . . to offend you? Does it not make sense, or—"

"It's okay, Emily," he said in a light voice that contradicted his expression. "I assume, knowing you as I do, that you're not suggesting we move in together."

"Not without getting married first," she said, wishing it hadn't sounded so defensive.

"It's alright," he said with a chuckle. "I was teasing you."

Emily glanced down, wondering why she sensed that his teasing was an attempt to cover something he didn't want to say. Never once in all the many hours she'd spent with him had she felt anything less than complete sincerity and honesty. She was about to accuse him of hiding something from her when he said, "Emily, there's something I need to tell you."

"Okay," she said, feeling even more nervous than he appeared. "I'm listening."

"Perhaps I should have told you sooner, but it's not something that's easy to talk about with someone you've just met . . . and everything else just evolved so quickly." He chuckled tensely. "I kept waiting for the right moment, but . . . I never wanted to sour the mood between us, or . . . perhaps I've hesitated telling you because I knew that it would change everything between us, and I didn't want to mar all we've come to share."

Emily's heart began to pound, as much from the darkening of his expression as from the seriousness in his voice. "Go on," she said when he hesitated too long.

"I did not expect something like this to come up in my life . . . now . . . after all these years." Samuel looked at the floor, then at her. "But there is a reason why I've worked my life out the way I have; the apartment I'm living in . . . the deal with the care center. There's a reason, Emily."

Emily felt her palms turn sweaty and her breath quickened, sensing what this might be about, but unable to grasp any concrete possibility. "I'm still listening," she said, hearing her voice quaver.

"Well," he said, clearing his throat and rubbing a hand over the top of his head, "there's no easy way to say it. I have a degenerative disease, Emily."

Emily allowed his words to sink in, and suddenly her brain felt clouded. "What are you saying?" she asked breathlessly. "What exactly does that mean?"

"I'm not going to bore you with all of the technical names and terms. I've had it for many years; the diagnosis is clear and official. At times it's worse than others, but my most recent tests—just over a month ago—show that it's taking a turn for the worse. Truthfully, much of the time I'm not with you, I'm in bed. It's only a matter of time—and not likely very long—before I will be confined to a wheelchair." He sighed and added, "I'm also not likely to live many more years, if that long."

Emily attempted to absorb what he was saying, but there seemed to be a cloud of fog that was intensifying in her head. In an instant a hundred memories assaulted her: the discovery of Michael's cancer, the endless string of treatments, medication, time in the hospital, the deterioration of his body, and finally his death. Could she live through something like that again? For a moment she felt tempted to be angry with him for not telling her sooner, but it only took another moment to understand why he hadn't. And how could she be angry? She took a good, long look at Samuel and briefly considered everything she knew about him. Before she'd ever met him, he had known this about himself, and yet he was so full of life, so positive, so *happy.* And he had to know that what his body had to endure before he finally reached the freedom of death could be hellish. She'd grown to care for him quickly and deeply, and her most prominent thought was her grief on his behalf. Still, she wasn't prepared for the emotion that burst out of her with no warning. She pressed a hand over her mouth and tried to turn away, but he caught her arm in his hand as he moved to sit next to her, and she found her face against his shoulder.

"Cry if you must, Emily," he said, holding her close. "But . . . please, cry *with* me. Don't hide your tears from me."

Emily cried long and hard, certain her concern for Samuel was linked to the heartache she'd endured from losing Michael. Again she asked herself if she could live through that again. She had a choice before her. There was no official commitment between her and Samuel. He'd arranged to be taken care of. She could walk away now and she felt sure he wouldn't blame her. She looked into his eyes while he wiped her tears, and the answer was clear. No, she couldn't walk away. She wasn't sure *how* she could endure losing another man to disease, but in her heart she knew that their being together was not a coincidence. He needed her, and she needed him, and somehow they would get through this. The prompting that had compelled her to come here and open this conversation now added to her confidence that this was the right course for her life.

Given her train of thought, she was completely unprepared to hear him say, "So you see, Emily, while I am deeply grateful for your friendship, it's easy to understand why I can't marry you."

Emily drew back, attempting to accept what she was hearing. "Easy?" she echoed. "*Why* can't you marry me?"

"Emily!" His expression became as astonished as his voice. "Did you hear what I said?"

"I heard you."

"Do you have any comprehension of what it means?"

"I've got a pretty good idea."

"This is not cancer, Emily. This disease randomly attacks the nervous system. I don't know from one day to the next how it might affect me, and it's only going to get worse. One day I could be blind, the next crippled. I could completely lose control of every muscle in my body. What if I can't walk or feed myself or get to the bathroom, or even speak? And it's more likely to happen sooner than later. Do you hear what I'm telling you?"

"I hear you," she said, "but it doesn't change how I feel about you."

"Forgive me, my dear, but how you feel about me is irrelevant. I'm grateful for how you feel about me, Emily. I am. But this is not how it was supposed to work out. I had finally reached a point where I was content to be alone; I figured it was better that way. I've made arrangements to be cared for—by people who can take good care of me and not get emotionally involved."

"What about Trent? Does he know?"

"Of course he knows. I've had the disease for years."

"Does he knows it's taken a turn for the worse?"

"Yes, he knows."

"And?"

"And what? He's pretty shook up over it. That's the biggest reason he's bringing the family for a visit, and then I will be grateful that his home is halfway around the world, and he doesn't have to be burdened with this."

"What makes you so sure it's a burden?"

"And what makes you think that it's not?" he countered, putting his hands on her shoulders. "I love you too much, Emily, to bring this new challenge into your life—and to your family." His voice softened. "I will be grateful for your friendship and—"

"Friendship?" she retorted, feeling wholly angry now. "Is that all this is to you? I'll drop by the care center once a week to see how you're doing?"

"Whatever you feel comfortable doing is more than alright with me."

Emily erupted with a sardonic chuckle. "Comfortable? I don't feel *comfortable* making a U-turn in this relationship because you don't want to be a *burden*."

Samuel let out a heavy sigh, then said with firm resignation, "I'm not going to marry you, Emily. You deserve better than that."

Emily stared at him in disbelief, wondering if she was going to scream at him or burst into tears. Deciding that neither was acceptable, she grabbed her purse and hurried out of the apartment. As soon as she had the car on the highway, the tears cascaded out of her in torrents. She was just past the edge of town when she had to pull over and cry until she got it out of her system enough to focus on the road. Long after her tears ran dry, she just sat in the car, staring at nothing, attempting to deal with the shock. She finally accepted that the shock wasn't likely to settle quickly and she needed to get home. During the drive, a few more stray tears crept down her cheeks while she wondered if she felt angry or hurt or just plain sad.

Arriving at the house she noticed Jess sitting on the veranda with his feet up. *Oh that's just what I need,* she thought, wanting only to get to her room before anyone could read the signs of strain in her face that she knew couldn't be hidden. A quick glance in the rearview mirror affirmed it; she'd been crying long and hard and she looked like it. Taking a deep breath, she just got out of the car and hurried toward the house, hoping a wave in his direction would suffice. But he stood and walked toward her, making it clearly evident that he'd been waiting for her.

"Hello, Mother," he said, meeting her at the top of the steps.

"Hello, Jess," she said.

"Samuel called," he said, and Emily sighed. "He said you left upset; he was worried about you."

"Well, as you can see I'm home safely."

"That doesn't necessarily mean you're alright," Jess said. His tone and expression made it evident that for all of the progress he'd made in accepting this situation, his defenses had been triggered. He was acting very much like a father figure again, and she wondered if he believed that Samuel had said or done something to hurt her.

Emily had to ask, "Did he tell you *why* I was upset?"

"No. And I resisted the urge to demand an explanation."

"Well, I can give you some credit for that," she said, attempting to move past him.

"So, why are you upset, Mother?" he asked. When she didn't answer he asked, "What did he do? If he hurt you in any way I'll—"

"You'll what, Jess? I am capable of handling this. Contrary to what you seem to believe, I am not some naïve teenager, and you are not the parent here."

"Okay," he said more gently, "I'm sorry. I'm just . . . concerned for you. After what happened the last time, what am I supposed to think? Does this have something to do with money?"

"It has absolutely nothing to do with money."

"Okay, so what did he do to upset you?"

"This is not as black and white as you seem to think it is," Emily said. "Samuel Reid is one of the most decent, honest, suitable men I have ever met. He has done nothing remotely wrong or inappropriate. He is tender and wise and sensitive and . . ." Emotion overtook her and she pressed a hand over her mouth. She found Jess's shoulder absorbing her tears, and felt his arms around her.

"And what, Mother?" he asked gently.

"He's dying," she muttered through her tears, crying harder.

Jess wondered if he'd heard her correctly. He took hold of her shoulders and looked into her face. "Did you say dying?"

"That's what I said," she muttered, wiping helplessly at her face.

"What . . ." he stammered. "How . . ."

"I can't talk about it right now," she said, and hurried into the house.

Jess watched her go, then sank into a chair. He pondered what little he knew of the situation and felt sick to his stomach. He'd finally accepted that this was a good step for his mother. She'd finally found someone to fill the void left by his father's death. And now this. *Dying?* Hadn't his mother already endured enough heartache? Enough loss? Enough death? And what about Samuel? If this was what it seemed to be, the man had to be at least as upset as his mother. Jess had grown to care for Samuel; they all had. And now what?

Recalling that he'd promised to call Samuel to let him know his mother had arrived safely, he went in through the library door and used the phone there, where no one would overhear. He dialed the number, and it barely rang before Samuel said hello.

"She's home," Jess said.

"Still upset, I take it."

"Yes, she is."

"Did she tell you why?"

"She managed to mumble a few words before she insisted on being alone." Jess swallowed carefully. "Please tell me this is not as bad as it seems."

"That depends on what you mean by *it*," Samuel said.

"She told me that you're . . . dying." Jess hated the way images of his father's death came to mind.

"Well, not right away, but that's the eventual outcome." He gave Jess a brief overview of the disease and his history with it, what the prognosis was, and his reasons for not telling Emily before now. He finished his explanation of the current situation by saying, "And that's why I can't marry your mother."

"I don't understand the connection," Jess said.

"Give me one good reason why I should be willing to become a permanent burden to your mother—and the rest of the family, for that matter." He sounded almost angry.

"If she loves you, then I would see that as reason enough."

"Well, I love her too much to—"

"You know what?" Jess interrupted. "You should be having this conversation with my mother."

"I was trying to when she left," Samuel said more quietly.

"Once she's had some time to adjust to the shock, I'm sure she'll be wanting to talk to you," Jess said.

"I'd come right now if I thought that was the case."

"Well, I can't guarantee it, but . . . I think she'll want to see you. Either way, maybe we could all stand to talk this through. And at the very least we can make sure you don't go hungry."

"You're too good to me, Jess."

"You've brought a great deal of joy into my mother's life," Jess said. "And for that I'm grateful."

"And what about the misery she's been confronted with today?"

"Today isn't over yet," Jess said. "Just get in the car; we'll talk when you get here."

"I'm on my way," Samuel said.

Once Jess hung up the phone, he sat and stared at it for several minutes before he went to find his wife. He needed her. She cried when he told her what Samuel had told him, and then she said the very thing he had thought upon hearing the news. "Hasn't your mother already had more than her fair share of struggles in this world? Hasn't she already lost enough loved ones to death?"

They talked until a knock sounded at the side door, and Jess knew it was Samuel. When he opened the door and their eyes met, Jess suddenly didn't know what to say. He reached out a hand, and Samuel took it firmly. A moment later Jess put his other arm around Samuel and they ended up sharing an embrace that startled Jess when he was unexpectedly reminded of his father. He was equally surprised by a rush of emotion that caught him off guard. Stepping back he forced a steady voice as he asked, "You okay?"

"That depends on whether or not your mother wants to have anything to do with me."

"I really don't think that's the problem," Jess said. "But I'll let the two of you work that out. Wait in the lounge room. I'll get her."

"Thank you," Samuel said, and he started up the hall. He turned back and said, "Jess . . . if she doesn't want to see me, tell her I understand."

Jess nodded and hurried up the back stairs.

Emily was startled from deep thought by a knock at the door. "Who is it?" she called.

"It's your son," Jess called back. "You have company. Your boyfriend is here to see you." He said it almost lightly, and Emily wondered if her news had made any difference in Jess's attitude.

Emily pulled the door open and said in the same light tone, "What makes you think I have a boyfriend?"

More seriously he said, "Because you love him, and I believe he loves you too. He drove a long way to see you; I think you should go talk to him."

"Yes, I suppose I should," she said, stepping into the hall. She was surprised to realize that she knew exactly what she needed to say.

Walking down the stairs with Jess at her side, he said facetiously, "Did you want me to hold your hand?"

"Thank you, but . . . I think I can handle this and . . ." She stopped walking, and he did the same. Pressing a kiss to his cheek, she said, "Thank you, Jess. I'm grateful for you and for the way you care. Truly I am."

"I just want you to be happy—now and forever."

"And I will be," she said, moving on down the stairs.

"He's in the lounge room," Jess said, and Emily went one direction at the bottom of the stairs, while Jess went the other.

Emily pushed open the lounge room door, taking a deep breath. Samuel rose to his feet, his expression expectant, almost afraid. "Before you say anything," he said quickly, "there's something I need to say. I'm just . . . so sorry, Emily. I didn't expect to find someone like you; I wasn't looking for this. It just . . . happened. And then, I kept thinking . . . this will move slowly. There will be plenty of time to stop it, to tell her, to . . . rearrange whatever might be getting arranged. I didn't plan to fall in love, Emily. And I'm truly, truly sorry for bringing this misery into your life. I keep thinking that I should have never asked you to dinner, or—"

"Samuel," she interrupted, stepping toward him, "it's alright." She took his face into her hands. "It was meant to be, my love." She kissed him, then said more quietly, "Now, there's something I must say. God brought us together, Samuel, to bless each other's lives. I will—"

"But how can this be a blessing to you, Emily? How?"

She pressed her fingers over his lips. "Listen to me, Samuel. We can't possibly know all that the future will bring, or the impact our choices might have on our lives—or the lives of others. While I know practically nothing about this disease or the way it's affecting you—or will affect you—the outcome is still variable. I don't know how it will all play out. I don't know how long you—or even I—will live. I only know that we are supposed to be together for whatever time we may have. I know it with all my heart. I will not deny what my heart is telling me I must do."

"And what is that?" he asked.

"We need to be together," she said firmly, "for as long and as much as possible."

"Emily, how can you say that when—"

"I'm prepared to take this on, Samuel, because I know in my heart that it's right. What if we had been married before the diagnosis was made, or before you knew it was getting worse?"

"That question is irrelevant. We weren't. We are in a position where we have a choice regarding the commitment we make."

"And I am choosing to commit my life to you and see this through."

Samuel turned away and gave an exasperated sigh. "I cannot bring this burden into your life, Emily. I cannot bring this burden to your children."

"I am willing to make you a part of my life and to take on whatever that entails. How much my children choose to become involved—or not—is up to them." He said nothing, and she added, "What if it were the other way around?"

He turned to look at her. "It's not the other way around, Emily. I am the one who will very likely need more care than a baby."

"And what if it were? What if I were in an accident tomorrow and became completely paralyzed? Then what?" He remained silent, and she insisted, "Answer the question! Answer it truthfully. I want to know."

Emily watched him squeeze his eyes closed, and his chin quivered as he said, "I would give everything I have to care for you and to share our life as much as it's possible."

"Do you credit me with loving you less than you love me?"

"No," he said firmly, opening his eyes. "I credit you with being more worthy of such love and dedication than I."

"Samuel, I love you. I know this is right. We were not brought together so that we could merely be . . . kissing friends. I know it beyond any doubt."

"How can you know it, Emily? How can you know that your own desire isn't clouding your judgment?"

"I just *know*," she said firmly, but with a quaver in her voice. His eyes widened skeptically, and she added, "I know beyond any doubt that this is the right course for me, for my life. And until you can tell me with the same conviction that it is *not* the right course for you, I will fight with everything I have to share as much of my life with you as I possibly can. And in order to do that, I want to be your wife." She sighed and added, "It's not up to you to determine what will be a burden or a blessing in my life, Samuel. I need you in my life, and I'm willing to take on whatever challenges may come with that."

Samuel was more quiet as he said, "Emily, can't you see that it's better for you if we don't marry? It's you that I'm concerned about. You that—"

"Did you hear what I said, Samuel?" He only stared at her, seeming stunned as she repeated, "Until you can tell me with the same conviction I feel now that this is not right for you, I will fight to have you in my life." She sighed deeply and added, "I'm asking you to pray about this, Samuel. We've talked about personal revelation, and you are entitled to it as much as anybody. If you do that, and you can look me in the eye and tell me that you know beyond any doubt that God does not want you to be my husband, then I will accept it—and we can be friends."

Samuel looked completely taken aback. A full minute passed while he seemed to be internalizing what Emily had said. She finally asked, "Will you do that . . . for me?"

"Emily, I . . . I've never gotten any such answer. How can I possibly . . ."

"If you try . . . with a sincere heart, you'll get an answer. Tell me you'll do it."

He sighed loudly. "I will . . . do my best."

"Thank you," Emily said gently as she stepped toward him. Putting her arms around his waist, she felt a deep relief when he returned her embrace with fervor. "I love you, Samuel," she said. "And we'll get through this . . . together."

"I love you too, Emily. And I'm grateful to know how you care, but . . ."

Emily drew back and put her fingers over his lips. "We'll talk again in a couple of days. In the meantime, we both need to give it some thought and prayer. Okay?"

"Okay," he said, pressing a kiss into her hair.

For a long moment Emily just held to him, attempting to comprehend how much he had filled a hole in her life—and how the news she'd been given today threatened to break her heart. But she knew that if he would only agree to share his life with her as far as it was possible, they could bless each other's lives and have a great deal of joy in whatever time they might have together. And maybe, just maybe, the disease would move slower and less aggressively than what he'd been told.

Feeling a need to adjust to all that had happened in one short day, she urged him to sit beside her on the couch, where they talked for nearly two hours. She asked him questions about this illness and listened while he told her in detail the symptoms and the prognosis. She cried some, but then, so did he. She walked him to his car when he was ready to go, then she went up to her room, telling her family only that she needed to be alone and she was starting a fast, so she wouldn't be eating.

Emily talked to Samuel on the phone for a few minutes before she went to bed, and again the next day for a short while. But she didn't see him at all for three days. She took advantage of the time to research the disease and learn as much as she could about it, knowing that being educated on the matter would aid her decisions. Deeply exploring her own feelings on the matter, she couldn't deny the grief she felt to realize this man she had so quickly grown to love was inevitably doomed to endure this horrible disease that would likely cut his life significantly shorter. But at the same time she felt deeply comforted, as if a part of her knew that if any woman could handle it graciously, she could. She'd been trained well in grief through her life's experiences, and she knew that God would see them through.

Emily talked with her family about the details of the situation and told them straight out that through fasting and a great deal of prayer, her conviction about marrying Samuel had only deepened. They expressed some of the same concerns that Samuel had, but each of them—except for Jess—admitted that they had quickly grown to care for Samuel and that they would stand behind Emily in whatever she chose to do.

"And what about you, Jess?" Emily asked, looking directly at him. "I want you to be honest with me."

"If you love him, Mother, and you know it's right, then I'm not going to question your decision. If you choose to make him a part of the family, then I don't have a problem with treating him like family."

Emily felt close to tears as she realized he truly meant it. "Thank you, Jess," she said. "Your support means a great deal to me."

"Well," he said, giving her a warm smile, "you supported me through some pretty tough things. Maybe it's time I repaid the favor."

Emily smiled in return and then glanced down until Jess asked, "So, what's wrong?"

"Well, I still don't know if he'll agree to marriage; I've hardly heard from him. I feel like it's right, and a part of me believes he'll come to that, but . . . another part of me worries that . . . he just won't."

"Give him time," Jess said. "Eventually we'll talk him into it."

But nearly a week passed since Emily had challenged Samuel to pray for his own answer, and she still hadn't seen him. They'd talked on the phone a number of times, but only exchanging brief bits of small talk. He admitted that he wasn't feeling well, but he hotly refused her repeated offers to come and visit him. She debated doing it anyway, but feared the drive would be a waste of time if he refused to let her in. And she didn't want to put him in a position that made him uncomfortable. Still, she missed him desperately and felt that this separation was ridiculous and senseless when every day that passed was a day they could have been spending together.

* * *

On Saturday morning Jess found his mother sitting at the computer but staring at the wall. Her somber countenance these last several days made him appreciate the joy Samuel had brought into her life, and at the same time he felt almost angry—with the circumstances if not with Samuel—for this pathetic turn of events.

"Hey you," he said, and she turned toward him, startled. "What's up?"

"Not much," she said, looking absently toward the computer screen. "I've been studying this disease on the Internet—again—attempting to become more educated, if nothing else. But I believe I've read just about all there is to read at least once."

"And what have you concluded?" he asked gently.

"Well . . . it could be tough, but there are many variables. Maybe it won't get as bad as he thinks. Maybe it will. Either way I truly feel I can handle it, but . . ." She sighed and left the sentence unfinished. "Anyway, I've also been catching up my journal, but . . . there's not much to say since I wrote in it last."

Jess sat down before he asked, "May I intrude?"

"Sure," she said. "What can I do for you?"

"I was going to ask you that."

Emily sighed. "I doubt there's anything that anyone can do. I can't force him to marry me."

"Well a man would have to be a fool to not want to marry you."

"Maybe he wants to. He's just . . ."

"Still a fool," Jess said, but Emily only sighed again.

"I don't know," she said, following a minute of miserable silence, "maybe it's better this way."

"According to whom?"

"I don't know," she said again and left the room.

Long after Emily had left the room, Jess contemplated the situation and what he wanted to do about it. He spent a great deal of time in front of the computer, studying the facts as his mother had been doing, while he pondered the more personal aspects of it for Samuel. He finally determined that his desire to pay Samuel a visit was valid and felt right. He just prayed that it would go well. He certainly didn't want to make things worse. But then, judging from his mother's mood, it couldn't get much worse. He knew his mother well enough to know that eventually she would come to terms with this, and she would fill her life with gratitude and giving, just as she always had. But it would never be completely right. Of course, life had never felt completely right since Michael had passed away. There was nothing he could do about that. But at the moment, it felt right for Samuel to be a part of their family. And he *could* do something about that. And God willing, he wouldn't flub it.

Chapter Ten

It didn't take much effort for Jess to figure out exactly where Samuel lived. But once he got there he began to wonder if just showing up at his door was a good idea. What if he was asleep or not feeling well? Still, he felt like he needed to see him. He'd driven to town specifically for this purpose. He nearly knocked at the door then wondered if a little strategy might be better. Instead he called on his mobile phone, but it took Samuel several rings to answer.

"You okay?" Jess asked.

"Relatively speaking," Samuel answered, sounding groggy.

"Did I wake you?"

"Not really. I was just . . . resting."

"Well, we're worried about you."

"No need for that."

"I'm not so sure," Jess said and knocked at the door.

"Listen, Jess. Could I call you back? There's someone at the door." His tone of voice implied that he was relieved to get off the phone.

"No need for that," Jess said, "I was just checking up on you."

"Well, I appreciate it," Samuel said and hung up the phone just as he answered the door to see Jess standing there, turning off his own phone.

"Hi there," Jess said, taking note of the plaid pajama pants and long-sleeved T-shirt Samuel was wearing, with bare feet. "I have an outfit just like that," he added, but Samuel didn't seem amused. Jess also noted the weary look about him, and he wondered if it was more to do with his health problems—or his emotional state. Or if one was contributing to the other.

"What can I do for you?" Samuel asked, and Jess noticed he was leaning rather heavily against the door.

"First of all you can sit down before you fall over." Jess stepped inside, took hold of Samuel's arm, and kicked the door closed, surprised to feel Samuel's inability to stand without support. He helped him to the couch and muttered, "It's okay, we're practically family."

"Is that why you think you can barge in here and take care of me like a baby?" Samuel asked, but his tone didn't sound altogether serious.

"Helping you to the couch hardly qualifies me as your nanny." Jess sat down on the opposite couch. "So, how are you? Bad day?"

"You could say that."

"I've been studying your disease on the Internet," Jess admitted.

"Now why would you do that?"

"So I can understand it better," Jess said. "Would I be right in guessing that you did a lot of overdoing in order to spend time with my mother and not let on to the problem? And now you're paying for it?"

Samuel just sighed loudly, and Jess went on. "And maybe, since it's a disease of the nervous system, and stress can aggravate it, the current issues between you and my mother have made it even worse."

"You're sounding a lot like my son."

"How is that?"

"He's always too smart for his own good," Samuel said, but he smiled when he said it.

"Well," Jess smiled back, "I came to petition for the position."

"What position?"

"Being your son."

Samuel's expression darkened. "Does your mother know you're here?"

"No, I'm being sneaky. She said you refused to see her. I thought if you refused to see me, I could just beat the door in or something."

"You wouldn't."

"No, I wouldn't, but I could threaten to."

"So, you're here. What can I do for you?"

"I told you. I'm here to petition to be your son."

Samuel's expression darkened further. "You can't be serious."

"Do I look serious?" Jess asked, his expression solemn.

"Well, perhaps you *and* your mother should reconsider. I didn't think you were all too pleased about the prospect of her remarrying, anyway."

"I wasn't," Jess said. "But it doesn't take a rocket scientist to see that you brought a great deal of joy into my mother's life. And this last week, she's not been very happy at all."

"I'm truly sorry for the misery I've brought into her life."

"The misery is from your choosing to not be involved in her life."

"Perhaps it's better that she get over it now, as opposed to later— after she's become disillusioned over having to care for a debilitated husband."

"You just don't get it, do you," Jess said.

"I'm afraid I don't."

Jess leaned forward and put his forearms on his thighs. He looked sternly at Samuel. "This life is not about choosing a path that will bring the least resistance or challenge or difficulty. It's about choosing the path that God wants you to take for the greatest possible learning and growth and experience. It's about giving and caring and sharing—not holing up alone when there are other options. There is no way of knowing from one day to the next what might happen to any one of us. There is no human being who is immune to the possibility of sudden illness, disease, death, disability. But we commit ourselves to each other in order to make the most of what we've got. And who knows? Maybe you've got a lot longer and lot more life left in you than you realize. And you can't tell me that the prospect of living the rest of your life with my mother wouldn't give you some marvelous, positive incentive. I know I'm being presumptuous and obnoxious, but I really believe you need to try and see a broader perspective on this."

Samuel said nothing at all, and Jess finally spoke again to fill the silence. "Did you do what she asked you to do?"

Still Samuel said nothing, and Jess came to his feet. He felt suddenly on the verge of getting angry and didn't want to stay long enough to have it come to the surface. "You at least owe her that much. Whatever your decision may be, she needs to know where she stands—not be left in this limbo with no closure. I don't care how sick you are, you can give this matter some serious prayer. I know you have it in you."

"How do you know that?"

"I just know," he said, and more silence fell. "Is there anything you need? Can I help you with anything while I'm here?"

"No, thank you, Jess. I'm fine . . . really."

"Will you do what she asked?"

Samuel nodded but looked skeptical.

"Good," Jess said, moving toward the door. "We'll expect to hear from you in a few days. If you need anything, you know where to reach me.

"Oh," Jess said on his way out the door, "there's a really great line in the Bible you might appreciate. Look it up. It says that it's not good for man to be alone."

Through the drive home Jess contemplated his conversation with Samuel, and he couldn't help feeling a little amazed that *he*—of all people—would be going out of his way to marry off his mother. Pondering how he really felt about this, he had to admit that he truly believed in his heart that Samuel was supposed to be a part of their family, at least while on this earth. And he prayed that it would all work out for the best.

Returning to the house, Jess wandered into the little family cemetery. He'd not been here for quite some time, but still, seeing his father's grave always took him aback. It felt strange—plain and simple. But he had adjusted. He'd never stopped missing him and wishing he could have stayed around longer. But still, he had adjusted to Michael's absence—something at one time he'd never believed was possible.

Squatting down beside the grave, Jess felt the sudden urge to talk with his father. It had been a long time since he'd spoken aloud to him. He didn't know if Michael was available to hear it, but it made Jess feel better as he began, "Hey, Dad. I sure miss you. I hope you're okay with all this. It seems that I am. I never thought I'd say that, but he seems to be a great guy. I think he'll take good care of her. If you know what's going on here, it would be nice if you could pull a few strings. We could really use a miracle, I think. I'll keep praying for one, and you see what you can do from that end. I love you, Dad. I'll see you again one of these days, but not too soon, I hope. I've got to raise my family. They're beautiful, you know. Yes, I'm sure you do." Jess pressed his hand lovingly over his father's name, carved in granite, then he headed to the house to check on that beautiful family, somehow knowing that Michael Hamilton was indeed aware of the happenings of his family, and that somehow, all would be well.

* * *

Emily began to feel that Samuel would simply never come around. She'd hardly even spoken to him for days, and when she did, he had practically nothing to say. She missed him desperately, and when she prayed that she would be able to just let go and move on with her life, it simply felt all wrong. But she didn't know what to do about it. Then out of the blue, he called on Wednesday morning, and simply said, "Can I see you?"

"Of course. Do you want me to—"

"I'll come out there, if that's all right," he said.

"That would be fine."

Little more than an hour later, Emily watched from the veranda as he stopped his car at the end of the drive and got out. Watching him walk toward her, she felt a heart-pounding fear that he truly would deny her the opportunity to be his wife. Seeing him again after all these days apart made her realize even more how much she had truly grown to love him and how desperately she wanted him to be a part of her life.

She stood to meet him as he walked up the steps. He reached out both hands, and she took hold of them tightly. "I'd forgotten how beautiful you are," he said and kissed her quickly.

Emily smiled and looked up at him, wondering where to begin. She was grateful when he said, "There's a great deal I'd like to say, so we'd do well to get to the point, I think." He motioned toward the chairs, and they sat down, facing each other. He looked slightly more gaunt than the last time she'd seen him, and it was evident that he'd not been feeling well.

When he hesitated Emily said, "And what might the point be?" She held her breath, thinking that she might prefer *not* getting to the point, if his answer left her disappointed. Until he said no, she had the hope that he might come to see her perspective.

"Well," he said, "there's only one way to say it, really." He took her hand and looked into her eyes. Emotion broke his voice. "I was wrong, Emily. For whatever time we have left in this life's journey, I want to share it with you."

Emily took a sharp breath and held it. She quickly recounted his words in her mind, trying to be certain she hadn't heard him wrong. She was almost ready to admit it was true when he added, "I'm asking you to marry me, Emily. And my deepest hope is that I can bring some measure of joy into your life that will compensate for the inevitable challenges."

"You already have." She eased to the edge of her seat and threw her arms around him.

He returned her embrace with strength and whispered near her ear, "I pray that you don't regret it." He took her shoulders into his hands and looked at her. "You can still say no, and I would understand."

"I can't tell you no," she said, touching his face, "because I know more every day that this is the right course for me."

"And what about your family?" he asked, only slightly skeptical.

"They are willing to stand behind me, whatever I decide to do. Even Jess."

He sighed. "Yes, I knew that."

"You did?"

"Well," Samuel leaned back slightly, "he came to visit me . . . on Saturday."

"I see," Emily said, wondering why he hadn't said anything. "And what did he have to say?"

"We can talk more about that later. Suffice it to say that he made it clear I needed to act like a man and do what you'd asked me to do."

"He said that?"

"Not in so many words. But I'm glad he said what he did. I think I was feeling a little bit too sorry for myself and perhaps even downright depressed. I can get that way when I don't feel well, which is something we need to talk about. But back to Jess. He also let me know that he was petitioning for the position of being my son."

"He said *that?*" Emily laughed in disbelief.

"Yes, actually, he did, and I believe he means it."

"Yes, I believe he does," Emily said, her voice almost dreamy.

"Are you sure you don't want to say no?"

"I'm absolutely sure that the answer is yes," she said, even dreamier.

Samuel took a deep breath, then he smiled. "Well then," he said, "we should plan a wedding. We haven't got time on our side."

"So, we'll make the most of every minute," she said.

"There's something else I need to say." Samuel's expression turned grave.

"I'm listening," Emily said, hoping it wouldn't be bad news.

"I've realized something else these last few days, and . . . I have to say how grateful I am for what you've taught me about God and about being able to get answers to prayers. A whole new way of thinking has opened up to me since I've met you, and I want to tell you how truly, truly grateful I am for what you've taught me. I also want to tell you that I would like to be baptized."

Emily became too emotional to speak. In a way, this news gave her more joy than knowing they would be married. For her and Samuel, their marriage would only last until they were separated by death. But this decision would bring eternal blessings to him; her joy on his behalf was beyond description.

While she was struggling to come up with something to say, he added, "I've learned enough about the gospel to know that it truly is possible for me to be with Arlene forever—just as you will be with Michael forever. So, I want to share what's left of this life with you, and in the next we will be deliriously happy with our eternal companions." Emily just nodded and hugged him again.

Emily threw together a simple picnic, and she and Samuel drove into the mountains where they were able to talk through this turn their lives were taking. Samuel shared details of how he had come to these decisions and of the spiritual conviction he'd gained through his prayer and study. They returned to the house late in the afternoon, and Samuel gladly agreed to stay to supper. Nothing was said at the table about Samuel's illness or their plans to marry, but Emily sensed it would be better to bring these things up when the children weren't present, constantly creating interruptions. She was pleased when Samuel said near the end of the meal, "I wonder if we could all talk for a few minutes later . . . when it's convenient."

"Of course," Jess and Scott said at the same time. Emily didn't miss the way Jess passed Samuel a little smirk.

"Once the children are down for the night, we can talk all you like," Jess said.

Samuel and Emily went for a long walk outside, further discussing their plans and feelings about the wedding and their life together beyond it. When all the adults, including Rhea, were gathered in the lounge room, Samuel thanked them for their time, then said, "I've come to a decision, and I would like you all to be the first to know— except for Emily, of course." He smiled at her. "She already knows." He scanned the faces of those in the room. "I'm going to be baptized."

Jess's heart began to pound. This was not what he'd expected to hear. In spite of Samuel's overt interest in the gospel, Jess had come to accept that the religious differences in this particular marriage were not such a big concern. He'd seen evidence of Samuel accepting and being involved with his mother's religious beliefs, and Jess hadn't thought much about it beyond that. The last time he'd spoken with Samuel, he never would have guessed that *this* had been churning inside of him as much as the issue of marrying Emily. But how could Jess deny his joy over this news? Whether or not Samuel ended up a literal part of the family or not, the fact that Emily's influence had brought him to this was glorious indeed.

Jess listened to the others express their joy on Samuel's behalf while his own joy fully settled in. Seeing the obvious happiness on his mother's face, he could only imagine how much this meant to her. Still, he couldn't help wondering where Samuel stood in regards to marrying Emily. And he felt concerned. He was brought out of his thoughts when Samuel said, "Jess, I have a favor to ask of you."

"Ask away," Jess said.

Even with the context of the conversation, he was still completely surprised to hear Samuel say, "I would like you to be the one to baptize me."

Jess felt momentarily stunned. He felt Tamra take his hand and squeeze it while he met Samuel's eyes across the room. "It would be an honor," Jess said. "Of course I'll do it. If you're sure you want me to do it. I mean, the elders who have been teaching you are—"

"They're wonderful young men, but they're not family," Samuel said.

Jess wanted to ask if that meant what he hoped it meant. He sensed the others wanting to ask the same, but Samuel quickly went on to say, "And Scott, I would like you to be the one to do the confirmation, if you're willing."

"It would be an unfathomable pleasure," Scott said.

"Good then," Samuel said with a little laugh. "Now that we have that out of the way, I would like to tell you that I've asked your mother to marry me."

The family did a repeat performance of their stunned surprise following the previous announcement, then they all expressed their pleasure at this turn of events. Everyone rose to their feet, exchanging embraces all around and expressions of congratulations. When Jess was facing Samuel, they shook hands earnestly, then shared a firm embrace. "Are you certain you're alright with this?" Samuel asked.

"I wouldn't have been beating your door down, begging to be your son if I weren't."

Samuel chuckled before he said more loudly, "There are some things we need to discuss, if that's alright." They were all seated again, and he went on. "You all know by now that I have a serious illness, and I am also hesitant to bring this burden into your family. I want to discuss the situation thoroughly, straight up front, so there's no question as to where I stand and what is to be expected. Your mother and I have talked this through extensively. We've agreed to make the very most of what we have and to deal with the situation the best we can. When my illness reaches a point where I need any more than minimal assistance, I don't want Emily—or any of you for that matter—carrying that responsibility. I have resources that can more than cover my care, and that's the way I want it to be."

"I believe I can speak for the rest of the family," Jess said, "when I say that we're not concerned about it."

"How can you speak for the rest of the family?" Samuel asked. "Do you know if they—"

"Actually, I *do* know," Jess said. "We had a family council and—"

"You had a meeting to discuss this?" Samuel asked, seeming disconcerted.

"We have family councils over everything of any significance," Tamra said. "There's no need to be alarmed."

"They had family councils over me," Scott said.

"And me," Rhea added with pride.

"If you can pass a family council," Scott added, "then all is well."

"I see," Samuel said with a little chuckle, but still seeming concerned. "And what exactly did you determine in this council meeting?"

Jess answered, "We will, as you said, take it on the best we can. We had a full-time nurse here in the home when my father needed one, and we did the same when his mother was terribly ill. I assure you we can afford it."

"I don't want *you* to afford it," Samuel said. "I have my own resources available, Jess. I will not be a burden to this family."

"Samuel," Jess said gently, "has it ever occurred to you that the opportunity to have you in our home and help you through this illness could be a blessing for us? Would you take away the opportunity for our family to receive those blessings because you're too proud to accept our help graciously?"

"Jess," Emily scolded gently, "please be more—"

"It's fine," Samuel said, putting his hand over hers. "I want your children to tell me how they feel and what they think."

"He's family, Mother. I'm not going to speak any differently to him than I would have spoken to my own father. I would hope that Samuel can take such candor as a compliment. If we didn't feel like you were a part of the family, we wouldn't be talking this way."

Samuel smiled. "I actually do take this as a compliment."

"So answer the question," Jess said. "Would you deny us the opportunity to bless your life, as you have blessed ours?"

"And how would I be blessing your lives?" Samuel asked skeptically.

Jess motioned toward his mother. "Look at her. She needs you. She loves you. And I know you love her. And," Jess lifted a finger, "you need her, too. You need to be a part of this family."

Jess saw tears come into his mother's eyes. She smiled at him, then at Samuel. It took Jess a moment to realize that the reason no one said anything was due to the fact that they all had tears in their eyes.

It was as if the Spirit had confirmed to all of them in the same moment that this was the right course for their family, and Jess knew from experience that when the Spirit spoke so strongly, it often meant that through the struggles ahead—whatever they may be—they would need to know beyond any doubt that this course was right. He decided to keep that thought to himself for the time being.

Conversation began again with unhurried, quiet inquiries directed at Samuel concerning his decision to become a member of the Church. The Spirit remained strong in the room as he openly shared his experience. Emily felt her heart overflow to bursting as she observed the conversation, thinking how well Samuel fit into her family and how right it felt for him to be there. She was surprised to hear that he wanted to be baptized right away, but Jess said that he felt certain it could be arranged.

Samuel mentioned that his son, Trent, and his family were coming to visit in a couple of weeks, and he wanted to be baptized before that time.

"Do you think he'll try to talk you out of it?" Emily asked.

"Not at all," Samuel said. "I simply want to spend as much time with them as I can, and I would like to have this done before they arrive. And then, if it's alright with you, I would like to plan the wedding at the very end of their visit, so that they can be here, but our honeymoon won't interfere with their time here."

"Sounds marvelous," Emily said with sparkling eyes that made Jess smile as he observed her. It truly was good to see her so happy, and in spite of life's continuing challenges, there certainly was much to be happy about.

They talked briefly about plans for the wedding. Emily told Samuel of the long-standing traditions in the family, and he was eager to go along with them. Samuel loved hearing how every wedding in the family, all the way back to Jess and Alexandra Davies, had taken place in the upstairs hall of the house—except for those that had taken place in the temple, of course. Emma and Tamra became visibly enthusiastic as they talked about food and guest lists and flowers.

"Of course you'll have the bishop marry you," Scott said. "That would be the standard under the circumstances."

"Yes, of course," Emily said, smiling at Samuel.

"Sounds delightful," Samuel said as he gave her a quick kiss.

Jess felt slightly taken aback to actually see this man kiss his mother, but he had to admit he really was okay with that; he was okay with all of it—a fact that surprised even him. He had to give credit to the Spirit in giving him the guidance and comfort he needed. As his life progressed, his experience with such things only deepened his testimony of how the Holy Ghost guided thoughts and feelings toward what was right and good. And he was grateful for such a miracle in his life.

The hour became late but they continued to talk and speculate over the future with Samuel becoming a part of the family. They made plans for Trent's visit and hoped that they could all do some things together. Samuel felt sure they would love to be involved with his new family, even though Trent hadn't yet been given the big news. The conversation came around again to Samuel's illness and his concern for Emily having to deal with that. Emma commented, "I hate to say it, but I can't stop thinking it. What if Mom dies before Samuel does?"

"I had the same thought," Scott admitted. "It's not likely perhaps, but anything can happen, and we should be prepared."

"If that were the case," Samuel said, "then I would insist on simply living at the care center. That was my original plan anyway."

"You know what I think?" Tamra said. "I think it's late, and we've already got way too much to think about. We need to just take this one day at a time. For now, let's just get through the baptism and the wedding and do our best to enjoy every minute of it."

"I couldn't have said it better myself," Emily said. "And since it's so late, I think we should put Samuel up in a guest room. I hate having him drive home at this hour. Jess, would you see that he has what he needs?"

"I'd be happy to," Jess said.

"Have I no say in this?" Samuel asked lightly.

"No, not really," Scott said with a chuckle. "But then, once you've spent the night and had breakfast with us, you might change your mind."

"No chance of that," Samuel said, tossing an affectionate glance toward Emily.

"You know," Emily said quietly to Samuel while the others were chatting as they worked their way toward the hall, "if I didn't live with all these people, we wouldn't have to have these family councils. If I lived on my own I'd just call them up and say I'm getting married, and this is when the wedding is."

"It's okay," he said, touching her face. "You have a wonderful family, and I feel greatly privileged to be a part of it."

Emily smiled and kissed him. "You've made me a very happy woman."

"It is I who am happy, I can assure you," he said.

Samuel told Emily good night and walked upstairs with Jess to one of the many guest rooms. Jess pointed out the private bathroom and the drawer filled with new toothbrushes and shaving items specifically for unexpected guests.

"I believe you should be able to find everything you need," Jess said, his hand on the doorknob. "If something comes up, I'm just down the hall on the left."

"Thank you, Jess," Samuel said, "for everything."

"It's a pleasure, truly," Jess said, then turned to leave.

"One more thing," Samuel said. He reached for the knapsack he often carried with him and tossed a couple of things on the bed. Jess noticed several prescription medications and a Book of Mormon among the items. There was also a large manila envelope that he picked up and handed to Jess. "I want you to have this."

"What is it?"

"It's self-explanatory, I believe," Samuel said.

Jess wondered if he should open it later, but he opted for now, and Samuel didn't protest as he opened the flap and pulled out a piece of paper. A glance told him it was a legal document; the notarized signature and format of the page gave it away. Without reading every word, he grasped the implication and couldn't help sounding terse as he asked, "What is this?"

"It's a prenuptial statement. It says that I have no access to your mother's money—ever."

"Why do you think I would want something like this?" Jess demanded quietly.

"So you don't have to wonder," Samuel said earnestly. "So no one in the family has to wonder. I'm well aware that your mother has more money than she could ever spend in the remainder of her life, and if she did not, I would do my best to meet her needs with what I've got put away. But this will keep the money from ever being an issue."

"And what about *your* needs?" Jess asked.

"I can assure you, my needs are more than sufficiently met, Jess. I was never wealthy, but I did well enough, and my future is comfortably taken care of. My money is set up in a trust fund to meet my needs for as long as I live, and whatever might be left goes to Trent. Since I won't be paying rent on my apartment, I will be contributing to *this* household." Jess opened his mouth to say something but Samuel put up a hand to stop him. "I'm well aware that this household runs just fine without any contribution from me, but I *will* help care for my wife. I will be paying for the wedding and the honeymoon and any other travel that we decide to do. And I won't accept anything less."

Jess took a deep breath and realized he had nothing to say. He truly admired and respected this man. And he couldn't deny that it was nice not to have to wonder. He slid the document back into the envelope and simply said, "You're a good man, Samuel. I'm glad you came to your senses."

"So am I."

"I really don't need this." Jess tapped the envelope in his hands.

"Just tuck it away, and we'll say nothing more about it."

Jess nodded and told him good night. He returned to his own room where Tamra was already sitting in bed, reading from the Book of Mormon. "What's that?" she asked, nodding toward the envelope in his hands.

"A prenuptial agreement," Jess said, and Tamra's brow furrowed. "It states that he has no right, ever, to Hamilton money."

"Why would he think such a thing was necessary?"

"That's what I asked him. He said so we wouldn't have to wonder. I know he's aware of what happened with Rick; I guess he didn't want money to ever be an issue. I really wasn't concerned."

"No, but . . ." She hesitated as if she was trying to put her thoughts into words.

"What?" he asked, sitting on the edge of the bed to pull off his boots.

"Well . . . maybe it's not an issue with Samuel, but . . . maybe it could be for his family. I mean, I know nothing about Trent or his wife or if Samuel even has other relatives. I'm not even implying that anyone would attempt such a ridiculous thing. But we've heard some pretty outlandish stories about the lengths people will go to in order to get their hands on somebody else's money. Maybe he's protecting your mother from any such possibility more than assuring her of his own motives."

"I hadn't looked at it that way," Jess said, "but you could be right. Anyway, it really doesn't need any more analyzing; I'll just file it." He kissed Tamra and added, "I love you, Mrs. Hamilton."

"I love you too . . . Jess Michael Hamilton." She touched his face. "You seem happy . . . at peace over this."

"I am," he said.

"And why is that?"

"I don't know; it just . . . feels right. Somehow I just believe that Dad approves."

"Really?"

"Really. I can't explain how I know that; I just do."

"You don't need to explain," Tamra said, kissing him again.

Chapter Eleven

After sharing breakfast with the family, Samuel agreed that he really did still want to go through with the marriage. In fact he seemed all the more eager. He admitted that he enjoyed the bustle of family activity, and it somehow made up for all the quiet years of raising one child and then being completely on his own.

Once Samuel had gone home to catch up on his rest and some other things, Emily put her wedding plans down on paper and took the opportunity to call her other children and let them know the good news. While some were more enthusiastic than others, they all expressed their love and support and promised to be there for the wedding.

Over the next few days, arrangements were quickly made for Samuel's baptism. While some minor challenges came up, Emily was well versed in expecting opposition and handling it. The event itself came together without a glitch. As Emily watched Samuel step into the waters of baptism, with Jess at his side, she felt a peace and joy that couldn't be described. It was almost as if she had taken care of her final and truly important task on this earth. She felt so perfectly content that she could have died and been happy. Still, she was going to be married soon, and she had much to look forward to. And Samuel needed her, just as she needed him. Now that she knew more about his illness and its effects, she became keenly aware of his struggles. He had to be careful not to overdo it, or he would be doomed to time in bed to recover. He was on several medications that had to be administered religiously or problems would intensify. But she quickly adjusted to being a part of his life—disease and all. She enjoyed just sharing restful days with him, talking, reading together, watching old movies, or even napping on separate sofas.

With days passing, Emily was pleased to see how quickly the wedding plans came together. She'd had enough experience with her children's weddings that it wasn't terribly difficult, especially when they wanted it to be a simple celebration with family and close friends.

Emily felt a combination of emotions at the prospect of meeting Trent and his family. Through her long talks with Samuel, she knew that Trent was a good man and that the relationship between Trent and Samuel was basically good. She also knew it wasn't perfect, that there were some minor challenges and disagreements between them— as there were in most families. She knew that Trent was aware of the changes in his father's life, and he'd been informed about the forth-coming wedding. But he'd said very little about it, and Samuel wasn't quite sure where Trent stood on the matter. While Emily knew that Samuel would not be swayed in his decision, she hoped that Trent would be supportive enough to not cause any new challenges.

On the day that Trent and his family were scheduled to arrive, Emily drove into town to be with Samuel. Trent would be renting a car at the airport and driving in, not wanting to put strain on his father. Not to mention the fact that Samuel's car would not hold all of Trent's family. Samuel had requested that Emily be there for the arrival. He couldn't wait for her to meet his family, and the other way around. When they finally arrived, Samuel and Emily walked out to the parking lot to meet them as they got out of the car. Emily stayed back while Samuel exchanged laughter and warm embraces with Trent and Julia and their children. She could see a resemblance between Samuel and Trent that hadn't been so evident in photographs. She could also see that the relationship between them was strong; their happiness at seeing each other was readily evident.

Emily got a quivery stomach as Samuel turned to make introduc-tions. She saw Trent's eyes light up pleasantly when he saw her. "So this is Emily," he said, reaching out both hands.

Emily took them as Samuel said, "This is her, my bride to be."

"It is such a pleasure," Emily said.

"Emily," Samuel went on, "this is my son, Trent, his wife, Julia."

"We have heard *so* much about you," Julia said, easing her husband aside in order to embrace Emily. "I can't tell you how thrilled we are to know that he's finally found someone."

Emily smiled at Julia, but she didn't miss something uncomfortable in Trent's eyes that made her wonder if, at some level, he disagreed.

Samuel eased the tension by hugging his grandchildren and introducing them to Emily. He raved about how much they'd grown and how adorable they were, then they all went up to the apartment where they sat down to eat the meal that Samuel and Emily had prepared. Emily wasn't surprised, but was pleased to realize how much she liked these people. Still, she sensed an undercurrent, however subtle, and she wondered if it had to do with her.

After the meal was cleaned up, the children went out to a play yard that was specifically for the grandchildren of residents. The adults sat down to visit, and Emily was surprised to hear Samuel say, "Okay, Trent. I can tell something's bothering you. And I need to know what it is. I'll not have our time together weighed down by some unspoken concern."

"I had every intention of talking with you," Trent said, as straightforward as his father. "But I did want to find an appropriate time."

"What's wrong with now?" Samuel asked.

Trent glanced warily toward Emily and then at Samuel. "Perhaps it would be better if we discussed this alone or—"

"There's nothing that can't be said in front of Emily." Samuel took her hand where they sat on the sofa. "She's family now, and there are no secrets between us."

"I understand," Trent said, "but . . . for the sake of tact, perhaps . . ."

"Are you concerned about hurting my feelings?" Emily asked.

Trent hesitated. "Perhaps."

"Well, I'm pretty tough," Emily said. "I would prefer that you just say what you have to say, and we can deal with the feelings accordingly."

Trent sighed loudly. "Very well," he said, directing his attention to his father. "I must admit that . . . while it's good to see you so happy, I can't help feeling a little disconcerted by all of this."

"I think that's understandable," Samuel said. "Your mother's been gone a long time. This is a big change for all of us. You haven't been around, so it makes sense that it will take some getting used to. Emily's children have had varying degrees of struggle in this adjustment as well. Their father hasn't been gone nearly so long, and it's a difficult transition."

"Okay, but . . ." Trent glanced at Emily as if he feared saying something wrong in her presence. "Are you really sure this is the right thing? Are you sure it's for the right reasons?"

Samuel gave a surprised chuckle, but before he could answer, Trent added, "I'm not questioning your judgment, Dad, but . . . are you sure you're doing the right thing?"

Samuel only sounded mildly irritated as he answered. "Now that sentence was an oxymoron if I've ever heard one. If you're not questioning my judgment, exactly what are you doing when you question my decision? Do you really believe that I am jumping into this impetuously? Do you think I haven't carefully considered every aspect of this situation?"

"I don't know," Trent said. "Have you?"

Samuel's loud sigh made it evident he was striving to remain patient. Emily gave his hand a gentle squeeze to offer silent support. "How about if you stop hinting and skirting the issue, and just come to the point. Stop talking in generalities, and just tell me what you're concerned about that you think I may have overlooked."

Trent looked down, then back up, as if summoning courage. "Well, I have two concerns. First of all, your health. Have you realistically considered the difficulties this could create for Emily and her family?"

Samuel sighed again. "I have considered it to the point that I was extremely reluctant to agree to this marriage. But I know beyond any doubt that it's the right thing to do. Emily and I have discussed the health issues extensively, and we have done the same with her children."

"Have you talked about the medications, and the—"

"Trent," Samuel interrupted gently, "I don't need to repeat every detail of all we have discussed. I can assure you that it's been covered."

Trent took a deep breath, as if he had trouble convincing himself of that. Emily felt that Samuel had read her mind when he said gently, "I realize you're just concerned about me, and I appreciate that, but you need to trust my judgement and give me the benefit of the doubt, son."

"Okay," Trent said. "Forgive me if . . . well, it's just . . ."

"I understand," Samuel said. "Now, what else is bothering you?" Trent didn't answer, and Samuel added, "You said you had two concerns. We've gotten past the health issue. What else?" Again Trent glanced at Emily, visibly concerned about speaking in her presence. "Just say it," Samuel insisted.

Trent said quickly, "Okay, I'm concerned about the money."

Samuel let out a sardonic chuckle. He and Emily exchanged a confused, almost comical glance. Emily wasn't certain what, if anything, Samuel had told Trent. "*What* about the money?" he asked.

"Well . . . forgive me, Emily," Trent said kindly. "You did invite me to speak candidly, and perhaps it's best to just get all of this out in the open. I know there was at least one woman my father dated who wanted little out of the relationship beyond financial security. I've heard of many marriages, especially those that take place in later years, that don't necessarily last long, and the divorce creates a financial disaster. I just want to be certain that my father's financial needs are met for the remainder of his life and that the money he has put away is there to meet those needs. Forgive me if this sounds insensitive, but perhaps some kind of prenuptial agreement would be in order, if only for the sake of—"

"It's already been taken care of," Samuel said, beginning to sound angry.

Emily turned toward him in surprise. "*What's* been taken care of?"

"I'll tell you later," Samuel said to her, then he turned to Trent. "I can assure you it's not a problem. Was there anything else?"

"How can you know?" Trent asked, sounding distressed. "I know you're in love now and you can't comprehend anything ever going wrong, but—"

"But what?" Samuel asked with practiced patience in his voice. "You're afraid that Emily is just some kind of gold digger who will leave me penniless and I'll be left on the streets with nothing? And you might have to take me in and meet my every need?"

Trent's eyes betrayed his agreement, but his voice was genuine and kind as he said, "You know we would if we had to."

"Yes, I know you would, but I can assure you that will *never* be necessary." He leaned forward and said earnestly, "Son, I didn't mention this because I didn't feel like it mattered, but under the circumstances I think you need to know—and then you can stop making a fool of yourself." Trent's brow furrowed, but he said nothing. Samuel lowered his voice to an almost comical whisper, "You grew up around here, son. Ever heard of Byrnehouse-Davies and Hamilton?"

"Of course," Trent said, not seeming to grasp the connection until his father added, "Meet Mrs. Hamilton."

Trent's eyes narrowed on his father, then on Emily, then they widened with obvious embarrassment. He squeezed them shut with a self-punishing grimace and a self-conscious chuckle as his father added, "The very wealthy Mrs. Hamilton."

"I am so sorry," Trent said to Emily with a good-natured laugh. "He never mentioned your last name, and . . ."

"It's alright," Emily said. "I can assure you we had similar conversations with *my* children. But I'm really not worried."

"There's no need to be," Samuel said, more to Trent, as if he intended for his son to know this fact without question. "I've already made it legal. I have no access or right to any of Emily's money, now or ever."

"When did you do this?" Emily asked Samuel firmly.

"Just before I agreed to marry you," Samuel said, looking directly at her. "Jess has the document."

Emily let out a breathy gasp. "Why would you—"

"Because it was appropriate," Samuel said firmly. "No one will ever have to wonder. There, that's all that needs to be said."

Emily opened her mouth to speak again, but Samuel put his fingers over her lips. "Enough," he repeated gently. "We can talk about it later."

Trent put a stop to any further protest when he said, "Again I'm sorry for bringing it up at all."

"It's alright," Emily said, forcing her focus toward Trent. "As you said, it's likely better to have such feelings in the open. Now you know where we stand. I would far prefer that you be open and honest than to let concerns fester. Think how much trouble you've saved by not stewing over whether or not I'm marrying your father for his money." She smiled impishly at Samuel, and he laughed softly before he gave her a quick kiss.

Trent and Julia went out to check on the children. Emily took advantage of their absence to say to Samuel, "And why didn't you tell me about this document you gave to Jess?"

"I didn't think it was important," he said. "You know I'm not marrying you for the money. It doesn't have to be common knowledge. But Jess is the man of the house, and I thought he needed to know. It's a precaution that can also prevent any of my relatives from coming out of the woodwork to cause a problem. It's just a technicality."

"Okay," Emily said, and kissed him.

A few minutes later the family all came inside to make plans for their time togther, then toward evening, they all went out to dinner. Before Emily returned home, Trent took Emily's hands into his, saying gently, "You must forgive me if I said anything to offend you. I can see how happy you've made my father. I only want the both of you to stay that way."

"You didn't offend me," Emily said. "I appreciate your being straightforward."

"Well then," he smiled, "there's only one drawback to this, as far as I can see."

"What's that?" Samuel asked with a comical scowl, appearing at Emily's side.

"We were going to talk you into coming to live with us for the rest of your life. Now I know that won't happen."

Samuel said with no hint of humor, "I wouldn't want to be a burden to you or—"

"It would *not* be a burden," Trent insisted, and Emily gave Samuel a sidelong glance.

"If you can convince him of that," she said to Trent, "I will be eternally indebted to you."

"He's just proud," Trent whispered purposely loud enough for his father to hear.

"Indeed," Emily added, winking at Samuel.

Through the next few days, Emily didn't see Samuel at all while he spent some time with his family, and she kept busy with wedding preparations. But she talked to him on the phone, and he said all was well and they were having a marvelous time. On Saturday Samuel brought his family out to the station for dinner. Emily was pleased to see that they seemed to mesh with her own family enough to visit comfortably. Samuel's three grandchildren truly were adorable, and not too far apart in age from Jess's children for them to play well together. The following day Samuel went to church with the family as usual, while his own family stayed at the apartment. He told Emily they were supportive of his beliefs, but he doubted they would ever embrace them. And while he longed to have them all be an eternal family as soon as possible, he believed that eventually all would come together as it should.

Over the next few days, Samuel continued to spend a great deal of time with his family, while Emily worked on finalizing wedding arrangements and spending time with her own family. Even in Samuel's absence, she felt a deep contentment. She felt as if her initial discontent and loneliness had driven her to take steps that had eventually led her to this point, and she was truly happy.

* * *

Jess couldn't help noticing his mother's happiness and contentment. In some ways he still found it difficult to think of his mother marrying again, but he was becoming accustomed to the idea. And there was no denying how much he'd grown to care for and respect Samuel. The reality of Samuel's disease was difficult to think about, but he agreed with his mother that they would deal with it as best they could, knowing that taking him into their family was the right thing to do.

Jess had to admit that he was actually feeling rather content. Life was good, and he was grateful. And then he got a phone call at work that threw him off balance. He tried to tell himself that it wasn't a major thing, but examining his feelings closely, he knew that it was, and he needed to be prepared. It took him a few hours to come to terms with it enough to even bring it up to his wife. He found her in the sitting room just off the nursery, reading a novel while the children played close by.

"Well hello," she said, pleasantly surprised.

"Hello." He sat down beside her and kissed her.

"What brings you here this time of day? You're supposed to be very busy elsewhere."

"Thankfully it's a slow day," he said.

"What's wrong?" she asked, her tone of voice indicating clearly that she'd picked up on his somber mood.

"Nothing . . . I hope; I mean . . . maybe it might be a personal definition of whether or not it's a problem, or . . ."

"Just say it," she insisted.

"I have an appointment with the stake president. You're supposed to go with me."

She actually smiled before she said, "You're not in trouble, are you?"

"Not that I know of," he said, not sharing her humor.

"Then . . . they're going to put you in the elders quorum presidency."

"Maybe, but . . . I think it's bigger than that. I could be wrong, but . . . I just have a feeling that . . . it's bigger than that."

"Oh boy," she said, all humor absent from her voice. "How much bigger?"

"How should I know? I'm not psychic. I just think . . . it's bigger."

Tamra hugged him tightly while she seemed to be contemplating the news, then she touched his face, saying gently, "Whatever they might want you to do, you'll do it beautifully. You're an amazing man, and I'm behind you one-hundred percent."

Jess smiled and touched her face in return. "*You* are the amazing one. What did I ever do to deserve such an incredible wife?"

"You married me," she said, and kissed him, making him laugh.

Jess forced himself to go back to work, but he couldn't help being preoccupied with whatever the stake president might want to see him about. When the time finally came for the interview, Jess found he wasn't surprised at all—but he did feel terribly inadequate and more than a little nervous. He knew it would be appropriate to tell his immediate family, but he wanted to tell his mother first. He just wasn't sure how to go about bringing it up. He found her alone in the family office late in the evening, typing at the computer.

"Oh, hello," she said brightly when she saw him.

"Hello," he said as he sat down. "What are you up to, Mother?"

"Just catching up my personal history," she said. "I actually have something new to write about now."

"So you do," he said. "So, how's it coming?"

"Almost done," she said, "until I have new adventures, at least."

"Whatever happens," Jess said, "make sure you don't die without recording your every adventure. I don't want to read your story someday and not know how it ends."

"Oh, you'll know how it ends," she said with a wink. "If I don't get a chance to write the ending, you can write it for me."

"No thanks," he insisted. "I'd prefer you do that." Emily turned to look at him more directly, and he asked, "So, how are you doing, Mom?"

"I'm great. How are you?"

"All things considered, I believe I'm doing well." Not wanting to give her a chance to question what he meant by "all things considered," he hurried to ask, "Are you getting everything arranged for the wedding, then?"

"I believe so," she said, giving him a brief summary of what she'd accomplished. She concluded by saying, "My only challenge at the moment is getting an appointment with the bishop. His executive secretary said it would have to wait until next week sometime."

Jess glanced at her abruptly, and his heart quickened as he attempted to grasp what that might mean in relation to himself. He'd been hoping for a way to open this conversation, and while he didn't feel entirely ready to say what he needed to say, he knew he'd never get a better chance than this. "I might be able to shed some light on that," he said.

"Really? Is he out of town or something? Have you spoken to him or—"

"No, actually . . . I hear they're putting in a new bishopric this Sunday."

Emily's eyes widened. "Really?" She chuckled softly. "I guess this bishop *has* been in a long time. So I may be talking to a new bishop, then. Where did you hear this rumor?"

Jess took a deep breath. "From the stake president."

"Really?" she said yet again. "When did you see him?"

"He called me in for an appointment." Her eyes widened further, and he added, "Don't say 'really' again. He really did. That's what I wanted to talk to you about." He took another deep breath. "They've asked me to be the new bishop, Mother."

Jess watched his mother's eyes, perhaps expecting to see some well-disguised skepticism or doubt. He certainly felt skeptical and doubtful. But he only saw perfect confidence and approval. Still, he had to admit, "I feel so completely . . . inadequate, so unequal to this. How can I do this, Mother?"

Emily smiled, and her eyes brimmed with a sparkle of moisture. "That's exactly what your father said when he was first called to be the branch president, and you were just a little boy."

"Okay, but . . . he was so . . . amazing."

"Yes, he was—still is, I assume. But no more than you, Jess. You have a willing heart, a strong spirit, a good head on your shoulders, and a great deal of compassion. Think what you could have to offer to struggling youth; you've been there."

"Yes, I've been a lot of other places in my life I'd rather not admit to, but—"

"Yes, you have. And maybe there's someone in the ward who is depressed or suicidal—and they need a bishop like you."

Jess was taken aback to recall that at one time he *had* been depressed and suicidal. "I never looked at it like that," he said.

"All you have to do is stay close to the Spirit and do the best you can, one day at a time, and you will be made equal to the calling."

Jess inhaled deeply, savoring her wisdom, feeling as if it might literally sustain him. What would he ever do without his mother?

"You know what this means, don't you," she said lightly, with a twinkle in her eye.

"What?" he demanded, suspicious.

"This means that *you* will be performing my marriage."

"Yes," he grumbled, "and I'm supposed to interview you and your prospective husband, as well. It's too weird; I'm not sure I can do that."

"Of course you can," she said, laughing softly. "I think it's marvelous. It will make this wedding all the more memorable—and amazing."

Jess grunted in disagreement and was glad when she steered the conversation elsewhere. They talked for a long while about this unexpected development in Jess's life. Calling upon her memories of Michael, Emily shared many more insights into Jess's new calling that he'd never considered. He felt grateful for his father's experiences and for the strength of this great woman who had stood faithfully beside him through terms as both branch president and bishop. When Jess finally told his mother good night, he felt a deep gratitude for having her in his life, and under his roof. What a great blessing she was to him! He found Tamra sitting up in bed, reading the *Ensign.* He sat close to her and talked again about his feelings of insecurity in fulfilling what he'd been asked to do. Tamra's faith and encouragement strengthened his own, and he felt doubly blessed to have such a wonderful wife. How grateful he was to have these two great women to strengthen and guide him! Perhaps he could survive being a bishop after all.

* * *

"Okay," Jess said, "this is absolutely the weirdest thing I have ever done." He looked across the desk at his mother and Samuel and couldn't hold back a little laugh. He'd officially been a bishop for about two days, and now he was interviewing his own mother and her fiancé regarding their upcoming marriage.

"I don't know about that," Emily said with a teasing smile. "I've seen you do some pretty weird things. I mean . . . remember that lip-sync thing you did when you were a teenager? And what about the—"

"Okay, Mother." Jess chuckled. "I get the idea. That's just the point. You know everything about me. You're my mother."

"Yes, I am," she said with pride in her voice.

"How am I supposed to be an ecclesiastical leader to the person who taught me everything I know?"

"You're doing just fine, Jess," Emily said.

"I'd have to agree with that," Samuel added.

"And what would you know?" Jess asked facetiously. "You haven't been a Mormon long enough to know whether or not I'm doing fine."

"I still think you're doing fine." Samuel's tone became completely earnest. "And just for the record, I want you to know that I will do everything in my power to keep Emily happy and secure and to put God first in our relationship, whatever might arise."

"Are you saying that to your bishop or your future stepson?" Jess asked, more seriously.

"Both," Samuel said firmly, but with a kind smile.

Jess was glad to have the interview over, but he had difficulty imagining himself actually performing the ceremony. With plans for the wedding well under control, he just tried not to think about it. In adjusting to his new calling, he had to admit that dealing with his mother's marriage was the least of his concerns.

In spite of the demands of being a bishop, Jess found time to spend with his family and also to get to know Samuel's family better. He was able to have a couple of good conversations with Trent and found that they actually connected rather well. While they had little in common, they shared a sincere desire for their parents to be happy, and they both agreed that this marriage was a difficult transition with the accompanying changes it would bring into both of their families. They discussed Samuel's illness and the possible challenges, the worst being that he could soon be facing disability and likely an untimely death. Still, it was evident that Samuel and Emily were incredibly happy together. Jess and Trent eagerly agreed that this was a good thing, and they hoped for their parents to share many happy years together.

* * *

The night before the wedding, the entire family gathered in the yard for supper. Jess had observed with delight as each of his sisters had arrived from out of town, how their varying degrees of doubt and concern had melted away upon observing their mother interacting with Samuel. It was impossible to see them together and not know that it was meant to be. He still felt an occasional twinge of sorrow to think of his mother being with anyone except his father. But in his heart he knew that Michael Hamilton approved of this union, and that it was a good thing. Still, he missed his father dreadfully and wished that he could be here to see the entire family gathered. But then, if he were here, Emily certainly wouldn't be getting married. As always with such thoughts, Jess felt it likely his father was aware of such family gatherings and that somehow his spirit was close, at least once in a while.

Late that evening, after most of the household had gone to bed, Jess felt restless and decided to wander downstairs, perhaps in search of a bedtime snack. Samuel and his family were settled into guest rooms for the night so they could all be here early and help with the final preparations for the wedding. Jess left Tamra reading in bed and started down the hall toward the stairs. A quick glance down the other hallway showed his mother's bedroom door to be ajar and the light on. Impulsively he changed his direction and peeked into the open doorway, then he almost wished that he hadn't. Emily was sitting on the floor near an open chest, with a number of things spread out on the floor. Jess knew that chest well; he'd helped her pick it out following his father's death as an appropriate place to store his belongings that she'd wanted to keep. And now most of those belongings were scattered around her. She pressed her hands lovingly over Michael's favorite denim shirt that covered her lap. There were tears on her face.

Jess felt momentarily tempted to leave her in peace and sneak away before he was noticed. But something stronger compelled him to intrude. He knocked lightly on the open door and she looked abruptly toward him.

"Sorry to disturb you," he said, stepping into the room. "Are you alright?"

"I'm fine," she said and seemed to mean it. "I just . . . needed a few minutes to say . . . good-bye."

"But not forever," Jess said gently.

"No, not forever," she replied softly, and her tears increased. Jess sat on the floor beside her and urged her face to his shoulder.

He held her while she wept for several minutes, then they sat in silence until he said, "Are you going to be alright?"

"Yes, of course," she said.

"You haven't changed your mind, have you?" he asked lightly, but with tenderness.

"No, of course not." She smiled, drawing a deep sigh. "I know this is the right thing to do. I'm very grateful to have Samuel in my life."

"He's a good man."

"Yes, he is," Emily said as she began to reverently place Michael's belongings back in the trunk.

They were both startled when Samuel said from the doorway, "What's this? A late-night party?"

"Maybe," Jess said. He wondered if his mother might feel self-conscious or embarrassed over her attention to Michael's belongings on the night before marrying another man. But she smiled toward Samuel and returned to her task as if nothing were out of the ordinary.

He thought that perhaps Samuel wouldn't notice exactly what she was doing, but he squatted close beside her and asked gently, "Reminiscing?"

"A bit, I suppose," she said. "Closing one door so that I can open another."

"An excellent analogy," Samuel said.

Jess watched them exchange a quick kiss and a warm smile. He felt a renewal of conviction that they were meant to be together, and he was grateful for the inner peace that had replaced his previous fears and concerns. He hoped that they would be truly happy and that their time together would not be too brief.

Chapter Twelve

Emily felt certain that Jess's performing the ceremony for her marriage simply made a good thing better. The Spirit was strong as he spoke from the heart about the power of love and the way he had personally witnessed the happiness that Samuel and Emily had brought into each other's lives. The exchanging of vows was accompanied by many sniffles in the room. Emily felt a little teary herself. While she knew beyond any doubt this was the best thing she could possibly be doing with her life, she couldn't help feeling the irony that this was the very spot where she had exchanged vows with Michael more years ago than she cared to count. She knew without question that Michael not only approved of this marriage, but he was also happy about it. Just as on numerous other occasions since his death, she felt immensely grateful for the knowledge she had that in spite of the barrier between them, she could still know where he stood on the things that really mattered.

Emily had mixed feelings about leaving for a honeymoon while her entire family was gathered together in her home. But they all assured her that they would see each other soon, and they all seemed genuinely pleased with the marriage. She was grateful for that.

Setting out on a honeymoon with Samuel, she had difficulty containing her happiness. She'd not been this happy since Michael's death had robbed her of this kind of companionship. The more time she spent with Samuel, the more she grew to love him, and she thanked God daily for bringing such a marvelous blessing into her life.

Together they did a great deal of sightseeing, taking the pace slow for the sake of Samuel's health. Being with him twenty-four hours a day, Emily more readily saw the signs of the disease that plagued his body. But they talked openly about it, and they were both determined to enjoy every possible moment together.

Extending their honeymoon several weeks, they spent time in each of their children's homes. Samuel had never been to the States, and he enjoyed the sightseeing as well as the opportunity to get to know Emily's children better, as well as their families. Taking it slow with long bouts of resting intermixed with their travel, they also went to England and spent some time with Trent and his family. By the time they returned to Australia, they had been married nearly six months. And what a glorious half a year it had been! Emily felt so perfectly happy that she often felt as if she would burst. Her children were doing relatively well, beyond the normal challenges of family life. And Emily felt a deep peace in knowing she had striven to remain faithful through her life. The only deterrent to her happiness was the growing evidence that disease was eating away at Samuel's nervous system. Through their months of marriage she had seen a steady decline in his health, which was the biggest reason Samuel facetiously declared that it had taken them six months to do a two-month honeymoon. Still, Emily was happy and felt extremely blessed.

As much as she had enjoyed their travels and the time they'd spent with family members who lived elsewhere, Emily and Samuel both heartily agreed that it was good to be home. Emily was so happy to see Jess and Emma and their families that she actually cried. And it was evident that they had missed her as well. Getting reacquainted with the family she shared her home with proved to be a joy in itself. The children had grown and progressed a great deal in her absence, and she enjoyed spending time with them.

Samuel quickly settled comfortably into the routine of the household. Their days developed a slow, comfortable pace as it quickly became evident that Samuel simply had little energy to expend. It seemed he had given everything he had to enjoying his travels with Emily, and now he was simply worn out. But Emily didn't mind. She enjoyed sitting on the veranda with him or taking a slow, brief stroll in the yard. She loved holding his hand while they watched the sun go down—or up. She loved holding him close at night or just holding his hand. One of her favorite times of day was after the lights were all out late in the evening, and they would just hold hands and talk until they drifted to sleep together. They often read together and shared long conversations, which helped fill the days when he simply couldn't get out of bed at all.

Emily was called to be the compassionate service leader in the ward, which filled her time with something she enjoyed greatly— serving others in need. She also found time to catch up her personal history with all the wonderful things that had happened since she'd married Samuel, and she filled scrapbooks with their memories while she stayed near him as he rested.

In spite of Samuel's health problems, he was able to travel to the temple with family members who were available so that he could be sealed to Arlene by proxy. Samuel's happiness was so blatantly evident that his physical struggles seemed temporarily irrelevant.

Just past Samuel and Emily's first anniversary, the decision was made for them to move into a bedroom on the main floor, so that Samuel could more easily get to the kitchen and lounge room and be with the family. Less than two months later he was mostly confined to a wheelchair. A nurse came to the house each day to help him bathe and to see to his medical requirements, and beyond that the family was able to help him with all that he needed. Emily was pleased to see the way her family had grown to sincerely love Samuel, and they truly enjoyed helping him. Samuel often asked Emily if she'd had any idea what she'd gotten herself into. But she would just smile and kiss him and assure him that their time together was among the best times in her life.

Through regular visits to a local specialist, Samuel's condition was monitored very carefully, and they were all deeply dismayed to hear that the disease was progressing rapidly. But they drew from one another's strength, attempting to be as positive as possible. Following a priesthood blessing that Jess and Scott gave Samuel, the symptoms actually eased up some, and Samuel felt quite well for several weeks. The timing was good since the entire family was coming a few days after Christmas. They were all celebrating Christmas day in their own homes, and then they were traveling to Australia to be all together for four days. It was the first time they'd all been together since the wedding, and Emily found herself greatly anticipating the event, as did Samuel. Even Trent and his family would be coming. It seemed the ultimate way to celebrate Christmas.

When the family was finally gathered together, Emily sat with Samuel's hand in hers, watching her children and grandchildren all working together to put on a big meal in the yard and to keep the little ones out of trouble. Trent's family intermixed with the others so beautifully that it all felt close to perfect.

"That's quite a posterity you've got, Mrs. Hamilton-Reid."

Emily laughed softly. "Between the two of us we have a beautiful family."

"Yes, we do," he agreed, and kissed her hand. And Emily felt as if her life were complete.

* * *

Jess supervised his children while they set the long tables outdoors, at the same time keeping an eye on Claire while she chased a kitten around the yard. The holidays to this point had been especially nice. Tithing settlement had gone smoothly, for the most part, and he'd been able to spend some wonderfully relaxing time with his family. He'd grown relatively comfortable with his calling as bishop, in spite of its ongoing challenges. And there was a certain tranquility about his life. He glanced toward his mother where she sat with Samuel on the veranda, observing the delightful chaos of the family, and the peace inside him deepened. Emily radiated happiness. She was a good woman, and she deserved to be happy.

An unexpected quickening of his heart caused Jess to stop and take note of what might have prompted it. For a long moment his surroundings felt distant while the gentle thought filled his mind that he should stop and take account of this moment. He turned and took in all that was going on around him: his siblings and their husbands were chatting and bringing food from the house; his children and nieces and nephews were laughing and playing together, and some were even managing to help out a little; and his mother and step-father were sitting close together, visiting and smiling contentedly. Jess took a deep breath and silently thanked God for all he'd been blessed with and for the Spirit's gentle reminder of how truly good life was.

Claire started to cry when she caught the kitty and it scratched her, startling Jess back to the moment. He sent the kitty toward the overseer's home where it lived, and gave Claire the comfort she needed. Then Tamra declared that it was time to eat, and everyone gathered around the long tables set out beneath the trees in the yard. It was a common tradition, but it seemed the tables kept getting longer.

A couple of days later, a large number of family members left for their homes, and tender farewells were exchanged. Jess's sisters had decided, however, that they were going to spend some extra time together. They'd been planning and making arrangements for many weeks so that they could send their husbands and children home in order to spend some quality time together as siblings. It only happened this way every four or five years, and Emily was thrilled for the extra time with her daughters. Occasionally Jess was invited into the circle of their activities, but for the most part he left them to chatter and giggle while he went about his business. Between seeing to his work at the boys' home, and his duties as bishop, he put a few stitches into each of the three quilts they tied, and he went with them to Brisbane to go through a temple session. Samuel and Scott were able to go as well, and it proved to be an incredible excursion. Sitting in the celestial room beside his mother, she took his hand and whispered, "I could die happy."

He turned to her, startled. "There will be no such talk," he insisted lightly, in spite of the uneasiness he felt over such a statement.

"No worries," she said with a smile. "I'm just . . . content, that's all."

"Well, I'm glad," Jess said, kissing his mother's brow. "You deserve to be."

Following a pleasant reprieve in this room built to represent heaven, Jess wheeled Samuel back to the men's dressing room and gave him the help he needed to change his clothes before they all went out to dinner together. They returned home exhausted but with memories to last a lifetime.

Early Saturday morning, Jess's sisters who needed to fly to the States finally had to say good-bye. They shared farewells with Emily and the rest of the family before Jess drove them to the hangar where Murphy was waiting to fly them to Sydney. Jess hugged them each tightly and watched them fly away before he returned home. He thoroughly enjoyed the remainder of the day. No meetings or obligations. The house was fairly quiet since all of the company had gone home except for Amee. She'd been going to fly out with the others and have her husband meet her at the Sydney airport, but she hadn't been feeling well and decided she'd do well to stick close to a bed and a bathroom. Making other arrangements wasn't a big problem, and so she'd stayed. Jess missed Allison and Alexa already, but he had fond memories of the time they'd spent together over the last few days. He spent the morning just hanging out with his wife and children, occasionally checking in on his mother and Samuel. She was sitting on the bed beside him, reading aloud from a thick novel. It was a typical scene these days, but Emily's happiness was evident, and Jess couldn't help being grateful for the companionship Samuel gave her, even in his deteriorating physical state.

After taking a long afternoon nap, Jess got a call from Allison. She and Alexa were still at the Sydney airport, dismayed to realize their flight arrangements had been wrong. They were both scheduled to fly back to the States in another week. After arguing with airline personnel, they had finally accepted that the expense and hassle of getting the flight changed simply wasn't worth it. They'd called home and had made arrangements for their families, and they were coming back to stay another week.

"Fortunately Murphy was getting something to eat in the airport and didn't leave before we realized there was a problem," Allison said. "So, we just wanted to warn you."

"Okay," Jess said. "We'll be watching for you. Tell Murphy to take good care of you."

"Oh, he always does," Allison said.

Jess was grateful for his nap because Murphy and his sisters didn't arrive until very late. He drove out to the hangar to get them, and once they were all settled in, he went to bed. He woke early on Sunday morning and went down to the kitchen, already dressed for church since he had the usual early bishopric meetings. He found his mother and sisters and Rhea all there, talking and laughing while they ate cold cereal. Samuel was at the table in his wheelchair, clearly enjoying the chatter going on around him. He had to admit that he enjoyed it himself. There was nothing quite like having his mother and all of his sisters together, and his sweet wife often among them. Typically, he and Scott just took it all in, grateful to not be the only men in the room. Samuel helped even out the numbers a bit, but the women definitely kept the conversation going. Jess actually felt quite glad over the delayed flight, but wondered how the husbands and children in the States were managing.

"Good morning," he said, getting a bowl for himself.

"Good morning," they all said in haphazard unison.

"Have you seen my wife?" he asked, taking a seat between Emma and Allison.

Emma reported, "She ate with the children while you were in the shower, and she's bathing Claire. Scott has bath duty with Laura this morning, so I'm making the most of it."

"How delightful," Jess said. "I think I'm behind on bath duty since I became bishop."

"She'll get even one of these days," Emily said. "She'll be president of something and you'll have *everything* duty."

"I'll look forward to it," Jess said with light sarcasm. "I think it might be easier than this bishop thing."

"But you're so good at it," Emma said. "I'm glad that . . ." She hesitated when Emily put a hand to her chest rather suddenly, and her expression revealed mild panic.

"What?" Jess demanded, and she looked startled to realize that everyone else in the room had noticed.

Emily quickly debated whether or not what she had just felt was something to be concerned about or, more accurately, something that her family should be concerned about. She searched her feelings and had to admit, "Something . . . doesn't feel right."

"What do you mean?" Allison asked, sounding panicked.

"I . . . don't know," Emily admitted. "Maybe I should just . . . give it some time and—"

"Or maybe we should take you to town and make sure there's nothing serious going on," Alexa suggested.

Samuel said firmly, "I think she needs to go to the hospital."

"There," Jess said, "listen to your husband. He's right."

Again Emily searched her feelings and didn't argue. "Okay," she said, coming to her feet. "Let's go."

"You take her," Allison said to Jess. "We'll bring Samuel." She turned to Samuel and asked, "Is that alright?" He nodded.

Jess was thinking he needed to say good-bye to Tamra when she appeared in the doorway. Emma gave a thirty-second explanation while Emily kept a hand pressed to her chest, her expression clearly showing pain. When a thought came suddenly in his mind, Jess had to believe it was a prompting. Regardless of whether it was or not, he decided that it was a better option. "I'm calling for an emergency helicopter," he said, reaching for the phone. While he was on the phone, Scott and all the children showed up in the kitchen, as if they'd been drawn there by some unspoken force. Once the call was finished, he watched his mother embrace everyone in the room, as if she intended to be gone for a couple of weeks.

"You'll be back before the day's out," he said to her, certain that whatever ailed her could be quickly corrected once she got to a hospital. But by the time the helicopter arrived, he was beginning to feel seriously concerned. The minute it took off, all of the adults piled into two vehicles; Samuel was already seated in one since he'd been anxious to follow Emily to the hospital, and Scott had helped him. Rhea had eagerly offered to watch all of the children so that they could hurry into town. She told them to stay as long as they needed. During the drive, Jess made calls on his mobile phone to let his counselors know that he wouldn't be attending any meetings, and they would just have to manage without him. He told them he'd call and check in with them later in the day. Once that was taken care of, he couldn't keep from feeling afraid. He expressed his concerns to Tamra, Allison, and Alexa, who were all in the vehicle with him. But they didn't offer the positive encouragement he was hoping for, and he wondered if they all shared the same foreboding that this was serious.

* * *

Emily became suddenly filled with anxiety as she was put into the helicopter and felt it rise into the sky. She felt cruelly torn from her home and loved ones and was terrified that she might never see them again. Preoccupied with the pain in her chest, she felt the fear settle in more tangibly until she found it difficult to breathe. Forcing her mind to prayer, she fought to breathe deeply and not let her fear keep her from feeling the comfort of the Spirit. Within minutes it was there, subtly soothing her fears and replacing them with a distinct calm. She knew that whatever resulted from this, it was part of God's plan, and the matter was in His hands.

Emily realized she must have lost consciousness when she emerged into a disoriented awareness of her surroundings. She was still in the helicopter, and the pain was still there. But she was more preoccupied with the dream she'd just had. She'd been sitting on the side veranda, surrounded by her children and grandchildren, when she looked up to see Michael sitting on his favorite stallion, watching her closely. He smiled at her and beckoned for her to join him. She hurried down the steps and onto the lawn where he was waiting. He held out a hand for her and raised her effortlessly onto the horse's back behind him. As she was seated, her eye caught some people standing at the highest part of the lawn. She recognized them as a small group of her loved ones who had gone from this world. Glancing in the other direction, she saw her family still gathered on the veranda, talking and laughing, apparently oblivious to her leaving. Except for Samuel. His eyes were starkly focused on her, his sadness evident. For a moment she felt torn, but he smiled and waved, and peace filled her. She knew he would be alright, and that in spite of his sadness at their parting, he shared her joy in being with Michael, just as he would one day soon be with Arlene.

Wrapping her arms around Michael's chest, she was struck by how thoroughly familiar he felt. She held to him tightly as he galloped away. She heard him laugh, and a thrill consumed her spirit. Oh, how she loved his laugh! Oh, how she'd missed him!

While Emily focused on the images of her dream, it was easier to ignore the pain she was feeling as well as her disappointment at realizing it had only been a dream. She couldn't deny that at the moment she would far prefer to leave with Michael. She felt ready. And while there were hovering concerns for the family she would leave behind, she knew they would be alright. She knew she would still be able to help comfort them when necessary. In her heart she knew they were ready too.

Emily was keenly aware of arriving at the hospital and of the medical procedures that were taking place. She wanted to tell them not to fuss and bother so much. She was ready to go and didn't want them to do anything to prevent that. Then she reminded herself that whether or not it was time to go certainly was not up to her. She simply tried to relax, focusing on praying for her loved ones—that whatever the outcome, they would be comforted and strengthened.

* * *

Jess pulled the Cruiser to a screeching halt in the hospital parking lot. They all got out and ran inside, where they were told they had to wait.

"But is she alright?" Jess demanded of the nurse at the desk.

"She's stable, and they're doing some tests to try and determine the problem. They'll send someone out to talk with the family just as soon as they have something to tell you."

Jess felt his wife's hand on one of his arms and his sister's on the other, silently reminding him to stay calm. He turned around to see Scott pushing Samuel through the door. He reported grimly, "We have to wait; they're doing some tests."

Samuel just nodded. Scott said, "I hate it when that happens." Jess wondered if Scott was remembering, as he was, the hospital vigil they'd shared when Emma had gone into septic shock following her kidney transplant. A few minutes after they were all seated, it became evident their thoughts were in the same place when Scott added, "I don't like the memories being stirred here."

"Me neither," Jess said.

"What memories?" Emma asked.

"You were unconscious, darlin'," Jess said, "and we thought we were going to lose you."

"Oh that," Emma said.

"But we're not going to lose Mom," Alexa said with a forced brightness to her voice. "Whatever it is, they'll figure it out and they'll fix it. She's still so young—relatively speaking—and healthy. She's got a lot of good years left in her."

Jess wanted to agree with her, but he couldn't find the words. Glancing around the room at his family members, he wondered if they all had the same thought. No one had anything to say. Did they all share this sense of foreboding that the outcome would not be favorable? He told himself that perhaps it wasn't a foreboding at all. Perhaps he was just paranoid, and everything *would* be fine, just as Alexa had suggested. Emily's chest pain was a likely indication that this had something to do with her heart. He'd known many people with heart ailments who had lived many years, managing the problem with medications and procedures to keep arteries clear and functioning. The fact that she'd received medical care at the first indication of pain seemed a positive point. Surely everything would be fine.

While he was trying to talk himself into that, a thought occurred to him, and he immediately voiced it. "We're all together." He glanced again at each of his siblings. "We weren't supposed to be together today, but we are." Through the silence that followed, it became evident that everyone had grasped the implication that he couldn't explain with words. It was as if some great event was about to occur, and their being together had been orchestrated by a Higher Power that could see a perspective far beyond their mortal comprehension. In that moment his brain felt suddenly foggy, as if a tangible barrier had come down between his conscious mind and the spiritual implication of the present situation. Had they truly been brought together as a family to say farewell to their mother? Or was their being together simply necessary to help her get through something difficult? It was too strange to chalk up to coincidence, and the thought of his mother leaving this world was simply incomprehensible, unacceptable—preposterous. Certain that there had to be some other meaning in this experience, Jess forced his mind to prayer, pleading with everything inside of him that this was not the beginning of a new trial in his life—and for those he loved most.

Hardly a word was said among the family while the minutes dragged. Jess wondered if their thoughts were all similar to his own, making it impossible to say anything that didn't either feel phony or morbid. When a nurse appeared in the waiting room, asking for members of the Hamilton family, they all came to their feet, except for Allison who remained seated beside Samuel, holding his hand. She told them that Emily was between tests and waiting for results; she was conscious and asking to see her family. While they normally only allowed two people at a time to be with a patient, an exception could be made so they could all go in and see her. Jess's relief in being able to see her was contradicted by an increasing uneasiness over the situation. Were they letting them all in at once because time was too brief? He immediately scolded himself for having such a thought and told himself to be more positive, to have more faith. Surely this was not as serious as it seemed and all would be well.

Scott pushed Samuel's wheelchair close to the side of Emily's bed while the others gathered around. Jess watched his mother take Samuel's hand as they exchanged a smile, but neither of them had anything to say. She looked pale and strained; her voice was weak when she finally said, "Everything's going to be okay, you know. I don't want you to worry—any of you." She turned to look at each of them, offering a faint smile.

Allison eased a little closer and took Emily's hand. "I love you, Mom," she said. "I couldn't have asked for a better mother."

Jess's already quickened heart began to pound. That sounded like a good-bye if he'd ever heard one. Was Allison feeling some kind of prompting to say such things? The foggy sensation in his brain increased as he watched each of the women exchange similar words with his mother, and careful embraces. Scott did the same, and then Samuel said to her, "I love you, my darling. Thank you for giving my life a happy ending."

Emily smiled at her husband. "It's the other way around," she said, and Jess wanted to scream. This was not an *ending*. It couldn't be! She couldn't leave them yet. He simply couldn't accept it, *wouldn't* accept it. He felt her eyes come to rest on him, the only one who hadn't yet spoken with her. She reached a hand toward him, and he eagerly took it. "There's nothing to worry about, Jess," she said as if she could see right through him. "Everything's going to be okay."

Jess wanted to demand what her definition of "okay" might be. If it was her time to go, and they all believed they would eventually be together again, and they all managed to get along without her until they joined her in the next life—that might be okay, but it certainly wasn't what he wanted. He noticed her grimacing slightly, and her eyes flickered, as if she might lose consciousness. He tightened his grip on her hand and she focused on him again. "Don't you leave us, Mom," he said, forcing a calm, gentle voice that belied the fears bubbling up inside of him. "We need you."

She gave a gentle laugh. "You can all manage just fine without me," she said, taking another glance around the bed at her loved ones gathered there.

Jess swallowed carefully and fought his urge to protest. He knew he couldn't talk her out of dying, but he felt more prone to believe that he was letting his imagination run away with him. Convincing himself that this was an easily solved problem, he pressed a kiss to her brow and said gently, "I love you, Mom."

"I love you too, Jess," she said as he drew back to look into her eyes.

Emily looked up at her son and saw him become blurry. She struggled to focus on his face, then wondered if she was seeing double. She turned again to look at the faces of her loved ones surrounding her, and a deep peace settled over her. Just before oblivion overtook her, she felt certain she had seen Michael's face among them.

Jess was closest to his mother and distinctly heard the last words she said before she slipped into unconsciousness, but he didn't want to believe the implication. His heart began to pound. He glanced over his shoulder one way, then the other, almost expecting to see something that he knew he wouldn't see. Then he leaned closer to his mother and touched her face. "Mother, no!" he said, wishing it hadn't sounded so harsh. She didn't respond, but he could hear her breathing and knew she was only asleep. "Mother, don't leave us," he said, sounding even more emotional. He was vaguely aware of the confusion and concern of the others in the room, but he was too preoccupied with the fear that he'd heard his mother's last words.

"What is it, Jess?" Scott asked, close to his ear, putting a hand on his shoulder.

He was trying to find words to explain when a nurse pushed her way between him and his mother to check on her. She then gently said, "She's lost consciousness. The doctor's waiting to talk to all of you. I'll keep an eye on her."

Jess immersed himself in his mother's presence as best he could and pressed another kiss to her brow before Scott urged him reluctantly from the room. They were all guided to a private consultation room where a doctor was waiting, dressed in surgical garb. He kindly explained the tests that had been done and the conclusion they'd come to. The report Jess had expected to hear, related to his mother's heart, was not the same as the words he heard the doctor speaking. But it was the word *aneurysm* that caught him and stuck in his brain. After the doctor had explained the need for immediate surgery, Jess forced a hesitant question to his lips. "What exactly is an aneurysm?"

"In this case," the doctor said, "one of the main arteries of the heart is bulging like a balloon; it's filled with blood." He went on to explain how it happens and how they were going to attempt to fix it, while Jess's uneasiness steadily increased. He felt he had to ask, "How many times have you done this procedure, Doctor?"

He looked directly at Jess, and his eyes were nothing but patient and compassionate. "Truthfully, I've been doing heart surgery for sixteen years, and I've done this procedure about that many times. Most people who get this never make it to the hospital alive."

Jess sucked in his breath and heard his loved ones express varying degrees of surprise and concern. He was grateful to hear Scott ask the question that he couldn't get out of his mouth. "What are her chances, Doctor?"

Following an unnerving moment of silence, the doctor cleared his throat quietly and said, "Realistically, I'd give her less than a forty-percent chance of coming out of the surgery."

A deathly silence followed.

"Someone will keep you informed," the doctor added. "I'll do everything I can." He turned and left the room, closing the door behind him.

It seemed minutes before anyone moved or made a sound, and then it was only the sound of sniffling and the women reaching for tissues. Emma finally broke the silence by saying, "I can't believe it. It's not possible."

"It's going to be alright," Samuel said gently, and all eyes turned toward him.

Jess couldn't keep from saying what he'd wanted to say to his mother, but hadn't dared. "'Alright' is relative though, isn't it? If she dies and we manage to get along without her and we know we'll all be together again someday, technically that's 'alright.' But it sure as heck isn't *my* definition of 'alright.'"

Chapter Thirteen

The lack of conversation that filled the surgical waiting room felt deafening. Typical hospital noises prevented complete silence, but no one had anything to say. Occasionally a surgical liaison came out to tell them that the surgery was progressing well, but they knew nothing of her actual condition. Jess kept glancing at the clock between discrete observations of his family members. He wondered if their thoughts were the same as his. Were they all fearing the worst and praying with everything inside that the outcome would be better than that? *Less than forty percent?* He couldn't believe it, couldn't comprehend it. He simply wasn't prepared to lose his mother. At least with his father there had been some warning, some time to adapt. The shock had come upon learning that he had terminal cancer; there had been many months beyond that to be with him and talk with him and have some kind of closure with the situation. But this! This was just too strange. She'd been sitting at the breakfast table one minute laughing and all was well, and the next there had been pain and fear and now he might never see her alive again.

Jess repeated the inner monologue that had already tromped through his brain several times. She would make it through this! She had to! And then he recalled the last words that had come out of his mother's mouth, and in the same moment he understood them. A moment later a thought struck him with such force that it took his breath away.

"What is it?" Tamra asked quietly in response to his quiet gasp. He shook his head in an effort to convince her that it was nothing, then his wife and every other aspect of his surroundings became hazy and distant as the idea he'd been given settled more fully into his mind—and then into his spirit. His mother was dying and he knew it. He knew it beyond any doubt. It was her time to go. In the same moment that he wondered why he would be given such an undeniable, profound witness of what was to come, the answer presented itself. The words appeared plainly in his mind. *You are not only the patriarch of this family—you are their bishop. They will need your strength to get through this. But have no fear; I will be at your side for as long as you need me.* With the words came a sensation that was startlingly familiar, even though he'd only felt it this strongly once before. *His father was standing beside him!* And the words in his mind had come from him.

Following Michael's death, Jess had studied and come to understand the principle of the ministering of angels. Moroni's explanation of the principle was something he had read so many times that it came easily to his mind now. . . . *Have miracles ceased? Behold I say unto you, Nay; neither have angels ceased to minister unto the children of men. For behold, they are subject unto him, to minister according to the word of his command, showing themselves unto them of strong faith and a firm mind in every form of godliness.* Jess knew that it was under the direction of Christ that angels were given direction and permission to minister to those on this side of the veil when it was appropriate. In spite of understanding the principle, Jess was stunned to realize that he had just experienced such a miracle. In the breadth of a moment he was struck with the enormity of that miracle and with the undeniable witness of the Spirit that what he felt was true, along with the harsh reality that his mother's life would not go beyond this day. Jess felt tears burn his eyes and trickle down his cheeks—a stark combination of incomprehensible peace and joy and unfathomable fear and pain. The spiritual sensation encircling him slowly eased, and he felt keenly aware of the earthly surroundings in which he had to cope and exist. Then he realized that every member of his family was staring at him, eyes wide with concern.

While he was struggling to know what to say, how much to say, Allison asked gently, "What is it, Jess? What's wrong?"

His tongue felt swollen in his mouth, and he could only shake his head, hoping they'd understand that he needed a few minutes to gain his composure. He was relieved when Emma said, "You know, I can't stop thinking about the time that Mom stayed up all night with me when I got that horrible food poisoning when I was fifteen. And I can think of at least a dozen other tragedies in my life when she was always there."

"If she wasn't there when the tragedy happened," Amee said, "she was always on the next plane to be there."

"Which makes it feel completely wrong for us to be sitting here like this without her among us," Alexa said, and Jess was grateful for the way this conversation had distracted the attention away from himself—even though he didn't necessarily like its context.

"That's precisely my point," Emma added. "It's all wrong."

"She's always been so strong," Amee said. "So . . . incredible. Whatever we come up against, I don't know how we can get through it without her."

"She'll always be with us, one way or another," Allison said, but Jess didn't like the way that sounded either.

He was relieved when Scott changed the subject by saying, "I'll never forget how easily she took me in like one of her own. It's like she took one look at me and knew I was a love-starved, motherless urchin. I can't imagine where I would be without her."

"I echo that," Tamra said. "She was everything my own mother had never been. She was amazing."

"What's with the past tense?" Jess asked, wishing his tone hadn't betrayed how upset he was. In spite of the peace he'd just felt, he was having trouble accepting the reality.

"Is," Tamra corrected vehemently. "She *is* amazing; she always will be."

"Amen," Samuel said, and Allison reached for his hand.

Hating the silence that descended, Jess broke it by saying, "I'll never forget how she sat by my bed day in and day out while I was recovering from that accident."

The conversation moved along as memories bounced back and forth, moving from the tragedies they had shared into some of the best times they'd had together. The time went more quickly while they reminisced, but Jess was still aware of the clock and was wondering what could possibly be happening. While he could hardly acknowledge that such a thought would even find root in his brain, he couldn't help wondering why the surgery was taking so long when she was just going to die anyway. And then he tuned in more fully to the conversation taking place around him. *This* is why, he thought. They needed this time to indulge in nostalgia and sentiment. Now while there was still hope, they needed to be reminded of all the good Emily had brought into their lives. Jess listened with a growing warmth about the memories that meant most to each of Emily's children. The life she had lived, the trials she had endured, and the faith she had exhibited were an inspiration to everyone present.

While the conversation went on, Jess couldn't help noticing that Allison was keenly aware of him, as if she sensed that he knew something he wasn't sharing. He knew it was only a matter of time before she questioned him. He only hoped that when the moment came, he would know what to say and how to say it.

A quiet lull came when it seemed that everyone had run out of things to talk about, and the clock showed that it had been nearly five hours since they'd spoken with the surgeon.

"I hate to admit it," Allison said, breaking the silence, "but there's a feeling here . . . around us . . . that's somehow . . . familiar."

"I had the same thought," Amee said, her voice almost wary, "but I can't quite place it."

"I can place it," Emma said, her tone heavy. "This is how it felt when Dad was dying."

A long moment of stunned silence preceded Alexa saying, "Just because we're all together and we're worried and upset does not necessarily mean that the same thing is happening here."

"Or maybe it does," Allison said. Her attention turned to Jess as she asked, "I couldn't help noticing that you heard what Mom said just before she lost consciousness, and it upset you." She paused and her voice softened. "What did she say, Jess?"

Jess only wondered for a moment if he should answer the question honestly and directly. And then he knew that he should. He also knew that the answer would change everything for them, just as it had for him once he'd come to accept and understand it. When he hesitated a moment longer, Emma asked, "Is it so difficult to repeat?"

"Yes," Jess said with a cracked voice. He watched the expressions of those around him become wary and afraid. He cleared his throat carefully and spoke in little more than a whisper, "She said . . . 'Oh, Michael, you came.'"

Jess heard a collective gasp, then a heavy silence descended until Alexa said with an edge to her voice, "That doesn't necessarily mean what you all seem to think it means. He could just be there to . . . comfort her through this."

Jess wanted to argue with her; he wanted to present the case of what he'd just learned through the guidance of the Spirit. But he knew that time would prove everything. He simply said, "Perhaps."

Alexa met his eyes across the room as if she could find something there to assure her. She finally said, "But you don't believe that."

Jess was contemplating how to answer her when he saw the surgeon approaching. Everyone's attention was drawn to this man as he approached, looking weary and strained. Jess wondered if his was the only heart pounding just as Tamra reached for his hand and squeezed it nearly as hard as he squeezed back.

The family all listened patiently while the doctor went into a detailed report of what he'd done through the course of the operation. Allison held one of Samuel's hands, while Emma held the other. The general conclusion came down to Emily's being on a heart-lung bypass machine, because the damage to her heart was too great for it to work on its own.

Allison asked the doctor, "Can she stay on that machine until her heart heals?"

The doctor's voice was gentle as he answered, "No, she cannot."

A moment of silence preceded Scott asking, "*Will* her heart heal?"

"No, it will not," the doctor said even more gently, his countenance brimming with compassion.

Jess found the strength to ask the question that he knew everyone else was wondering. "Are you saying that she is dying?"

The doctor's tenderness was not diminished by his straightforward manner. "I'm sorry to tell you that she is."

He remained quiet for a couple of minutes while family members responded with varying degrees of emotion and shock, but it was evident he'd delivered bad news before. He simply waited until Samuel asked with a broken voice, "What now, Doctor?"

"She will not regain consciousness. Once she's cleaned up from the surgery, she'll be taken to a room where you can all be with her for as long as you need." He went on to offer his condolences and asked if they had any questions for him. He answered them kindly and with patience before he stated a final "I'm truly sorry," and walked away.

Jess crumbled into the chair where he'd been sitting before the doctor's arrival. Crying silent tears, he held tightly to Tamra's hands and listened with swelling shock as the others expressed their own disbelief and anguish. He kept thinking of the words that had come to his mind in preparation for this. He felt a strange, bizarre kind of comfort in knowing that it was meant to be. It was indeed her time to go.

By the time they were allowed to be with Emily, she was already gone, and her hands had turned cold. Jess found it strange to compare his father's death to these moments that felt so surreal and dreamlike. There was more visible emotion now among his loved ones, as the shock was difficult to comprehend. By the time Michael had passed on, they had all been well prepared and had grieved a great deal. His death had actually brought a certain peace, and even some relief. But now, with Emily, Jess could only think that twenty-four hours ago there had been no sign of this, no forewarning that death was at the door. He was grateful to be surrounded by his sisters—all of them—and couldn't help marveling at how they had all been kept here when three of them should have returned to their faraway homes. He appreciated the conversation that came between bouts of emotion, where they all agreed that in spite of the shock, they couldn't deny an underlying peace and much evidence that this event had been planned and orchestrated from the other side of the veil—just as their father's death had been.

They spent a few hours going in and out of the room where Emily lay as if she were sleeping. They each took a turn alone at her side, saying what needed to be said with a certainty that she was close enough by to hear them. While his sisters were preoccupied else-where, Jess sat down beside Samuel and put a hand on his arm. "You okay?" he asked gently.

The sadness in Samuel's eyes provoked fresh emotion in Jess when he had believed that he was all cried out. "It's difficult to see her go,"

Samuel said. "For me, our time together was only temporary, and I always knew that. She's with Michael again, as she should be, and one day I will be with Arlene again."

"Yes, you will," Jess said, fondly recalling his opportunity to be with Samuel as he'd gone through the temple for the first time, and at a later time, when he had been sealed to his first wife, with Emily standing in as a proxy.

"The separation is just . . . hard," Samuel said.

They sat together in silence for many minutes. Jess couldn't think of anything to say that might console Samuel's grief—or his own. Samuel finally said, "But I meant what I told her; she gave my life a happy ending. I have no regrets. She's an amazing woman."

"Yes, she is," Jess said. "She always will be. And I know that *you* gave *her* life a happy ending. But yours isn't over yet."

Samuel said nothing, but Jess saw in his eyes that he didn't agree. It was as if he had nothing left to live for. Jess's heart ached for him, but he didn't know what to say. Amee sat close beside Samuel and took his hand, and Jess took the opportunity to sit near his mother and hold her hand, trying to ignore its coldness. His emotions vacillated between a horrific shock that made him want to scream and throw a childish fit, and a deep peace that filled every cell of his being.

When the hour became late and they all had no choice but to leave the hospital, and to leave Emily behind, Jess felt himself gravitating more toward the desire to scream and protest. Arrangements had been made with a local funeral home, and they would all see Emily again in a few days, prior to the funeral. But it all felt so wrong. Just yesterday they had all been talking and laughing together, and now she was gone—with no warning, no opportunity to be prepared. And while Jess felt immeasurably grateful for the undeniable experience he'd had that had let him know beyond any doubt it was her time to go, the shock of losing her was equally undeniable.

Jess held the shock close with the hope that it would protect him from an unreasonable outburst. Driving home through the darkness, he listened as if from a distance while Tamra and two of his sisters discussed their disbelief, expressing feelings that he couldn't bring himself to say aloud. Alexa questioned his silence, but Tamra just squeezed his hand as if she understood perfectly.

It was nearly midnight when the two vehicles arrived home. He was relieved when Scott offered to help Samuel to bed and see that he had all he needed. The moment Jess was alone in his own bedroom, that numb sense of shock rushed out of him in a wave. He crumpled onto the edge of the bed and heaved his anguish into the open air. His mother. Gone. He couldn't believe it. And while there was no denying the comfort he found in knowing this separation was not forever, it was a stark separation nevertheless. He felt cold and lost and alone. He'd been a man for many years now, a husband and father, in charge of the estate, and a bishop. But he felt like an abandoned, helpless child. *An orphan.* And the child inside him cried as he hadn't since the loss of his father.

Tamra found him curled up on the bed after she'd checked on the children. She wrapped him in her loving embrace and cried with him, sharing his grief with perfect empathy and understanding. He felt completely safe and less alone and deeply grateful to have her there. He thought of his sisters and wondered how they were coping. Emma had Scott, but the others were separated from their husbands by many miles.

Jess finally felt his anguish ebb into silence, but even with the complete exhaustion that consumed him, he lay awake staring into the darkness. He felt certain that Tamra was asleep with her head against his shoulder until she muttered quietly, "Talk to me, Jess. I know you need to be strong for the others, but not for me."

"And how did you know that?" he asked, his voice hoarse and strained.

"I could see it in your face," she said gently. "You're not only the patriarch of the family, you're also the bishop."

Jess gasped to hear the same words that had been impressed so clearly into his mind earlier at the hospital.

"What is it?" she asked, leaning up on one elbow. When he didn't answer, she pressed a hand to his face. "Jess, what's wrong?"

Jess considered how to tell her. He'd been given a sacred experience and he knew better than to treat it lightly or speak of it too freely where it wasn't appropriate. But she was his wife, his soul mate, his eternal companion. She was right when she said that he didn't need to put up a façade of strength for her. *She* was his strength. And he needed a place where he could be completely honest and open, or he would never get through what lay ahead.

"What?" she asked again, her voice soft with concern. And he knew it was right to tell her.

"That's exactly what my father told me," he said in little more than a whisper.

Through the silence he sensed her attempting to understand what he meant. Then she rolled over and flipped on the lamp on the bedside table. She turned back to face him. "When?" she asked.

Fresh emotion slipped into his words. "He . . . was there—in the waiting room . . . with us. I felt him close to me, and . . . the words came so clearly to my mind . . . that I had to be strong . . . that I was not only the patriarch of the family, but also their bishop. But . . . he let me know that he would be with me for as long as I needed him."

Tears streamed down Tamra's face before she wrapped her arms around Jess and wept freshly. "Oh, Jess," she murmured close to his ear, "you knew."

He drew back and took her shoulders into his hands, looking into her eyes. "Knew what?"

"You knew . . . before the doctor came out; you knew she would die."

Jess hated the way her words drove a gaping hole into the blanket of shock attempting to protect him from the full impact of reality. He squeezed his eyes closed and felt hot tears leak between his eyelids as he nodded his head. "Yes, I knew," he muttered.

Tamra said nothing more. As if she sensed the burden he carried that he could never quite articulate, she just held him tightly, and again they wept together until exhaustion overtook them.

Jess came awake to the sound of the phone ringing. He squinted against bright morning light and knew he'd slept late. It took him two rings to remember why he felt so disoriented and exhausted and another to realize that his mother had been in the kitchen yesterday morning, talking and laughing, and now she was gone. One more ring and he surmised the possible reasons that someone might be calling *him* as opposed to anyone else in the house. Either he was late for work, and his staff at the boys' home was wondering why he hadn't shown up, or his counselors in the bishopric were wondering why he'd not checked in with them the previous evening as he'd told them he would after they'd agreed to cover his meetings. He wished he'd thought to make a couple of calls last night and avoid having to make explanations this morning. The phone stopped ringing, and Jess knew that someone elsewhere in the house had answered it. With any luck it wouldn't be for him after all. He was alone in the bed and wondered how long ago Tamra had gotten up to deal with the children. Then the door came slowly open, and she peeked her head into the room.

"Hi," she said with a compassionate smile.

"Hi," he replied.

"The phone's for you," she said with apology. A child began to cry in the distance, and she quickly handed him the phone before she scurried away.

Jess cleared his throat and picked it up, not wanting to face *anything* today. "Hello," he said, and the voice of his first counselor responded.

"I just wanted you to know that we've got everything covered for as long as you need. And whatever you need me to do for the funeral, you just let me know. The Relief Society ladies are on their way out right now, and we'll be out in a few hours . . . to see what we can do."

"Thank you," Jess muttered, forcing the question from his brain to his lips. "How did you know?"

"Scott called me last night," he said. "Anyway, I don't want you to worry about a thing. I'm your slave for as long as you need me."

Jess swallowed the lump in his throat and simply said, "Thank you, but . . . slavery is illegal around here, last I checked."

"Just don't tell anybody."

Jess got off the phone and hung his head as fresh tears burned his eyes. His mother was gone. He just couldn't believe it. Tamra returned after seeing that the children were minding their manners. She came with a tray of breakfast and insisted he eat it, whether he wanted to or not. He *didn't* want to, but he did it anyway. While he ate she caught him up on the calls that had been made and on the arrangements that were underway. The boys' home was under control, and the closest circle of relatives had been informed. And he learned how his three out-of-town sisters had coped without their husbands. They had all three slept in the same king-sized bed, crying and holding hands amidst some snatches of rest.

Once Jess had eaten, he gave his wife a tender kiss and thanked her for the way she held him together. With tears in her eyes she simply said, "I love you, Jess, and we'll get through this; I'll be right beside you all the way."

Jess forced himself into the shower, but ended up sobbing while hot water ran over his face. He finally pulled himself together after spending many minutes on his knees, but he still hesitated before stepping from his bedroom into the hall, suddenly fearing that he might not be up to whatever he had to face through the coming hours. Then the words came into his mind, as clearly as they had the previous day. *Have no fear; I will be at your side for as long as you need me.* Tears of a different kind stung Jess's eyes. He felt completely humbled and thoroughly in awe that he would be given such tangible evidence of life beyond the veil. He knew his father was at his side, and he felt relatively certain that his mother couldn't be far away either. And with that knowledge he drew back his shoulders, uttered a silent prayer of gratitude, and headed down the stairs.

First off, Jess found his children. He hugged them and held them and talked with them about what had happened with their grandmother. When the children were occupied elsewhere, he found his sisters visiting with members of the Relief Society presidency. After the visit ended, his sisters all huddled together and cried; he found it difficult to know what to say in the face of their overt grief. So he just gave them each a hug before he searched out Samuel after being told that he'd not yet made an appearance. Scott had gone to help him earlier and had taken him some breakfast, but he'd refused to come out of his room. Jess personally took a lunch tray to the room Samuel had shared with Emily and found him sitting in his wheelchair, looking out the window.

"How are you?" Jess asked, setting the tray down.

"No worse than anyone else," Samuel said.

Jess moved a chair closer and sat to face him. "I know you made it clear a long time ago that I would always be the head of the household," Jess said, "but I think I'd like to relinquish that position to you."

Samuel gave a subtle smile. "Oh no. You can't delegate that responsibility. And why would you want to? You're doing just fine. Your family members look to you for good reason."

Jess hung his head. "I don't know how to help them understand this when I don't understand it myself. I feel as if I'm supposed to have the answers, but I don't have them."

Samuel sighed loudly. "I think you have more answers than you're letting on to."

Jess looked up sharply and met Samuel's piercing eyes. "You and I both know it was her time to go. Great comfort can be found in such knowledge."

"Do you feel comfort, then?" Jess asked.

"I do," Samuel said as contradictory tears leaked from his eyes. "I also feel unimaginable sorrow."

"Yes," Jess admitted, "I feel the same . . . in both respects. But what's to be done?"

"Only one thing," Samuel said. "We move on; it's the only thing she would want. She knew it was coming. She was ready to go."

"She knew?" Jess asked, wishing it hadn't sounded so sharp.

"Oh, not consciously," Samuel said gently. "But . . . I think that perhaps . . . she sensed that it was close."

"And you? Did you sense it?"

"No," he said firmly. "I was completely unprepared. It's looking back . . . recalling little things she said . . . that makes me think she knew."

Their conversation was interrupted when Emma came to tell them that the counselors from the bishopric had arrived. Samuel urged Jess to go and visit with them, but later that afternoon when Jess called a family meeting, Samuel arrived with Scott pushing the wheelchair; he held a book and a large manila envelope on his lap. The room was especially quiet, since some of the children had been taken to stay at the homes of friends in the ward, and the others were upstairs with Rhea, who had eagerly volunteered to watch them. Following the standard opening prayer that began any family gathering, Jess looked around at the solemn faces of his family members while he prayed for the words to say. He felt impressed to utter his most prominent thought. "I cannot begin to express my gratitude for the fact that all of my siblings have been together through this. In my opinion, that fact alone is evidence of the love of our Father in Heaven. I'm grateful that I didn't have to call you—any of you—the minute you got home and tell you to turn around and come back for a funeral." Jess sighed and took Tamra's hand. "I'm grateful too for my incredible wife, who is always by my side through whatever life brings upon us." He looked directly at Scott and Emma, who were also holding hands. "And I'm grateful to be sharing this home with my sister and her family; and I'm grateful she married my best friend." He turned to Samuel. "And I'm grateful for you, Samuel— for the added light and joy you've brought into our home."

Jess sighed again more loudly and wondered only a moment how to go on. "I know you'll agree that this is one of the most difficult things we've ever faced as a family. But we've proven that we can survive, and we will go on and live in a way that she would want us to. I want you to know that I know, beyond any doubt, that it was her time to go. The matter was—and is—in God's hands."

"And she is with Michael now," Samuel added with firm serenity.

"Is that difficult for you?" Amee asked him.

Samuel gave a sad smile. "In a way, yes. But in the eternal perspective, I know she is where she will be eternally happy. And one day I will be equally happy with my Arlene."

Amee took Samuel's hand and squeezed it. Jess loved the way his sisters had grown to love Samuel so completely.

They discussed what had been done so far to arrange for the funeral and burial and what still needed to be done. They divided lists of people who still needed to be called, and together they wrote Emily's obituary while Allison typed it on her laptop computer. When all was done except for planning the actual funeral program, Samuel opened the book on his lap that Jess now recognized as his mother's journal. "She told me many times," Samuel said, "that she had a letter in the back of her current journal with some requests for her funeral."

"She told me that too," Jess said, and all of the others said the same. "But I'd forgotten. Why don't you read it, Samuel?"

Jess noticed how Samuel's hands were doing better than average as he opened the letter with only minimal help from Amee. He cleared his throat and read, "'Dear Family, If you are reading this, then I am either dead, or you're snooping. Either way it's okay. I want you to know that I love you all, and I will be watching over you. In fact, I suspect that if I am dead and you're reading this, I'm probably very close by.'"

Jess hurried to wipe away a surge of tears and realized the others were crying too, but there was a peacefulness in the room that couldn't be denied. He felt it likely that she was close by.

Samuel continued to read. "'I have a few preferences that I would like for my funeral. Of course, by the time I get to the other side such things will probably mean little to me, but humor me anyway.'"

Samuel read the list, which began with having all of her grand-children sing "Families Can Be Together Forever." She then specified certain speakers and musical numbers that included every member of her family in one way or another. After the list had been read, Jess glanced around to see equally stunned expressions on everyone's faces. He wasn't so surprised about being asked to speak himself, since he'd spoken at his father's funeral, but he wasn't prepared for her request that he conduct the funeral as well. It was standard for the bishop to conduct a funeral within the ward—unless it was a family member, and then that responsibility fell to someone else. He had to admit that with his own fragile emotions, conducting the meeting did not suit him. But he could see that at least three of his four sisters were not happy with their assignments, either. Amee was the first to express herself. "Why would she do that? She knows I hate to talk in public."

Jess was struck abruptly with a thought, and he just as quickly shared it. "Perhaps she felt impressed to initiate something that she believed would bring about growth in all of us." Only silence came in response, and Jess wondered if they all felt, as he did, that the idea was true. It was certainly her style.

No one complained further about their assignments for the program. They went on to plan it out in detail.

"Oh," Samuel said in the midst of the discussion, "there's a P.S. here. It says, 'I want to be buried in the dress that's in the top of my cedar chest.'"

"What dress?" Alexa asked.

"I guess we'll have to go see," Allison said. "But I have a hunch. We'll go look when we're done here."

When they had finished going over the program, Samuel said, "She also left this." He motioned to the large, thick, manila envelope on his lap. He asked Amee to open it and distribute its contents. Inside Emily had a handwritten letter to each of her children, their spouses, and her grandchildren. And one for Samuel. Those for family members not present were set aside. Jess and his sisters agreed that they each preferred to read their letters privately. The meeting was adjourned, and Jess went with his wife and sisters to their mother's bedroom, where Allison knelt in front of their mother's cedar chest and reverently opened it. Lying on top, wrapped in white tissue, was a new set of temple clothing, and beside that was a lovely white dress with lace trim around the collar and hem and cuffs. The lace was handmade, and while Jess was trying to figure why it looked familiar, Allison said, "When she stayed with me last, she had me help her with this. It's made from one of the tablecloths that Grandma made."

"You mean Michael's mother?" Scott asked.

"That's right," Allison said. "You know how Mother gave us all a set of linens when we were married? Things that had been made by our grandmother and great-grandmother."

"And some by our great-great-grandmother," Tamra mentioned. "How could we ever forget? They're magnificent."

"Well," Allison said, "there was one piece left; this tablecloth. And Mother had the idea that she wanted to make a temple dress out of it. But apparently it hasn't been worn yet."

"It's beautiful," Alexa said, holding it against her.

"It seems she had everything carefully planned," Emma said.

"She just wanted her death to be organized," Scott said lightly, "just like everything else she did."

"I sure miss her," Allison said with a sniffle, laying her head on Jess's shoulder.

He put his arm around her and echoed, "I miss her too."

For the next couple of hours, they all sat together on the floor and explored the contents of their mother's cedar chest and the memories represented there. They found blessing gowns and dried wedding flowers. There were scrapbooks and baby books and boxes filled with cards and letters. And a number of miscellaneous keepsakes; Emily had attached a little note to each one that explained its meaning to her. The laughter they shared as they reminisced and discussed their mother's life felt almost unnatural to Jess as he considered that they were dealing with her recent death. Until he considered the undeniable peace that he knew they each felt. The separation was difficult, the shock was hard to accept, but they had the gospel, and they all knew, beyond any doubt, that she lived on. And under the circumstances, eternity was such a profound blessing.

Chapter Fourteen

That evening at supper, no one had anything to say. The children were noisy as usual, but for the adults, Emily's absence was stark. They had reminisced and analyzed until there simply seemed to be nothing more to say. Near the end of the meal, Samuel said, "When we're finished here, I wonder if I could talk to you—Jess and Scott."

"Of course," Jess said at the same time Scott said, "That would be fine."

Scott tossed Jess a concerned glance before their attention was drawn to the children's antics. When supper was over, the men went to the family office, and Samuel asked that they close the door.

"What can we do for you?" Jess asked once they were all comfortable.

Samuel looked down and sighed deeply. "Now that your mother is gone," he said quietly, "I don't want to intrude upon your hospitality any further and—"

"Intrude?" Jess interrupted. "You haven't intruded upon anything."

"Amen," Scott said. "We love having you in our home; you're family. If you're trying to tell us that you should leave now, you can forget that idea straight up front."

"I'm with Scott," Jess said. "We've just lost our mother. We don't want to lose you as well."

Samuel sighed again. "Your graciousness means so much to me, really. And you've both been wonderful to help me. But there was a great deal that your mother did for me every day, things that you've been doing for me since . . . she left us, but . . ."

"Did we not manage fine when she would leave for the day now and then?" Scott asked.

"And what about when she left town for those three days last month to help that friend of hers?" Jess said. "Didn't we take good care of you?"

"You did, yes," Samuel said. "I'm certainly not complaining about the care. You're both very capable and willing—and I'm grateful. But you both have very full lives. You have jobs, families, Church callings." He glanced at Jess. "You're the bishop, for heaven's sake."

"Yes, it is for heaven's sake, I believe," Jess said with a little chuckle. "But those things are irrelevant to the issue, as far as I'm concerned. You're family. I know I speak for the entire family when I say that you are not a burden to our household. We can have a nurse come more regularly if that would make you more comfortable, but we really don't want to have you staying in some care facility when you have people who love you, people who benefit from your presence in the home."

Following a tense minute of silence, Scott leaned closer to Samuel and asked, "Is there a reason you don't want to be here? If so, please talk to us about it."

Samuel became emotional, and they gave him a couple of minutes to compose himself. "The memories . . . are difficult," he admitted. "Everywhere I turn, there's something to remind me of her. Of course, that's a bittersweet thing. I know you all have the same challenge, and . . . in a way, it's nice to be reminded of her in so many ways." He sighed and wiped at his ongoing tears. "I think that I could actually still do some good at the care center. I'm not physically capable of much, but . . ."

"Mom was going with you two or three times a week to spend volunteer time there," Jess said. "That can still be arranged. You don't have to live there to keep doing some good."

"So, have we convinced you of your stupidity yet?" Scott asked. "What can we say to make you realize that we really do want you here? That your being here is not a burden?"

"But I *feel* like such a burden," Samuel admitted. "Your mother took very good care of me, but . . . in a way, she had nothing better to do. She had no responsibilities that drew her elsewhere. And the companionship we shared while she helped me was a highlight for both of us."

"And you don't think we could all benefit from some companionship?" Scott asked.

"You're just all so busy," Samuel said, "and I don't want to—"

"Okay, how about this," Scott said. "You've told us you're not comfortable with having the women help you with certain things. Since your wife is no longer with us, we'll hire a nurse to come during the days while we're both working, and one or the other of us will be available otherwise. And don't even bring up the money. That stopped being an issue for us a long time ago."

"And if my condition worsens?" Samuel asked. "If I need more care than either of you can—"

"Then we'll reevaluate," Jess said. "But for the moment, that's not the case."

Once again Samuel sighed loudly. "Let me give it some thought. Perhaps we should at least get the funeral behind us before we start making any big decisions."

"Good idea," Jess said. "But I think we'll just plan on your staying, because you won't be able to think of a good reason not to."

"Not to mention," Scott said lightly, "you can't leave without one of us helping you leave, and we're not going to do it. So there."

Samuel chuckled. "You've got me on that one," he said.

They all remained in the office for more than an hour, talking through this turn of events and how it had affected each of them. Jess's respect and admiration for Samuel grew as he expressed genuine appreciation for all that Emily had brought into his life and for the time they had been able to share together.

It was very late before Jess found the opportunity to be alone with the letter his mother had written. He treasured her handwritten words on the pages folded together and marveled at her tender feelings as she expressed her love and confidence in him. He read it three times and cried long and hard with a mixture of peace and sorrow, then he tucked it into his journal, next to a copy of his patriarchal blessing.

Through the next few days, funeral arrangements were fine-tuned, and family began arriving from all over the world. Sean O'Hara and his family came as well. Sean had been like a son to

Michael and Emily since Jess's early childhood, and it wouldn't be right for him to be absent from such an event. Samuel's son Trent was among those who stayed in the home, and it was evident that Samuel was truly grateful that his son was able to come for the funeral, even though Julia and the children had needed to remain at home. Jess felt the strengthening of family bonds as his sisters' husbands and children came, and the family network became readily evident as they gathered for prayer each night.

When it came time for the family to gather at the funeral home prior to the viewing, Jess felt especially grateful for the loved ones surrounding him. They all shared the same grief and heartache and the same peace and gratitude for all that was good in their lives, most especially the gospel.

Jess was amazed at the people who came to pay their last respects to Emily Hamilton, although he realized he shouldn't have been surprised. She was an incredible woman who had had a profound impact on everyone who knew her. Just as with his father's death, the life they had lived was evidenced by the people who loved and respected them.

But there was one particular face that appeared among the crowd that caught him off guard. By the way she looked directly at him from across the room, he knew she had come to see *him*. It took him a moment to determine the familiarity of her face. She'd aged since he'd last seen her. At one time she had lived nearby and had been a very big part of his life. But she had moved a few hours away, and he'd not seen her for years. And now she had traveled those hours to be here for Jess.

She approached him and stood directly in front of him. For a long moment he just looked into her eyes, reviewing memories, accepting changes, marveling at the perfect peace he saw there when she, herself, had lost much in her life. Her son had been Jess's best friend for many years, and he'd been killed in the accident that had left Jess in a coma. She'd also lost her husband to an unexpected heart attack not many years ago. Just one look into her eyes let him know that she understood. She wrapped her arms around him and hugged him with a tightness that seemed to replenish something he'd lost— the warm and giving embrace of a mother, unrushed and heartfelt.

She took Jess's face into her hands and spoke in a gentle voice. "I made arrangements to come the moment I heard. I needed to see you face-to-face and let you know that my heart is with you." Tears glistened in her eyes as she added, "You've always been like a son to me, Jess, and no matter what, no matter the miles or the years, you will always find a mother in me."

Jess could only nod and attempt to swallow the knot in his throat before he hugged her again, even more tightly. She had lost a son; he had lost a mother. And even if he never saw her again, the bond of love he felt in that moment was eternally sustaining. They sat close together on a sofa and talked quietly for several minutes before Jess felt compelled to return to his place in the receiving line to greet other visitors. They promised to keep in touch, and he was glad to know that she used e-mail, which increased the likelihood of them maintaining contact. He thanked her profusely for coming and hoped that if his words could not express the depth of his gratitude, that she would sense it in her heart.

As the crowd thinned and the viewing began to wind down, Allison nudged Jess with an elbow and said, "Do you know those people, over there by that huge bouquet of gladioli? I don't think they went through the line; they're just kind of . . . hovering."

Jess focused on the couple who he guessed to be in the age range of his own parents. "No," he said easily. "Never seen them before."

"They look familiar," Allison said, "but I can't place why."

"Well, maybe you should go talk to them and figure it out," Jess said.

"No need," Allison added as the couple moved toward them. Jess glanced around to realize that everyone except him and his three older sisters had moved elsewhere; they were the only ones standing near the casket.

Allison clutched Jess's elbow, and he asked, "Are you suddenly nervous, or what?"

"Yes, but I don't know why," she said quietly.

"Hello," the gray-haired gentleman said, extending a hand, first to Jess, then to Allison. "You probably don't remember us," he said directly to Allison. "It's been a long time, but . . . I'm your Uncle David—David Hall, and this is my wife, Louise."

Jess noted that Allison looked disoriented, while he felt completely baffled. He told himself that her relatives would be his relatives and he should know these people. And then it clicked. Technically they had different fathers, although it was easy to forget when Allison's blood father had died long before Jess was born. He was aware of Alexa and Amee hovering close by, attentive to the conversation. They too shared the same father with Allison. The idea felt suddenly a bit unnerving.

"David . . . Louise," Allison said with pleasure as the memory obviously came to her. "Why it *has* been a long time. I remember coming to stay at your home when Grandma was staying there, and then . . . for her funeral."

"That's right," Louise said with a smile.

"And we did see the three of you," David added, his eyes taking in all of the girls but passing over Jess, "at that big family reunion in Idaho, but that's been . . . what? Ten, twelve years ago?"

"Something like that," Allison said, giving them each a quick embrace. "You remember my sisters, Amee and Alexa."

"Of course," Louise said, and greetings were exchanged among them.

Allison then added, "And this is our brother, Jess."

"A pleasure to meet you," David said, but there was something subtly skeptical in his eyes.

"Yes, it is a pleasure," Louise added, more kindly than her husband.

"Well, I can hardly believe you've come all this way," Allison said. "It's a long way to travel for a funeral."

"It is," Louise said, "but we've been talking about a vacation to Australia for years and had the money put away. When we heard about your mother's passing, we just hurried and made the arrangements so that we could be here."

"Well, it's awfully nice of you," Allison said. Amee and Alexa made noises of agreement and offered kind smiles, but Jess sensed their lack of enthusiasm. They'd both been babies at their father's death, and these relatives likely had little meaning in their lives. Allison had been older and had kept in closer touch with that side of her family, but still, that wasn't saying much. It was evident she'd only seen these people a few times in as many decades. Now that greetings had been exchanged, a tense silence descended, as if they had absolutely nothing to say to each other.

"So, how was your trip?" Allison asked, and Jess glanced around in search of an escape.

"Oh, it was long!" David said. "But good, all things considered."

They chatted for a few minutes about their sightseeing agenda, while Allison gave some recommendations. Jess exchanged a discreet glance with Amee and Alexa that made it evident they were equally bored and then relieved when Louise said, "Well, we mustn't keep you. We know you must all be exhausted, and with the funeral in the morning you have another big day. We just wanted to give you our condolences. It must be difficult. She really wasn't very old."

"No, she wasn't," Allison said. "But we know it was her time to go, and there is great peace in that."

"Indeed," David said, "and isn't it wonderful after all these years to know that your parents are finally together again." Jess felt himself bristle, wondering if the implication was what it seemed to be. David left no doubt on that count when he added, "Why, it's been since you girls were babies. Ryan and your mother must be so happy to be together, at last."

While Jess was contemplating an answer that met the defensive anger he felt, Allison's hand appeared on his arm with a not-so-gentle squeeze, as if she sensed his feelings and was determined to help keep him quiet. In the same moment she shot her sisters a discreet, cautioning glare. He noted their wide-eyed astonishment and felt some comfort to realize he wasn't the only one stunned here.

"Indeed," was all Allison said. "Well, thank you so much for coming. We should be rounding up our children and getting them home."

Polite farewells were exchanged before David and Louise moved away. There was a long moment of stunned silence before Amee said hotly, "Well, I'm not sure what to think about that."

Jess was glad to hear her express his own thoughts, since he didn't want to say anything too boldly against their blood father. But still, it seemed apparent to him that, in spite of certain technicalities that had yet to be overcome, Emily's eternal companion was Michael Hamilton. They had evidence that Michael had come for her when her spirit left this world, and Jess deeply believed they were together. Still, there was no denying that Emily had been sealed to Ryan Hall, and following his death she had married Michael Hamilton, but had not been able to be sealed due to her previous sealing. They also all knew that once Emily and Michael had both passed on, that following a certain waiting period, they could be sealed together, and all else would be worked out on the other side. At his parents' request Jess had promised that the sealing would take place as quickly as possible, and now that Emily was gone, they could actually put a date on the calendar for the event.

While Jess had initially struggled with the fact that his parents weren't sealed to each other, and his own mother was sealed to a man he didn't even know, he had long ago come to terms with the issue, knowing that it would all be worked out in eternity, as long as the proper ordinances were in place. Jess had heard his mother talk about her previous husband, making it clear that while she cared for him and respected him, he was not her eternal love. It was evident that while Ryan Hall had certain good qualities, and he'd made some positive contributions to Emily's life, he had also spent many years treating her badly and having no interest in living the gospel or honoring the covenants he'd made in the temple. On the other hand, Michael Hamilton had lived his life honoring his wife and living the gospel fully. Emily felt certain that she and Michael would be together forever, because they had lived for those blessings. Jess felt in his heart that she was right. But David Hall's words, freshly ringing in his ears, combined with the disconcerted expressions on his sisters' faces, were unsettling—to say the least.

"Well, I know what I think about that," Allison said, interrupting Jess's thoughts. "These people have had practically no contact with our family, and they simply have no idea what they're talking about. They're well meaning and kind, but there is an eternal perspective here that they just don't understand. Excuse me; I need to find Ammon and the kids. I'm exhausted."

Allison walked away in search of her husband. Alexa and Amee both stood there looking a bit dazed, perhaps concerned. "Hey, she's right," Jess said, then went to find his own family. But he had a feeling the matter wasn't settled.

It was late before everyone arrived back at the house and the children were all finally in bed. Getting the children settled under normal circumstances could be a challenge, but when all of their cousins were staying under the same roof, it was usually like a circus. He could well imagine his mother observing the chaos with a smile on her face. Thinking of his parents observing the antics together put a smile on his own face. Until he recalled what David Hall had said. Crawling into his bed, he felt angry to realize that he was actually giving the comment any thought at all.

"What's wrong?" Tamra asked, climbing into bed beside him. She leaned against the headboard and rubbed lotion generously on her hands.

"My mother just died," Jess said. "Her funeral is in the morning."

"I'm well aware of that," she said with a light scowl toward him. "I mean . . . what *else* is wrong?"

Jess let out a loud sigh. "My sisters' uncle showed up this evening."

"Your *sisters'* uncle?" she asked, pausing a moment, then adding, "Oh. That would be . . . your mother's first husband's brother."

"Yeah," he grumbled. "Say that three times fast without tripping over your tongue."

"I'd rather not. So what did your mother's first husband's brother have to say that's put such a scowl on your face?"

"He said that it was nice to know that Ryan and my mother were finally together again after all these years."

Tamra looked at him, clearly aghast, before she said with perfect confidence, "Well, he obviously doesn't know this family well enough to know that's not the case."

"But my mother *is* sealed to Ryan Hall," Jess pointed out, hating the cynical tone he heard in his own voice.

"And eventually she will be sealed to your father, and she will be allowed to make a choice. And we know, because she knew beyond any doubt, what that choice will be."

"But what if there are factors we don't understand?" Jess asked. "What if she *does* end up with Ryan?"

"I think that your mother probably holds a certain respect for Ryan and cares for him, and perhaps he is among those who might have greeted her when she passed over. But your father is her true love."

"But . . . what if—"

"Jess," Tamra interrupted, giving a sigh that indicated she was trying to be patient. "I think you're stewing over something that is irrelevant at the present, something that you know in your heart will all work out for the best. And I think we all know what that best will be. Yes, there's a lot we can't possibly understand from our perspective, but I also know that we have the guidance of the Holy Ghost, and as a family we have all felt the evidence of Michael being close to your mother in many ways. I think this is opposition attempting to upset you when it's important for you to be focused and close to the Spirit tomorrow." She ended with a soft laugh.

"What's funny?" he questioned indignantly.

"Well, listen to us. Only in a Mormon family would such an issue cause such a stir."

"Well, it's a Mormon issue," Jess said.

"And one that we need to exert a little faith over," Tamra insisted. "So get some sleep. We have a big day tomorrow." She kissed him and settled her head onto her pillow.

"We're burying my mother tomorrow," Jess said sadly.

"It doesn't seem real," she said, taking his hand. "It just . . . feels like she's gone to the States for a visit or something, and she'll be back one of these days."

"I had the same thought," Jess said. "It never felt quite right around here when she *did* go off to the States—or anywhere, for that matter. It always felt better when she was here . . . at home."

"It's going to be a tough adjustment," Tamra said.

Jess turned to look at her and touched her face. "At least I have you. I am more grateful than I could ever tell you that I have you."

"The feeling is mutual," Tamra said. Jess bent to kiss her, then he reached over to turn off the lamp before he settled into the bed.

While sleep eluded Jess, the issue of whether or not his parents would be together forever consumed his mind. How could he not recall how thoroughly upset he'd become when he'd first learned there was a problem? Unable to find a sealing certificate among the family records, he'd gone to his parents for an answer, expecting the problem to have a simple explanation. At the time, his father had known he was dying of cancer. To this day, the memory of those conversations chilled Jess deeply.

"I have a question," Jess had said in a tone of voice that made Michael and Emily both turn toward him with startled eyes.

"Yes," Michael drawled, setting his book aside.

"I can't help wondering why there's no evidence in our family records of the two of you being sealed together."

Michael and Emily exchanged a long, anxious gaze. Emily's eyes remained focused on Michael as he turned to face Jess and said firmly, "Sit down, Jess."

"I'm fine," he insisted and remained standing, but Tamra sat on one of the sofas.

Michael cleared his throat and said, "There can be no records for something that never happened, Jess. Your mother and I are *not* sealed together."

Jess sat down. He stared into his father's eyes, as if he could find the answers just by looking there. For a long moment everything he believed in, everything he had known to be true and firm, suddenly felt like it was sliding into quicksand. He couldn't even begin to fathom what could justify such an obvious oversight. A harsh silence settled over the room until Jess managed to sputter, "But how . . ."

His mother's voice startled him, and he snapped his head toward her. "I can't believe you don't know about this. We've had family discussions about this, Jess. Where were you? I mean . . . I know you were there physically. Were you so detached from the family through those rebellious years that you didn't hear what was being talked about?"

"Maybe I was," Jess admitted, "because I sure don't remember *anything* ever being said about *this*. How can a Latter-day Saint family with access to a temple have such an important piece missing? It makes no sense."

Michael sighed and once again shared a long gaze with Emily. "Okay, well," he said, "I guess we'd better start at the beginning." He shook his head and briefly rubbed a hand over his face. "I really hate this story," he added, reaching for Emily's hand. Jess reached for Tamra's in the same moment.

Michael cleared his throat again, then took a deep breath. "When I met your mother, Jess, I was not a member of the Church. The more I learned about it, the more I respected and admired your mother's beliefs, but I was not willing to embrace them for myself. I was quite adamant that my life had been good, and I saw no reason to change it. I felt quite confident that she would be willing to marry me anyway. But in the end her convictions on marrying in the temple overruled."

Michael let out a heavy sigh and leaned his forearms on his thighs. "There are no words to describe the devastation I experienced when she left me. I went through many stages of grief, anger, resentment . . . and ten years later, I still hadn't completely gotten over it. That's when our paths crossed again, and I learned that your mother's temple marriage was not necessarily good. Ryan had become inactive in the Church and didn't treat her very well. All those feelings of anger and resentment magnified immensely. I asked your mother to leave him and marry me. I was willing to take her daughters on as my own, and we could begin a new life together. But she chose to stay and honor those covenants she had made with him. Ryan made some positive changes before he was killed, and I joined the Church—of my own will, mostly because I had been left so in awe of your mother's convictions and commitment, even in the face of such obvious challenges."

Jess tried not to sound frustrated as he said, "I knew most of that already. But what has it got to do with—"

"I'm getting to that," Michael said. "Your mother married Ryan in the temple, Jess. She is sealed to *him,* and he is dead, and she cannot be sealed to another man in this life."

Jess struggled to breathe, then he abruptly sat up straighter and blurted, "So, who am *I* sealed to?"

Michael's tone was even as he stated, "Your mother. You were born under the covenant."

"And who are *you* sealed to?"

"My parents, my grandparents, my—"

"So, let me get this straight. *You,* my father, are sealed to a long line of ancestors. But my mother is sealed to a *different* man, a *different* family, and there is a huge crack down the middle of *this* family. My half-sisters are sealed to their blood father, but Emma and I have no eternal connection to *you.* And James and Tyson, who are already on the other side—who are *they* sealed to? A man that none of us even knew! Do I have that straight?"

"Technically, yes," Michael said, and Jess groaned. "But let me explain some things that took me a long time to figure out. First of all, you have to understand that the sealing ordinance is a wonderful and mandatory part of the plan. But it's not so important *who* we are sealed to, but rather that we *are* sealed. Secondly, there are certain limitations in this life, where rules must be established in black and white for the sake of order. But on the other side, everything will be made right according to how we live for those blessings."

"I'm lost," Jess said, his voice strained.

"So, I'll give you an example. Your great-great-grandmother, Alexandra Byrnehouse-Davies, had a similar situation. She was married to Richard Wilhite. He died, and she married Jess Davies. When we did her temple work, she was sealed to both men even though she can only be married to one on the other side of the veil. But the choice will be made there as to which one she will be with throughout eternity. But sealing a woman to more than one man can only be done following death. We all feel strongly that it will be Jess Davies, because he was the father of her children, and she was only married to Richard for a brief time, whereas she spent the bulk of her life married to Jess. Reading their journals, you can feel the intensity of the love they had for each other, as if it had been foreordained. Your mother and I have similar feelings about each other. And once we are both gone from this life, we're counting on our children to have the sealing performed on our behalf, so that everything can be made right on the other side."

"So, what are you saying?" Jess asked in a voice that expressed how deeply this was troubling him. "That there's a fifty-fifty chance you'll end up married to my mother on the other side?" He shot to his feet and added, "How can you just . . . sit back and accept something . . . so completely *ludicrous?*"

Michael shot to his feet as well. "Now, you listen to me, son, and you listen well." He lifted a finger and leaned closer to Jess. "Don't go assuming that this has *ever* been easy for me to accept. But just because it's been one of the greatest difficulties of my life, don't think for a moment that any part of God's plan is *ludicrous.* He knows what He's doing, even if you don't understand it. You have no idea the grief I have suffered over this issue and the grief I brought to my family because I was so hesitant to accept it. When I finally came to my senses, and humbled myself enough to *ask* God for the answers, instead of just assuming that I had it all figured out, He let me know beyond any doubt that I would be blessed with what I lived for in this life. I have committed my life, my heart, my soul, *everything* to loving your mother, caring for her and for our children. And I *know* beyond any doubt that we *will* be together—now and forever."

"How can you believe that when your wife is sealed to another man?"

The ensuing silence made it evident that Emily was crying. Jess and Michael both turned toward her then back to face each other. Michael's voice was quiet but firm as he stated, "I don't believe, Jess. I *know* it. There are aspects to this situation that cannot be explained with any degree of logic. It's a spiritual matter, with many complexities that took me years to fully understand. You have to get your own answers, and there's only one place you can get them. But you'll never get answers when you're angry. Trust me on that one. I learned it the hard way. And until you get those answers, trust me when I tell you that we *will* be together forever—as a family."

Jess blew out a long breath and looked at the floor. Half a minute later he said, "I'm sorry if I upset you, Mother. I need some time." He turned and left the room.

It was quite some time later before Michael found Jess sitting in the carriage house. They talked of many trivial things, as if nothing in the world was wrong, until Jess just came out and said, "I really thought you'd come out here to talk to me about . . . what we'd been talking about in the house."

"It can wait," Michael said.

"No, I don't think it can." Jess drew a ragged breath. "I'm having a rough time with this, Dad. I don't know what else to say."

"Well, what I wanted to tell you . . . what I *need* to tell you is that . . . I know exactly how you feel. When I asked your mother to marry me—after her husband had died—I just assumed that we would be sealed. When I learned how it works, I was devastated. I tried to put it out of my head and enjoy the life we had together, but it created more challenges for me than I care to get into. Eventually it took a lot of prayer and soul searching and a number of complicated puzzle pieces coming together for me to finally understand the big picture. And a day came when I knew that your mother and I were meant to be together, and as I lived for that blessing, it would be mine."

"But . . . the ordinance isn't there," Jess protested. "Without the sealing, there's no guarantee."

"Even with the sealing there's no guarantee, Jess. Let me tell you something your mother told me she'd learned through her first marriage. Except for the last few months of Ryan's life, Emily was terribly unhappy. She'd married him in the temple with the faith that they would be happy together. But he did many things to hurt her. Not physically. But emotionally she became a shadow of the woman I'd once known. She told me that she'd learned temple marriage is a wonderful thing, but it's really only a technicality. The reality of temple marriage comes through the ins and outs of everyday living. It's enduring to the end committed to someone you love and living worthy of those eternal vows. I'm not a perfect man, Jess. I have my weaknesses and I'm keenly aware of them. But I can say that from the day I married your mother, I did everything in my power to be a good husband and father. I made mistakes—some big ones. But I did my best to make restitution. I always tried to improve and grow for the sake of making my family better and stronger. My family has always been my top priority, along with living the gospel. The Atonement is there to make up the difference for my shortcomings after all I can do, and because I know I've done my best, I know with all my heart that we will be together forever—all of us. I can't tell you how I know, Jess. I just know, and I know it beyond any doubt. Through the years, that knowledge has settled more deeply into me."

Jess didn't want to keep arguing, but he still felt so uneasy about it. He had to say, "But, it's all so . . . abstract."

"Yes, it is. That's what faith is all about. If the principle of eternity was tangible and we could touch it, we wouldn't need faith to believe it's true."

Jess thought about that for a minute before his father added, "It will likely be many more years before your mother leaves this life, Jess. But when she does . . . when we're both gone . . . I want you and Allison to make certain it gets done. Once you see that we are sealed by proxy, everything will be as it should be. Promise me."

"Of course," Jess said firmly.

"Well then, now I can die in peace."

Jess brought himself back to the present, hesitant to leave behind such clear memories of his father. At times it almost felt as if Michael truly were beside him again, sharing his profound wisdom, the experience of his years, and the life he'd lived. And now Michael's words had reminded him of exactly what he'd needed. His mind wandered through the events of the past few days, ending with the reality that tomorrow was indeed his mother's funeral. Silent tears crept into the hair at his temples while he stared toward the ceiling, wondering how he would ever manage without her. He knew that somehow he would. He'd managed without his father, when he'd many times believed that such a thing simply wasn't possible. And in that moment he couldn't deny that in some ways this wasn't as difficult as it had been to lose his father. Perhaps the very fact that he'd survived losing one parent gave him the confidence that he could get beyond losing another. And he knew they were together. It had been difficult at Michael's death to observe his mother's loneliness; but now they were beyond that separation. In spite of what David Hall had said, Jess truly believed that his parents were together. He sighed as he imagined the joy they might be feeling to be reunited, and then he drifted off to sleep.

Chapter Fifteen

The funeral turned out to be as perfect as a funeral could be. Jess began his day with fervent prayer and then refused to give another thought to issues that Tamra had declared to be irrelevant at the present. And he felt sure that she was right. He managed to keep his composure while conducting the meeting and giving a brief talk about the influence his mother had had on his life. He felt that each of his sisters did a tremendous job with their assignments, and the song that was done by the grandchildren was beautiful beyond description.

Within twenty-four hours of the funeral, the household became almost eerily quiet. Trent had stayed on to spend some time with his father. And Jess's sisters were staying another few days, but their husbands and children had returned to work and school. He was grateful to have his siblings all together as they continued to adjust to this loss in their lives. They shared meals and a few outings and long talks that helped them come to terms with Emily's absence. The night before his sisters were scheduled to leave, Amee admitted, "Beyond the fact that I'm simply going to miss her, there's only one thing that really bothers me."

"What's that?" Jess asked.

"It's what . . . old what's-his-name said."

"You mean David," Allison clarified.

"Yes, him," Amee said with scorn.

"I told you before," Allison said, "he is simply not close enough to the family to understand the big picture. Our father was a good man in many ways; he also had some challenges. I know, because

Mom told me—and because I remember evidence of it myself—that Ryan Hall did not live up to those temple covenants. He made some positive steps before he died, but he spent most of their marriage treating her very badly and not even going to church. A temple sealing is contingent upon living for those blessings, and I don't think that he did. Of course, we can't possibly judge from our mortal perspective, but I know our parents—and the circumstances they lived through—well enough to know the desires of their hearts. Our mother loved our father in a very real way, but she didn't love him the way she loved Michael. I know that with all my heart, and I think the rest of you know it too."

Amee made a disgruntled noise, and Alexa said, "It would just be nice to know . . . if they really are together. I mean . . . I can't imagine her with anyone but Dad . . . Michael. But then, I never knew my real father. Just because my perspective is narrow doesn't mean it's right."

"But it *is* right," Emma insisted.

"I just wish we could know," Alexa repeated.

"I think you're all worrying about something that will take care of itself," Samuel said, and they all turned toward him.

Jess had honestly forgotten he was in the room, while Trent had gone into town to pick up a few things he needed. Jess was grateful when Allison said, "Oh, we're sorry, Samuel. Such conversation must sound terribly insensitive to you."

"No, not really," he said. "You're not discussing anything that your mother didn't discuss with me freely. There were no pretenses between us about the eternal scheme of our relationship. We accepted that it was until death, and we were grateful for the time we had. It's okay, really. But I think I might be able to shed some light on what's bothering you."

"How's that?" Amee asked eagerly.

"Well, I know exactly how your mother would explain it," Samuel said with a gentle smile.

"How?" Alexa asked.

"You can hear it in her own words," he said. "I've been reading her journals. I actually read some of them while she was still alive; she told me I was welcome to. But I found something just last night that I found especially fascinating, mostly because it was recorded twice in different ways. If one of you would go and get the two books that are open on my bed, I can find the passages."

Emma hurried from the room and came back with the books. Samuel's hands were giving him trouble, but with Emma's help he found the right page in one of the journals; the other was set aside. "There," he said to Emma. "Read starting right there."

Emma sat down and cleared her throat before she began to read Emily's words. "'I had a dream last night that I know beyond question is the answer to my fasting and prayers. It was—'"

"Wait a minute," Jess said. "When was this?"

Emma turned to the first page of the journal, and he could see her mind working. "It would have been before she married Dad."

"Okay, go ahead," Jess said.

Emma began again. "'It was so incredibly real and vivid, almost like a movie playing in my mind, and when I woke up the images remained very clear, but more important was the way it made me feel. I'm not saying that the dream is some representation of what literally took place in another time, but I do believe it was given to me to help me, in my narrow mortal perspective, to grasp a concept that I needed to understand. I know now beyond any question that marrying Michael is the right thing to do. I know that everything that's happened in our lives to this point was not coincidence or happenstance. It was all part of Heavenly Father's plan, right from the beginning. So the dream goes like this . . .'"

"Wait," Samuel said. "She describes the dream here in detail, but years later, when she was pregnant with the twins, she writes of how Michael was struggling with the very thing you're talking about now. He was questioning his eternal place with Emily, knowing she was sealed to Ryan. She writes in her journal of how she had recalled the dream vividly, had gone back to read about it in her journal, and then how she had repeated it to Michael in the form of a story. And that's how she recorded it the second time—in the form of a story, a fairy tale of sorts." He motioned to the other journal. Emma picked it up, and he helped her find the right place. "Okay, read here," he said, then he chuckled. "You're going to love this."

Emma began to read this story-like dream that their mother had recorded before she was born. "'In a faraway place, a world was being planned, and all of the spirit children of a great Father were brought together to help bring this wonderful event to pass. There was a man—a prince among men. He was a valiant, noble spirit, and he worked closely with the Father in many things. He fought valiantly in the war between good and evil, where the free agency of these spirits was challenged by the prince of darkness.

"'As this great world was being brought together and plans were set into motion to send the spirits down, each in their own time, the Father brought this man to his side and asked his heart's desire. "There is a woman," he told the Father. "I love her with all my heart and soul, and I wish to be with her forever, whatever the cost may be." The Father was pleased with the valiant one's wish, and He asked for this woman to be brought to His side also. He placed her hand in his and promised them eternity if they would take the roundabout course that would bless the lives of others through their earthly existence.

"'The Father talked to them of the pain and difficulty they might endure, and of the way their promises to each other might appear to be for naught. He told them of their potential, of the children they would have, and He told this young man of the mission he was fore-ordained to accomplish. For he would go forth in a time and place where there was much to be done, and into circumstances that would allow him the means to do it. But he would be born into a situation that would make it difficult to find the road he must travel. Still, the Father promised him divine guidance and an instinctive ability to find his way, provided he lived worthy of it.'"

"This is incredible," Allison said as Emma stopped to draw breath.

"Keep going," Amee insisted.

Emma continued to read. "'And there was another man, one who struggled with his faith, who had not been so firm in his convictions through the fight for free agency. He had chosen to follow the Prince of Peace, but his heart was often unsure. The Father saw potential in this man and believed that his earthly existence would better prepare him for a mission he would fulfill when he returned to the Father. But this man needed some extra help, and it was requested of the valiant one that he and this woman he loved, for a brief time on earth, sacrifice some of their time together to give this man the chance he needed. Of course, they agreed, and the Father promised them incomparable joy in return for their sacrifice.'"

Emma stopped reading as she was overcome with emotion, then Jess realized that everyone in the room was crying as they had evidently picked up on the same meaning that he had. Jess asked himself if his own feelings were the result of a touching story told by his mother while the grief of her loss was so close. Or was the Spirit somehow verifying that there was some spiritual truth woven into his mother's tale? He concluded with some degree of confidence that it was more the latter, and he felt relatively certain that, without any words exchanged, the others were feeling the same way. They all shared amazed glances before Emma gained her composure and moved on. "'The valiant one left for earth before the other two, giving them a few minutes to get acquainted before they followed. The valiant one was born halfway around the world from the others, but as promised, he was blessed with the instincts he needed to seek out a path that would bring them together.'"

Once again Emma struggled to keep her composure, but the others waited in silence for her to continue, each consumed with their own emotion. "'The valiant one struggled much through his years of searching for the path the Father had planned for him. He often became confused and afraid, and the prince of darkness worked especially hard on him, drawing on his weaknesses and blowing them into enormous stumbling blocks. At times he even came to believe that he was not valiant at all, but eventually he came to find his place, and find his worth, and once he was reunited with the woman he'd loved long before he was born, they lived happily ever after.'"

Emma sniffled loudly. "Oh my gosh," she said. "That is the most amazing thing I've ever read—with the exception of the scriptures, of course."

"Did you feel what I felt?" Allison asked quietly.

"What?" Jess asked, as if to test her.

"As if . . . it's true."

"Yes, I did," Amee said firmly.

"What did she write after that?" Alexa asked after blowing her nose with a tissue.

Emma wiped her eyes and found her place. "'And that's how I know that Michael and I are meant to be together forever. I know that I was somehow given the miracle of a glimpse into the life we lived before this one, where I saw Michael and me together with the Father. Even if it didn't happen exactly as I saw it, I believe it was given to me in a way that I could understand. While I loved Ryan and I'm grateful for the years we shared and for all I learned, and especially for our beautiful daughters, I know that his part in this plan is for a different purpose than Michael's. Our Heavenly Father knows and sees all things from beginning to end. Somehow He knew that Ryan would not choose to honor his temple covenants as he should have and that if Michael and I lived righteously, we would be blessed for our choices. I have felt the truth of these things over and over in my heart. In spite of the struggles we are facing now, I know that somehow we will be together forever as we live for those blessings.'"

"Wow," Allison said. "And just think of how far they've come since then. If that was written when she was pregnant with you, Emma, I know Dad was struggling a great deal. But things became better after that. He *was* valiant . . . in everything he did."

"Yes, he was," Alexa agreed. "And he loved our mother with his whole heart and soul."

"I think of the service they gave togther," Amee said, "and the missions they served."

"And now they're together on a new kind of mission," Emma said, sniffling again. They all agreed.

* * *

The family remained together and speculated for a long while about what it might be like on the other side of the veil, intermittently expressing their appreciation for the gospel in their lives that gave them a greater understanding of feelings and experiences and principles that to most people in the world would make no sense.

When the conversation began to run down, Jess said, "Thank you, Samuel. We're sure glad you were reading her journals and that you took the opportunity to share them with us. It's evident we all needed that very much."

"I'm just the messenger," he said humbly.

"Well you came with the right message at the right moment, and we're grateful." The others made varying indications of agreement amidst their ongoing emotion. "It's a privilege and an honor to have you in our home, Samuel, and I hope you'll stay indefinitely."

Samuel cleared his throat tensely, drawing all eyes toward him before he sighed loudly and said, "Actually . . . that's something I wanted to talk to you about."

"What?" Emma demanded as if he'd already admitted to criminal activity.

"Now, don't get all upset," Samuel said. "It's just that . . . Trent has invited me to return home with him. I've prayed about it, and in spite of certain reservations, I believe it's the right thing to do. I want to spend some time with my grandchildren."

Grueling silence stretched on until Jess said, "Well . . . that's certainly understandable, but we hate to see you go."

"How long will you stay?" Emma asked.

"I'm not certain. As silly as it might sound, I want to die here. Arlene is buried in this area, and I want to be with her. So if my condition starts getting much worse, I'll probably come back."

"And stay with us?" Emma asked with overt hope.

"That depends on how bad off I am," he said. "We'll cross that bridge when we come to it."

No one seemed to have much else to say, which made the timing of supper excellent. Trent came in just as they were gathering to eat, and they all talked and laughed through the meal—just as a family should. Jess looked around at his loved ones and marveled that he could be so blessed. In spite of the loss they had suffered, he felt such a profound peace that he hardly felt he had room to hold it all. And he was grateful.

* * *

The silence of the house that had descended when most of the relatives had gone home deepened considerably when the remainder of them left. It was difficult for those remaining in the home to say good-bye to Allison, Amee, and Alexa, even though they knew they would see each other regularly. It was even more difficult to say good-bye to Samuel. Because his health issues were not minor, by any means, they had no idea when—or even if—they would see him again.

Jess was grateful, as always, to have Tamra at his side and to be sharing this old family home with Scott and Emma. And to have Rhea around as well; she was a delight to all who knew her, and her support through these challenges had been amazing. They all agreed that even though they had a houseful of children and there was always something going on, it seemed strangely quiet after all the hustle and bustle of so many people being there for the funeral. But the most difficult adjustment was Emily's absence. Everything just felt less than right with her gone, but it was nice to live in the same home with people who shared the same grief and were willing to talk freely about the changes and the struggles.

Days slipped into weeks that wandered into months. Jess kept in close touch with his siblings through regular phone calls and e-mails. He recognized a frequency of contact that hadn't been there prior to their mother's death. There was even a new depth of sharing feelings and struggles and just the little events of everyday life. He had to admit that a growing closeness to his family members was a silver lining in the loss of his mother.

Jess also kept in close contact with Samuel, and even with Trent. In fact, Jess and Trent came to know each other rather well through regular e-mails. Samuel's health continued to take a course of ups and downs, but overall he was maintaining rather well. And then word came that he'd taken a turn for the worse, and he was insisting that he return to Australia—and he wanted to go to the care center. Jess—and every other member of the family—tried to talk him into coming back to stay in their home, but he had made up his mind, and he wouldn't change.

Trent, Julia, and their children accompanied Samuel on his journey home, and they all remained close by for a couple of weeks. They eagerly accepted the Hamiltons' hospitality and stayed at their home while they helped Samuel get settled into the care center, and they went back and forth regularly in between having some vacation time.

Jess was as glad to see Samuel again as the rest of the family, but there was no denying how much he had deteriorated in the months since they'd seen him, and Jess feared that he wouldn't last much longer. Still, it was good to be with him again, and the family quickly began habits of visiting him regularly. Trent's family's departure back to England brought difficult farewells for them and for Samuel; they all knew it was likely they'd never see Samuel alive again. Once Trent and his family had left the country, Jess and Tamra, and Scott and Emma increased their visits to Samuel, making certain that hardly a day went by when he didn't get some company. Occasionally they even talked him into an excursion to spend a few hours at the house, but even that quickly came to a halt as his condition worsened even further. And then, on a rainy morning nearly eleven months from Emily's death, the care center called Jess very early to tell them that Samuel had passed away in the night. For Jess, Samuel's death brought back some of the emotions he'd struggled with in losing his own father. But now, just as then, there was an underlying peace. Samuel was with Arlene again after nearly thirty years, and he felt certain that Emily was also there to greet him. And Jess felt certain that Michael would have met him with great pleasure and gratitude.

Jess began to feel a nervous excitement as the date approached for the family to gather in the temple and do what Michael and Emily had asked of them many years earlier. Arrangements were made and plans were put into motion, and then life became so hectic that he gave the matter little thought.

When a series of challenges set in and didn't let up, Jess began to wonder what might be going on. Then he realized that the date scheduled for the family to meet at the temple was edging closer. Details had been arranged for the event. Allison and Alexa and their husbands were flying in from the States, and all of the adults in the family would be meeting at a hotel in Sydney. It was the same hotel where the family had met for weddings and other special events that had taken place in the Sydney Temple. More recently, a temple had been built closer to home, but the Sydney Temple had great memories and long-time traditions for the Hamilton family.

Jess had been greatly anticipating this particular family gathering ever since his mother's death, but he'd become so thoroughly busy

the last several weeks that he'd honestly lost track of the passing of
time. Of course, there had been plenty going on to keep him
distracted. Nearly every member of the household had been on
antibiotics for illness at least once, little Michael had broken his arm,
and Jess had needed to deal with a number of challenges in the ward
that fell under his stewardship as a bishop. A nasty legal case had
come up regarding one of the boys in the boys' home that had taken
a great deal of Jess's attention, and Scott had discovered that one of
his assistants in the stables had been embezzling. But they'd dealt
with each crisis the same way they always had—one day at a time,
with prayer and an attempt to stay close to the Spirit and to remain
levelheaded. Jess couldn't say for certain if the challenges were the
result of the forces of opposition attempting to keep them from
getting to the temple, or at least to keep them from getting there free
of stress and anxiety. Or perhaps it was simply a string of bad luck.
Maybe a combination. The reasons for all the struggles really didn't
matter. He was determined that, no matter what, they *would* get
there, and they *would* keep their promise to see that the ordinance
was completed.

When the day finally arrived to set out for Sydney, a dozen things
went wrong before they were finally in the air and on their way. Scott
offered a beautiful prayer just before they took off, with Jess piloting
the plane. They knew the children were all in good hands with the
arrangements that had been made. Rhea had been left in charge, with
some assistance available from sisters in the ward. It was a beautiful
day, and all was well. Jess found it a pleasant flight while he visited
with Tamra, Emma, and Scott. Even though they all lived in the same
house, the demands of jobs, children, and Church callings often kept
them from really having quality time together. They arrived at the
hotel in Sydney to find that Allison, Amee, Alexa, and their husbands
were already there and settled. Half an hour later Sean and his wife,
Tara, arrived as well. They had all agreed that while Sean was not officially a member of the family, he was close enough. Such a monu-
mental event could not take place without Sean being present. All six
couples went out for a fine dinner, then went back to the hotel where
they talked and laughed until nearly midnight, when they finally
went to their separate rooms to try and get some sleep.

Jess found sleep especially elusive as he contemplated what would take place in the temple in just a few hours. He pondered all he knew of his parents' history, and how, according to the dream his mother had recorded in her journal, that history had likely begun long before either of them had been born. He contemplated the struggles he knew his parents had endured. Now that they had both passed on, he had studied both of their journals extensively, learning things about them that only surprised him by the reality of how much they had struggled in their lifetimes. And yet, they had both been thoroughly valiant, shining examples of striving to do what's right and live according to God's will in spite of the challenges. He admired and respected them both beyond words, and he loved them beyond belief.

Jess thought of all the grief that his parents—especially his father—had fought with related to the very issue of their not being sealed together. And now, in not so many hours, that missing ordinance would be in place, and whatever happened from that point on would be sorted out on the other side of the veil. Jess felt certain that he might never know the outcome until he was able to pass through the veil himself. But he'd promised his parents that he would do this for them, and it was a promise he was eager to keep. He would actually be standing in as a proxy for his father, and Allison would be standing in for their mother. When Jess had been just a child and Michael had been struggling with the issue, he had asked Allison if she would do the sealing following their deaths, and she had agreed. Now, all these years later, the opportunity was finally at their doorstep.

Jess finally slept and had a bizarre montage of dreams. He couldn't remember their content once he awoke to the light of day, but he had the feeling that he'd dreamt of his parents. He couldn't help hoping that might be an indication that they were close by. As they hurried to get ready and get to the temple for their appointment, it was easy to forget the enormity of what they were doing. But as they were all gathered in a beautiful sealing room, everyone dressed in white, the reality began to set in. The sealer performing the ceremony had been made aware previously of the unique situation they were dealing with and how much it meant to the family. But he'd been told nothing more concerning the family or its background. Naturally then, it came as a surprise when he said with reverence, "You have brothers who have passed on? More than one?"

Following a long moment of stunned silence, Jess said, "That's right. Our brother and his wife were killed in an accident several years ago, and we have another brother who died in infancy."

The sealer only smiled and said, "Isn't it a marvelous blessing for a family to be gathered in its entirety for such an event?"

While Jess longed to sense whatever the sealer might be sensing, he wondered how many times in his life loved ones had been close by and he simply hadn't known. The thought was a bit unsettling, yet comforting somehow.

As Jess and Allison knelt on opposite sides of the altar on behalf of Michael and Emily, Jess felt an unexpected surge of emotion. While holding his sister's hand, he used his free hand to quickly wipe tears from his face and realized that Allison was doing the same. He heard some sniffling in the room, but kept his focus on the sealer at the head of the altar. As the ceremony began, Jess felt such a profound burning in his chest that he could barely speak the words he needed to say. Once they were spoken, a knot of emotion tightened his throat and moistened his eyes. A silence filled with awe and reverence infiltrated the room. Jess heard a sniffle break the silence and turned to see the sealer with tears in his eyes. There was no need for words to be spoken. In truth, any words might have detracted from the sacred silence surrounding them. Jess could never fully explain how he knew, but he knew beyond any doubt that Michael and Emily were both present, as well as many others who were affected by this glorious event. He knew his parents were together and that the ordinance that had just been performed on their behalf had been accepted. Jess pondered for a moment on how his parents had lived their lives in a way that had entitled them to these blessings, and now they were seeing the fulfillment of all they had endured as they had lived the gospel fully.

Jess was hard-pressed to keep from bawling like a baby as the truth of what he felt penetrated every cell of his being. He turned to meet, one by one, the eyes of every member of the family. The emotion shared by everyone else in the room made it evident that they had all felt it; they all knew it was true. They gathered close together in the little room, sharing a group embrace while tears flowed and expressions of joy remained silent. Only Allison spoke, and what she said simply said it all. "They have come full circle, and there can be no better ending to a love story than that."

ABOUT THE AUTHOR

Anita Stansfield has been writing for more than twenty years, and her best-selling novels have captivated and moved hundreds of thousands of readers with their deeply romantic stories and focus on important contemporary issues. Her interest in creating romantic fiction began in high school, and her work has appeared in national publications. *Gables of Legacy: Full Circle* is her twenty-fifth novel to be published by Covenant.

Anita and her husband, Vince, are the parents of five children. They and their two cats live in Alpine, Utah.

The author enjoys hearing from her readers and can be contacted at info@anitastansfield.com. She can also be reached by contacting Covenant at: www.covenant-lds.com.